NO MORE SECRETS

A James Acton Thriller

Also by J. Robert Kennedy

James Acton Thrillers

The Protocol
Brass Monkey
Broken Dove
The Templar's Relic
Flags of Sin
The Arab Fall
The Circle of Eight
The Venice Code
Pompeii's Ghosts
Amazon Burning
The Riddle
Blood Relics
Sins of the Titanic
Saint Peter's Soldiers
The Thirteenth Legion
Raging Sun
Wages of Sin
Wrath of the Gods
The Templar's Revenge
The Nazi's Engineer
Atlantis Lost
The Cylon Curse
The Viking Deception
Keepers of the Lost Ark
The Tomb of Genghis Khan
The Manila Deception
The Fourth Bible
Embassy of the Empire
Armageddon
No Good Deed
The Last Soviet
Lake of Bones
Fatal Reunion
The Resurrection Tablet
The Antarctica Incident
The Ghosts of Paris
No More Secrets

Special Agent Dylan Kane Thrillers

Rogue Operator
Containment Failure
Cold Warriors
Death to America
Black Widow
The Agenda
Retribution
State Sanctioned
Extraordinary Rendition
Red Eagle
The Messenger
The Defector

Templar Detective Thrillers

The Templar Detective
The Parisian Adulteress
The Sergeant's Secret
The Unholy Exorcist
The Code Breaker
The Black Scourge
The Lost Children
The Satanic Whisper

Kriminalinspektor Wolfgang Vogel Mysteries

The Colonel's Wife
Sins of the Child

Delta Force Unleashed Thrillers

Payback
Infidels
The Lazarus Moment
Kill Chain
Forgotten
The Cuban Incident
Rampage
Inside the Wire
Charlie Foxtrot

Detective Shakespeare Mysteries

Depraved Difference
Tick Tock
The Redeemer

Zander Varga, Vampire Detective

The Turned

NO MORE SECRETS

A James Acton Thriller

J. ROBERT KENNEDY

UnderMill Press

This is a work of fiction. Names, characters, places, and incidents are products of the author's imagination. Any resemblance to actual persons, living or dead, is entirely coincidental.

ISBN: 9781990418495

First Edition

For Robbie Coltrane.

Hogwarts misses you.

NO MORE SECRETS

A James Acton Thriller

"Quantum computer technologies can't be hacked, and in theory, its processing power can break all encryption."

Larry Karisny
Director of cybersecurity think tank ProjectSafety.org

"The goal of post-quantum cryptography (also called quantum-resistant cryptography) is to develop cryptographic systems that are secure against both quantum and classical computers and can interoperate with existing communications protocols and networks."

US Department of Commerce's National Institute of Standards and Technology

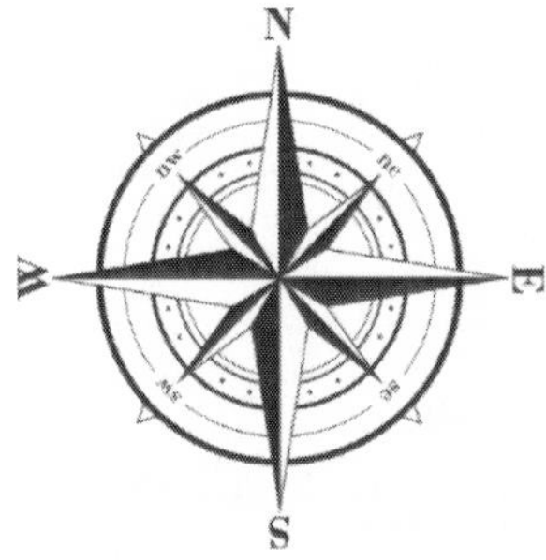

PREFACE

Most people have heard of Quantum Computing, but few realize the potential advancements it could lead to, and fewer still understand how it works. While ultimately speed is a factor, it is the fact it works in a fundamentally different way than current computers that gives it such potential to change our future so dramatically.

It can rapidly perform combinatorics calculations.

Something, again, few people understand.

But this capability could lead to rapid advancements in chemical and biological engineering by quickly modeling different combinations of chemicals and their interactions with each other, including diseases, that could lead to new medicines we haven't even conceived.

Other areas include artificial intelligence, financial analysis, and large-scale manufacturing optimization. Big problems solved quickly, including those we can't even imagine yet.

These advancements all have the potential for good, but with the good, also comes the bad, and the same can be said for Quantum

Computing, the most obvious being the fact it has the capability of easily cracking most encryption in use today.

Should our enemies succeed first, it could tip the balance of power for decades to come.

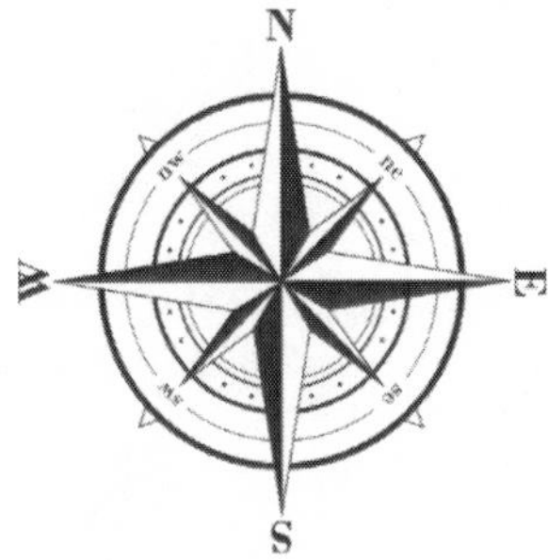

South of Tall el-Hammam, Jordan

Ten Years Ago

Archaeology Professor Laura Palmer sat on her haunches, staring at the newly exposed wall, the scorch marks clearly evident even after thousands of years, the sands of time having preserved evidence of the final destruction of what she was certain was the ancient biblical city of Sodom.

People had been searching for the fabled Sodom and Gomorrah for centuries, if not millennia. It was believed that if they existed at all, they were in the Jordan River Valley near the Dead Sea, exactly where they now were. The dig was considered a wild goose chase, and she had fought long and hard unsuccessfully to obtain funding. So she had turned to her benefactor for help—her ridiculously wealthy brother.

Charles Palmer had made a fortune in telecommunications, recently selling his company for hundreds of millions of euros. He had more money than he knew what to do with, and though older than her, it wasn't by much. She was at the beginning of her career as an academic, and he was already retired, or so he would have the world think.

He was working on something, something he was excited about, something he refused to discuss. It was why he had sold his company. He didn't want to be wasting his time on the mundane day-to-day tasks of running a large corporation. He wanted all the hours of the day available to him for his research.

He had immediately granted her request, funding the dig entirely, then it was merely a formality taking on a partner from the University of Jordan. It was a small dig, her and a Jordanian professor, half a dozen students each plus about a dozen local hires to do the grunt work and keep things running. It was her first major dig, and she was loving it. It was everything she could hope for, and when her brother had called asking if he could join her, what was already perfection in her mind became bliss.

She loved her brother as any younger sister would, but they rarely saw each other, and their interests were wholly divergent. He was on the cutting edge of technology, and she spent her time studying objects created by man thousands of years ago. Their parents had died too young, so they only had each other in this world, and she was always ecstatic to see him. In all their years, this would be the first time they had worked on something together.

Her brother waved at her with a smile that reminded her of her late father. She returned the wave then he disappeared inside a tunnel they had carved into a ridge they were now convinced was the result of an asteroid impact. The Bible described Sodom and Gomorrah and the

Cities of the Plain being destroyed by God's fury, by fire and brimstone. Modern scientists believed the cities could have been destroyed by an earthquake with mass casualties and destruction that led to the abandonment of the fabled sinful communities, but if that were the case, why the description? Why were the descriptions of hellfire burning the city and not the ground shaking it into rubble?

When she had read the history as related in religious texts, she had always been curious about the description of the destruction and why it didn't match any of the modern theories. When evidence of an impact crater, almost lost to the winds of time, was mentioned in an obscure journal, its epicenter pinpointed to this region, it had her curiosity piqued and her quest for funding began. Her brother had paid for satellite imagery that was being analyzed by experts to see if there was any evidence of ancient cities within the blast zone, and while they awaited the results, they were digging test holes at the edge of the blast crater searching for debris.

And she had finally found it. A dried timber buried in the sands, scorched as she might expect something to be when exposed to the blast wave of an asteroid impact. It was squared at the edges, clearly used in construction, and once she had it back in London, she would have it carbon-dated to see when it had been cut down, then the residue examined to see what caused the damage.

They could have their answers in short order, but she wasn't willing to wait, and excavation had continued around the area the timber had been discovered. Leading to her prize find—the shards of a large earthenware vase, intricately painted with a skill level far beyond what one would expect from several thousand years ago. And the subject matter? Scandalous. Further proof, in her mind, that they were indeed in Sodom.

A shout echoed from the nearby tunnel and she shot to her feet as she recognized the fearful cry as that of her brother. One of the locals rushed out of the opening as the ground shook. A plume of dust blasted from the tunnel and she screamed as she shielded her eyes and covered her mouth. She rushed through the billowing dust toward the entrance when somebody grabbed her.

"No, Professor, it's too dangerous! We have to wait!" It was Jagmeet Sharma, one of her students.

She struggled against him, though her determination to break free waned with the realization that he was right. It would be foolish to blindly charge in. She grabbed the walkie-talkie off her belt. "Charles, can you hear me? Are you all right?" She let go of the push-to-talk button and listened, the only response static. She repeated her call then froze. She could hear her voice nearby. "Everybody, turn your radios off!"

Sharma let go of her, turning his off, and several others indicated they had done the same. She repeated her call and again heard her voice just ahead. A gentle breeze pushed most of the dust away and she could just make out what was left of the tunnel opening ahead. "Charles, do you hear me?"

Again, she heard her own voice. She rushed forward, Sharma not stopping her this time, repeating her call, closing in on her voice. It had to be her brother's radio, which meant he must have been blown out of the tunnel and could still be alive, though injured and unable to respond.

Sharma pointed. "Over there!"

Her head darted in the indicated direction and she gasped. She rushed forward, stumbling over the debris scattered across the area, and dropped to her knees, grabbing the radio off the ground. It was beaten and scarred, but still functional, which wasn't necessarily surprising as they were military grade provided by her brother's former company.

She dropped the radio. "Charles!" There was no response as her eyes scanned the area, finding no evidence of her brother. She rose and headed for the entrance. "We have to get in there! We have to find him!"

Sharma grabbed her again. "Look at it, Professor, it's completely caved in. It's too dangerous."

"We can't just leave him in there! We have to find him!" she cried, tears flowing freely as she resigned herself to the fact Sharma was right—it was too dangerous. She collapsed to her knees and clasped her face as she sobbed.

Her brother was dead, and it was her fault.

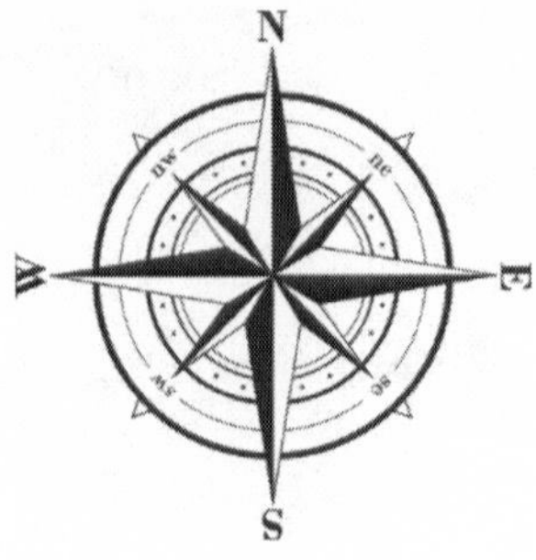

Lot Residence

Sodom

1649 BC

"I swear, husband, your constant agitation is going to bring this family to ruin."

Lot regarded his wife Idit. "My agitation, as you call it, is merely concern for my fellow man. You've seen how things are. Sodom has become a haven for sinners. I may not have been born here, but this is now my home thanks to you, and I weep at what it's become. You're blind to it because you've never seen anything different, yet I've seen other cities. With the possible exception of Gomorrah, Sodom is by far the worst. Do you realize that within three days' ride, there are towns and cities not dominated by brothels and gambling establishments, where the men work a hard day then go home to their loving families as opposed to drink and carouse with women they barely know? It's been happening here for so long that people believe this is normal, that this is the way things are supposed to be, but it's not. We need to open their eyes to what's going on around them. Make them see that there's a better way that will bring them closer to God. Otherwise, I fear everyone here will be condemned for eternity if they don't change their ways."

His wife pursed her lips as she stared at him in the fading light then over at the bed their two daughters were sleeping in. They were the reason he had decided action must be taken. They were twelve and ten, yet he had already seen men leering at them. The perversion in this city knew no bounds and he was determined to save his daughters from the sinful ways of their neighbors.

"And just how do you expect to make a difference?"

"By speaking out."

"And what good has that ever got anybody? At best, you'll ostracize us from the entire community. At worst, you'll get yourself beaten to death by one of those sinners."

He gestured at his daughters. "And what of them? Don't you think we need to make sure they grow up in a better world?"

His wife took his hand. "And I pray to God every night that they do. But these things are bigger than one man. Surely God is the solution to this, is He not? God should be the one to make the sinners change their ways."

Lot shook his head. "No. God provides guidance. He rewards the good and punishes the wicked. He doesn't magically wave His hand and turn the sinner into a pious man. If that were His desire, He would have done so already and there'd be no wickedness in this land. The fact there is, is proof that God is judging us when we face Him on our deathbeds. He wants men to look after themselves, to make the right decisions, the good decisions, and to take their own actions against those who would do evil. I believe all men can easily be led astray, especially when they have no example to follow, like here in Sodom. I think you'd be hard-pressed to find fifty good men, pure of heart, among the denizens of this city." He grunted. "In fact, I think you'd be hard-pressed to find ten."

She squeezed his hand. "Oh, it's not all that bad. I know there's one good soul in this house. Surely there are more within a city so large."

He smiled weakly at her. "And that's the problem, isn't it? My own wife believes that surely there are ten good people within this city as if that's a good thing. Just ten. There should be thousands. The majority of people here should be good, yet here we are talking about ten."

She withdrew her hand, offended. "And would you include me in that ten?"

"Of course. But when we die and are judged worthy, will we spend eternity together, alone, with none of our neighbors to share it with?"

"This is so depressing. Why must we talk of this every day?"

"Because it's important, but you're right, enough of such talk. We must discuss business affairs for a moment. Canaan was in today asking when the vase he commissioned would be ready."

Idit smiled and rose. "I finished it earlier today. I merely need to fire it. Do you want to see it?"

"Of course, you know how much pleasure it brings me to see the fruits of my wife's artistic labors."

She headed into her workshop at the back of their small home and reappeared, rolling the vase on its bottom lip, the earthenware vessel he had crafted for her to paint a large one about shoulder height on a full-grown man. She put it by the fire, the dancing flames revealing her intricate artwork. They sold earthenware goods. It was a family business inherited from his wife's family, handed down for generations. Bowls, pitchers, carafes, vases, urns, anything that could be made and fired in a kiln were on offer.

It was a respectable profession that barely provided for their family, but things had taken a turn for the better since they began offering custom work that went beyond form and function. His wife was a brilliant artist, and it was one of the things that had attracted him to her. Anybody who could create things so beautiful had to have a kind soul. Her work was in high demand and was improving their station with each commission, but as he gazed upon the artwork, his chest tightened, his stomach churned, and his jaw dropped.

"What villainy is this?"

Her eyes shot wide. "What, you don't like it?"

"Like it? It disgusts me!" He slowly circled the vase so he could see the entire creation filled with debauchery. Men and women writhing in passion and pain, the details graphic, intimate, with nothing left to the imagination. "How could you paint something like this?"

She shrugged. "That was the job. He described exactly what he wanted, so I created what he wanted. You don't like it?"

"Of course I don't like it. This is exactly what I've been talking about! This glorifies the sin that consumes Sodom."

She sat back down, folding her arms. "You knew what the commission was, yet you took it. He said he wanted to immortalize a party at his home."

Lot threw his hand at the vase. "He never said anything about this!"

"Not to you, but when I took the commission, I spoke with him about the party. He described an orgy that had taken place at his home the week before. He even gave me the names of those who were there so that their faces could be immortalized along with his."

Lot leaned closer to the vase, peering at the images and gasped as he recognized several of the faces as senior members of the community, as fellow businessmen. He slowly rounded the handmade creation when bile filled his mouth at two faces he recognized. "What is this?" he whispered.

His wife moved forward to see what he was looking at and chuckled. "I thought it would be funny. I can change it if you want."

"Funny? You think putting our faces on this as if we participated in such debauchery is funny?"

She shrugged. "Well, it's the fact that we never would that makes it funny. Besides, no one would recognize us."

He grabbed the vase and lifted it over his head then hurled it at the fireplace. It shattered and Idit cried out as she sprang forward.

"What have you done?"

"What have I done? How can you ask that? You know how I feel about such things!"

Her jaw clenched as she shot daggers at him. "You realize how much work I put into that? You realize how much he's paying for that? That could have fed this family for a month, but now because of your ridiculous puritanical beliefs, we have to either cancel the commission and risk our reputation, or I have to redo all this, which means I can't work on the next commission. You need to get control of yourself! This obsession of yours is hurting our family. It's hurting your daughters."

He glanced over at the girls, now sitting upright in their bed, tears in their eyes at the rare sight of their parents fighting. He pointed at them. "I do this for them."

His wife spat. "No, you do it for yourself. I love you, husband, but sometimes you have to accept that there's nothing you can do about those around you, and learn to live with that reality." She walked away. "I'm going to bed. If you know what's good for you, don't touch me."

He opened his mouth to say something but stopped himself and instead stared at the flames and the shards of what remained of the vase, his wife's lecherous artwork taunting him. She was right. It was a commission. He should have known what kind of party it was they were asked to immortalize.

And he wasn't certain why he was so enraged by it. Perhaps it was because it was incredibly graphic and had come out of the mind of his beautiful wife. Many of the things depicted, they had never done themselves, and it made him wonder if she had done them with someone else? Had Canaan described them in detail to her? Had those descriptions excited her? Had she put their own faces among those twisted in ecstasy because she wanted to be part of such an event, because she was bored with him, or because she wanted to do such things with him?

Whatever it was, it made him see her in a different light. Was she just as sinful as those he railed against? Was his own home tainted? He couldn't be sure, he could never be, but there was one thing he was certain about. There was no time to waste, because if the sins of Sodom had broken through these four walls, God's wrath couldn't be far behind.

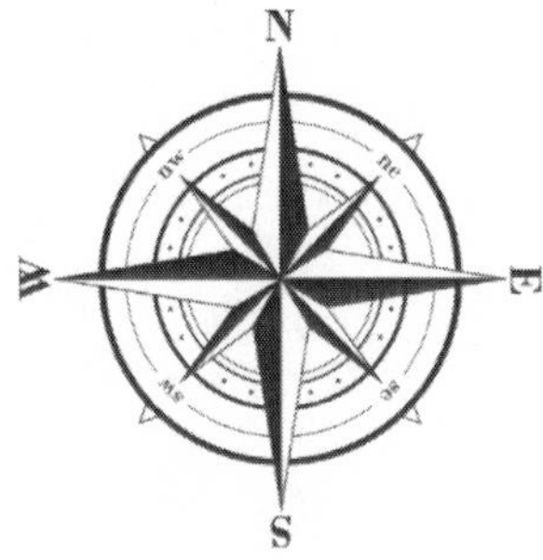

St. Paul's University

St. Paul, Maryland

Present Day

Tommy Granger thanked God every day that Dean Gregory Milton of St. Paul's University had given him a second chance at life. He had made some bad choices as a teenager, his hacking abilities renowned in dark circles, culminating in him breaking into the Department of Defense. He had boasted of his success and was quickly arrested.

Apparently, you couldn't trust hackers to keep a secret.

But now he had a new lease on life, thanks in no small part to the man he was about to see. He tapped on Archaeology Professor James Acton's office door, excited though nervous. He had done something he wasn't sure he should have, and was about to ask permission after the fact.

"Come in."

Tommy opened the door and poked his head in. "Do you have a minute?"

Acton beckoned him inside. "Of course, as long as it's not more paperwork."

Tommy stepped in and closed the door behind him, eying the stacks of paper on the professor's desk. "Haven't you guys heard of electronic forms?"

Acton grunted. "This is the Archaeology Department. We do everything old school."

"You do realize that doing things electronically is quicker? All this paperwork you're complaining about could probably be completed in half the time."

"Perhaps, but a thousand years from now, when your descendants are digging up this office, and there's no paper to find"—Acton picked up a page in front of him and shook it—"how will they ever know what the food budget was for the Peru dig last quarter?"

Tommy chuckled and sat in a chair in front of Acton's desk. "You're right. Knowledge like that could change the course of history."

"Exactly. I'm saving mankind's future." Acton leaned back. "So, what is it you wanted to talk to me about?"

Tommy shifted, slightly uncomfortable. "It's about Professor Palmer's brother."

Acton's eyebrows rose. "Charles? What about him?"

"Well, it's coming up on the tenth anniversary of his death."

Acton's head slowly bobbed. "Yes, I suppose it is. What of it?"

"Well, I saw this thing on Insta where someone put together a montage on the anniversary of their father's death. It was photos, video clips, images of newspaper articles, all set to music. Mai thought it was very moving and I have to admit, so did I, and it got both of us wondering if Laura would appreciate something done about her brother. I know she never really talks about him, at least not in front of us, so I wasn't sure if it would just stir up bad memories."

Acton scratched at three days' growth, the paperwork obviously consuming him for some time. "She doesn't talk about him much, that's true, but when she does, it's always with a smile. I think she'd be touched. You're right, it might bring back bad memories, but I think she'd appreciate the gesture regardless. I would suggest, however, whatever montage you put together celebrates his life and doesn't mention his death."

"Of course," agreed Tommy. "I'd never put anything in about what happened in Jordan." He paused. "What *did* happen in Jordan?"

Acton frowned. "A horrible accident. They had excavated into the side of a ridge and one of the support beams gave way and the entire ridge collapsed on him. They believe he was killed instantly."

"Believe?"

"Well, it was too unstable to go in and retrieve the body, and when they called for help from the Jordanians, they immediately shut down the dig, revoked the license, and expelled Laura and all the non-Jordanians."

Tommy's stomach churned. "You mean they never recovered the body?"

"No. I know it's always bothered her that she was never able to give her brother a proper burial."

"But I thought they had the funeral? Didn't that old Austrian guy say he had been there?"

"Well, there was a funeral, but there was no body to bury."

Tommy folded his arms. "Maybe I shouldn't do this."

Acton disagreed. "No, I think you should. I think it's a good idea. And it has been ten years. I think she'd appreciate it, especially something tastefully done that celebrates his life. He accomplished so much in such a short time, more than most people could ever dream of in a lifetime. He was brilliant. To think what he might have accomplished if he had lived another thirty or forty years. He could have changed the world." He sighed, staring off into the distance. "I would kill to know what he was working on when he died."

"What do you mean?"

"Laura said he was working on some project that had him extremely excited, something that could change the world, but he refused to talk about it to her. It was why he sold his company so that he could devote his time to whatever this project was, but he died before he could finish it."

Tommy's curiosity was piqued and he made a note to look into Palmer's background. "Fascinating," he murmured.

Acton regarded him. "What?"

"Nothing, just that there are so many of humanity's greatest minds that have died far before their time. It makes me wonder how far ahead we could be if the great minds of our society had lived out full lives."

"It does make you wonder," agreed Acton. He leaned forward. "So, how are you going to put this montage together?"

"I was thinking of doing something a little different. Typically, people are taking family photos and whatnot, but I figured she's seen all that, and of course, I'd have to ask her for it or have you root around in her things to find the photos. I'm just going to run my little software program that I wrote to crawl the web and look for his face. It'll pull any photos that friends or family have posted, newspaper articles, everything."

"How long would that take?"

Tommy shrugged. "Well, in theory, forever, but I'll confess I've had it running now for weeks, and because of who he was, it's coming up with all kinds of great stuff. He was a bit of a celebrity, so there are cool shots of him at charity functions, caught on the street, spotted in restaurants, things that she's probably never seen."

Acton placed his elbows on his desk, clasping his hands in front of him. "That sounds exciting, actually."

"I think it's going to be awesome. I just wanted to make sure you thought it was okay before I started filtering through things and putting it together." Tommy paused. "How long do you think I should make it?"

Acton shrugged. "Not too long. I find that's the problem quite often these days. People put together something that's good and then they think more must be better. No more than five minutes."

Tommy frowned. "I could probably put together something hours long with what I found already."

"Like I said, more is not necessarily better. But here's what I would do. Put together the highlight reel, set it to a song, like I said about five minutes long, then give her the rest of the images on a memory stick so that she can go through them when she feels like it."

Tommy liked the idea. "Sounds good to me." He gestured at the stacks of paper. "Are you sure you don't want me to print off all the photos instead?"

Acton flipped him the bird. "Get out of here, wiseass. I've got work to do."

Tommy chuckled then rose. "Can we bring it by tomorrow night?"

"Sure. Why don't you two come over for dinner? I'll barbecue. We'll have a few brewskies and then you can spring your surprise on her."

Tommy paused at the door. "Spring sounds so negative. How about we go with share?"

Acton laughed. "You're right. Let's go with share." He flicked his fingers toward the door. "Now get out of here. I really do have work to do."

Tommy left and closed the door behind him, feeling much better about the surprise he had been working on for weeks. He couldn't wait to show Laura what he came up with, but he also couldn't wait to do a deep dive into her brother's background and maybe discover just what was this secret project he was working on before he died.

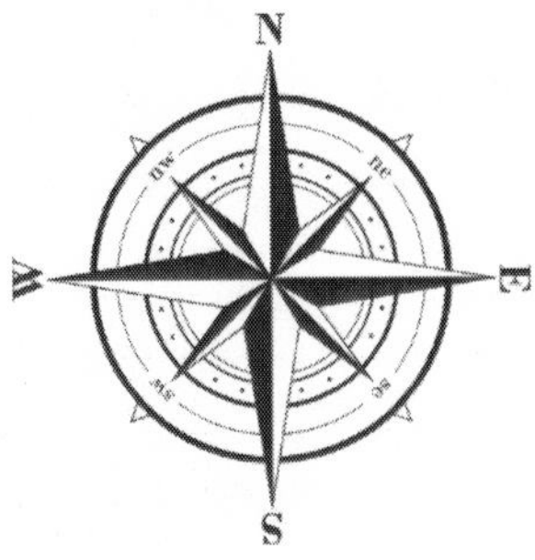

Lot's Shop

Sodom

1649 BC

"I apologize for the delay. It's entirely my fault. I was admiring my wife's work when it slipped out of my hands and shattered on the floor."

Canaan frowned at Lot. "I never thought you were clumsy, Lot. Could it be that the subject matter shocked you?"

Lot's cheeks flushed and he shifted his feet.

"You've always been a bit of a prude." Canaan regarded him as if making a decision on just how outraged he should be. He suddenly smiled. "I'll tell you what. I'll forgive you, and you can keep the commission on one condition."

Lot tensed, certain he wouldn't like any condition placed upon him by a man such as Canaan, a brothel owner who had made his fortune off the fronts and backs of women.

"I'm having a party next week. You've seen what they're like if your wife's reputation as an artist is merited. You're a good-looking fellow and your wife is stunning. I want you two to be my guests."

Lot swallowed the painful lump in his throat, jealousy consuming him at the thought of his wife at one of these parties, handed around like some plaything, her body writhing in ecstasy, the mother of his children moaning with pleasure. Bile filled his mouth and his fists clenched. "I'm afraid we'll have to politely decline."

"I'll double the commission."

Lot refused.

"I'll triple it."

Lot's eyes widened. It would be the largest by far they had ever been paid for a single work of art. It would secure their entire season, assuring his family generous meals until the next harvest. He closed his eyes and they burned.

Then he said something he couldn't believe. "We'll attend, but we won't be participating." He flinched as a hand cupped his nether region and squeezed.

"Oh, my friend, you'll be participating in things you never imagined." The hand was removed. "And trust me when I say, you might not participate, but your wife definitely will, if her reaction to my description of the last party is any indication." Canaan laughed and patted Lot on the cheek. "Who knows, my friend? You might just discover you have another side that you never knew was there. Come and find out. Join us and I'll pay you triple." He leaned closer. "And truly join us, and I'll pay you five times what I was going to."

Canaan departed, leaving Lot's heart pounding. He rushed forward and barred the door then receded into the rear of his shop, his entire body trembling. He hadn't said yes, but he hadn't said no. And the amount of money on offer was huge, but the cost was simply too high. He thought back to the image his wife had painted. It depicted men with women, men with each other, and women with each other. The faces he recognized weren't with their partners. It was a free for all of lust and gluttony, and what horrified him the most was that he could see his wife in the midst of such a thing reveling in the pleasures. And as he imagined it, his jealousy turned to rage and shame, for a small part of him desperately wanted to experience what it must be like to just once let himself go.

He closed his eyes and wept as he realized Canaan was right.

He was no better than those he condemned.

God, please help me. I beg of you.

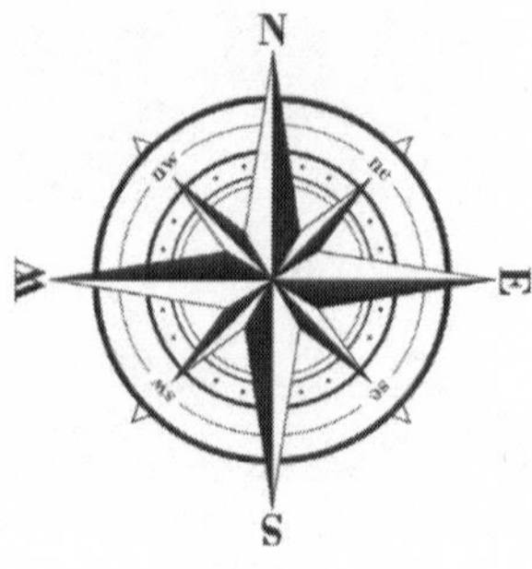

Acton/Palmer Residence, Overlook Village Gated Community

St. Paul, Maryland

Present Day

Professor Laura Palmer slowly drew the shish kebab skewer through the tines of her fork, depositing its contents on her plate. Grilled peppers, onions, and zucchini mixed with marinated pork was one of her favorite things her husband grilled, though she'd never admit to him that steak wasn't. The man was red meat obsessed, and while she loved a good steak as much as the next girl, she did love her vegetables, and this was the only way they were ever making it onto his grill.

Tommy picked up on the unusual choice, holding up a speared piece of pork. "Steak too expensive now, Professor?"

James grunted. "Everything's too expensive now, but I thought I'd grill something I know my wife likes."

Laura cocked an eyebrow. "I like steak."

"Yes, but you *love* grilled pork and vegetables."

She grinned. "This is true. My man knows me well." She held up her fork with a perfectly charred wedge of green pepper. "And I do love my veggies."

"And so do I."

She rolled her eyes. "Deep fried doesn't count."

"Hey, Kentucky Fried Chicken is still chicken." James leaned forward, striking a pose she recognized meant a story was coming. "Did I ever tell you about when I was in college, I used to date this girl and every time she would come over we would order this combo box. It had chicken wings, chicken fingers, deep-fried zucchini, french fries, all the normal stuff. But it also had deep-fried carrots, peas, and string beans."

Tommy stared at him. "Deep fried peas?"

"Yep, everything in the box was deep fried and everything except the fries had batter. It was awesome. But when we had both put on ten pounds after two months of dating, we discovered that just because vegetable was an ingredient didn't make it healthy."

Tommy's fiancée, Mai Trinh, giggled. "I guess not, but oh my goodness deep fried food tastes sooo good."

Laura reached out and squeezed Mai's forearm. "Not a lot of deep-fried food in Vietnam?"

"Oh, we fry a lot of food and some things are battered, but not like you Americans do it. We had Popeyes the other day, and I swear there was more batter than chicken."

James moaned. "I know, that's what makes it so good."

Laura shook her head. "And so bad for you."

James shrugged. "Hey, you only live once. It might as well be enjoyable."

"And short." Laura held up a red pepper. "And I find this equally enjoyable."

James' head lolled to the side toward Tommy. "And yet I still married her."

Laura gave him a look. "Yeah, like you could resist me."

"Trust me, it wasn't your favorite foods that attracted me to you."

"What did attract you to her?" asked Mai, and Laura cringed before the response was even out of her husband's mouth.

"A couple of cheeks and the twins."

Tommy snorted as Mai's eyes narrowed. "Huh?"

Tommy leaned toward his girlfriend. "I'll explain later."

Laura sighed. "I'm hard-pressed right now to remember why I was attracted to you."

"Before or after you saw me naked for the first time?"

Tommy sprayed his beer and even Mai laughed aloud. She sighed. "God, I hope we're like you two when we're your age."

An eyebrow shot up James' forehead. "Our age? Ugh, I feel so old."

Mai's jaw dropped. "Oh my God. I'm so sorry!"

Laura batted a hand. "Ignore him. He found a gray hair this morning and he hasn't stopped going on about it."

Tommy leaned closer, eying James' head. "I don't see any gray."

James gave a toothy smile. "Think lower."

Tommy squeezed his eyes shut. "Please tell me you're talking about your chest."

"Sure, let's go with that."

Even Laura laughed. "All right, now I remember why I married you. You make me laugh."

James eyed her. "Before or after you saw me naked for the first time?"

She tossed her head back, a good belly laugh ensuing. "I'll never tell."

They finished their meal, the conversation easy, comfortable, just the way good friends should enjoy each other's company despite the age difference. Mai Trinh had helped save their lives in Vietnam, and they both now thought of her as a daughter and Tommy like a son, children they would never have themselves thanks to the wound Laura had received in France.

She closed her eyes for a moment. France was a cursed country for her. She had lost her ability to have children, and thanks to events in Paris barely a month ago, they had almost lost Tommy and Mai. While she loved the country, the history, the culture, she wasn't sure if she would ever go back again.

James rose. "Tommy, help me clear the table, and ladies, please bring our drinks to the theater." He said the last two words with a snooty British accent.

Laura regarded him. "Are we watching a movie?"

James and Tommy exchanged glances. "I wouldn't call it a movie."

"You two are up to something."

James shrugged. "I'd tell a woman who didn't laugh at my junk the first time she saw it, but you'll just have to wait."

Mai giggled and Laura sighed. "Fine, don't tell me." She grabbed her glass of wine and her husband's beer then headed for the theater located in their new ridiculously large home. It was one of her favorite features, the massive projection system and Atmos speakers so enjoyable in the absurdly comfortable reclining chairs, they hadn't gone to a movie theater since they moved in.

James and Tommy joined them moments later, and Tommy did something at the computer that controlled the system as James stood in front of her. "This is Tommy and Mai's project, so I'm just going to park my ass and let the kids do the talking."

"For a change."

He stuck his tongue out at her then sat beside her, taking her hand. She leaned against him as Mai stood in front of them and Tommy joined her.

"Just what's going on?"

"You'll see, but just remember, no matter what happens, I told them this was all right, so blame me if I was wrong."

Now Laura's curiosity was killing her. What could he possibly be talking about?

Tommy clasped his hands in front of him, fidgeting. "Nobody said there'd be public speaking."

James rolled his hand. "We're all friends here. You can do this."

Mai took her fiancé's hand and gave it a gentle squeeze. Tommy smiled at her and began. "Professor Palmer—"

Laura leaned forward slightly. "Laura."

Tommy flashed a weak smile. "Okay, Laura, as you know, well, of course, you know, I mean…" He growled. "I'm not good at this."

"No, you're not." James laughed. "Forget the formal speech. This isn't a presentation. This is a gift."

Tommy paused. "You're right, it's a gift. Laura, this is our gift to you as the tenth anniversary of your brother's death approaches."

A lump formed in her throat and tears flowed freely as she bit down on her knuckle, struggling not to sob at the mention of her beloved brother. Next week would be ten years since the tragic accident, and as the date approached, she had been thinking more about him.

James leaned closer. "Are you all right?"

She nodded and indicated for Tommy to proceed.

Tommy smiled awkwardly. "Well, this is, umm, a celebration of his life." Tommy and Mai stepped aside, both clearly uncertain about continuing, but James again rolled his hand.

"Go ahead, it's all right."

Tommy pressed a button on the remote control and Laura cried out involuntarily as a photo of her and her brother appeared on the screen, slowly zooming in toward their laughing faces as Sarah McLachlan's "I Will Remember You" played over the speakers. The image transitioned to another of the two of them together when they were younger, and she laughed at the rabbit ears she was giving him as he stared at the camera so seriously. The tears ran but a smile spread as the good memories flowed.

James handed her a tissue and she dabbed her eyes dry as the montage continued, many of the photos and clips familiar, but so many were things she hadn't seen before. "Where did you get these?"

"I used my software to crawl the Internet searching for his face. A lot of it's from improperly secured social media pages, news websites, business and celebrity websites. I just let the bot go for a few weeks. I had it running in the background on half the university's computers."

James eyed their young friend. "Wait a minute. Is that why everybody's machines were running slow?"

Tommy grinned. "Are you going to turn me in?"

James laughed. "No, but I wouldn't let Greg find out. You might be looking for a job no matter what the reason was behind it."

Laura listened to the exchange but couldn't tear her eyes away from the screen, devouring every moment. It was emotionally taxing, but worth every tear, every shake of her shoulders. She thought of her brother every day and suffered with the knowledge that she was responsible for his death, despite assurances from everyone that it was simply a tragic accident. The tunnel was collapsing whether her brother entered or not, and whoever was in it at the time was dying, then someone else's sister, mother, or daughter, instead of her, would be grieving. And none would be blaming themselves for their loved one's death.

They were right, of course, but her brother wouldn't have been there if it weren't for her, and he wasn't trained for such things. She had asked herself countless times over the years what his final moments were like. Had he heard the timbers creaking? Had he ignored the warning signs, his inexperience having him heading deeper into the tunnel rather than turning around and getting out while there was still time, like the worker who had escaped only moments before the collapse?

The montage ended and James tapped the button in the control panel built into the arm of the chair, turning the lights back on.

Laura clapped as she sniffed. "That was wonderful, you two. Absolutely wonderful."

Mai's hands were clasped in front of her chin. "It didn't upset you too much?"

Laura rose and gave Mai a hug then Tommy. "Only in a good way. I haven't cried like that over my brother in years."

Tommy held up a USB key. "I found thousands of photos. The montage was only some of the highlights. I thought you might like to have them."

She took the memory stick and gripped it in her hand. "Thank you, Tommy."

He shifted awkwardly, his eyes drifting to his feet. "Just be careful. They're not filtered, so…"

"So, there could be things referring to his death?"

"Exactly."

She drew in a breath, gripping the memory stick tighter. "I understand. Thanks for the warning." She gave them both one more hug then turned to James. "Since we're here, why don't we watch my brother's favorite movie?"

James smiled. "And just what movie would that be?"

"Terminator 2. He loved that franchise. I told you how he was obsessed with computers. He couldn't get enough."

James chuckled. "Whose side was he cheering for?"

Laura gave him a look. "Haha."

Tommy cleared his throat. "I don't know if you want to hear it, but I did a little digging, and your brother was, well, rather remarkable."

Laura sat. "Well, I know he was brilliant."

"Yes, but no offense, you're not exactly into computers, so you might not realize how brilliant he was."

Laura gave young Tommy the stink-eye. "I'm not exactly a Luddite."

Tommy sat with Mai, his cheeks flushed. "I didn't mean that, but knowing how to use a computer and truly understanding it, are two very different things."

Laura agreed, waving a hand. "I'll grant you that. What was my brilliant brother involved in?"

"Well, he was way ahead of his time. Near the end, his focus appeared to be artificial intelligence and quantum computing."

James leaned closer, lowering his voice slightly. "And just whose side did you say he was cheering for?"

Laura swatted him. "Quiet, I want to hear this. Go ahead, Tommy, tell us about what you found out." She sat back and for the next fifteen minutes Tommy regaled them with what he had found out about her brother, most of it going over her head, though she grasped enough of it to realize that her brother's brilliance wasn't just a proud sister's opinion, it indeed was the truth.

What you could have accomplished had you not died.

Laura lay on their bed, utterly exhausted. It had been an unexpectedly wonderful day. She always enjoyed it when Tommy and Mai visited, but the montage of her brother had been entirely unexpected, and hearing about her brother's work for the first time from someone who understood it, could explain it, had been a revelation. He indeed was brilliant, apparently had strong feelings against unregulated artificial intelligence research, but more importantly, had been an expert in quantum computing, concerned about the implication if the Western world's enemies were first to the punch.

She flipped through the photos on her tablet, Tommy having set up their home network so that the USB key was now a shared drive, allowing her to see the images from any device attached to their Wi-Fi. There were thousands of images, many of which she had seen before, far too many covering his funeral, causing the tears to flow again, yet she kept swiping her finger across the screen.

James entered the bedroom from the bathroom. "You're going to make yourself sick going through that. You need to take a break."

She rolled into a seated position and crossed her legs, continuing to flip through photos. "I can't stop myself. It's painful but cathartic. I haven't allowed myself to really *feel* about my brother in years. I've tried to suppress the emotions, the guilt, the loss, but just seeing this all at once, it's so raw. If I close my eyes, I can picture that day, every moment of it, as if it were happening to me right now. He was so excited to be there, and I was so excited for him to be finally working with me on something. I was so young and naïve. It wasn't until years later that I realized there was no way in hell anyone was ever granting me funding for a dig at my age. If it weren't for him, we never would have been there. He helped kickstart my career. And if it weren't for him, I wouldn't be where I am today." She clasped her hands over her face as a new font of tears erupted. "I just wish he was here to see how my life turned out, how happy I am, and how much good his legacy has brought."

The bed shifted as James sat beside her and he wrapped an arm around her, drawing her close. "I like to think he is here with us, watching down on his little sister."

She sniffed and looked up into his eyes. "He would have loved you like a brother."

James smiled. "Of course he would, you know how lovable I am."

She giggled. "James, you always know just what to say." He kissed her forehead and squeezed her tight. She extricated herself and continued flipping through the photos, stopping at one of her brother emerging from a theater. "They never gave him a moment's rest. He couldn't even go to a movie without someone taking his photo."

James leaned in then snatched the tablet from her hands. He zoomed in on her brother's face. "Are you sure this is him?"

"Of course, and Tommy's software program flagged it as well, which means the facial recognition points match."

James zoomed out then back in on the marquee visible behind her brother, revealing the movie playing. "Do you see what movie is playing?"

"Terminator."

"No, Terminator Genisys."

She shrugged. "I'm sorry, I'm not familiar that much with the franchise. That was my brother's thing."

James stabbed a finger at the tablet. "Hon, don't you realize what this is, what this means?"

She shook her head. "I have no idea what you're talking about."

"Terminator Genisys came out years after your brother died."

She stared at her husband blankly, still not making the connection. "What do you mean?"

"It means if this photo is real, your brother is still alive."

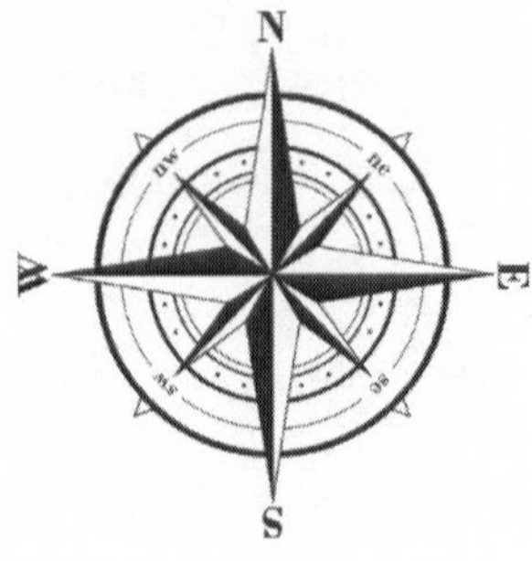

Lot Residence

Sodom

1649 BC

Lot rushed from the room and out the back door, vomiting on the stone of the rear courtyard. His wife's reaction had been exactly as he had feared—she had expressed shock at Canaan's offer, but he could see it in her eyes.

She was tempted.

She wanted other men touching her, pleasuring her. Anyone but her husband. It made him sick. He gasped in a breath and tears filled his eyes at the betrayal. Yet was it a betrayal? She hadn't done anything, at least not yet, and he found his thoughts drifting to what it must be like to just not care, to give in to all your carnal desires. Was he any less guilty than her? And was the fact that he was so tempted despite his intense jealousy mean he was as bad as those he vilified on a daily basis?

He heard someone behind him and a hand was placed gently on his back. "What vexes you, husband?"

He couldn't face her. "You want to go to the party, don't you?"

The hand was removed. "What? What would make you say such a thing?"

It wasn't a denial. "I could see it in your eyes. You're tempted."

"Only because of the money! You know we're heading into the slow season. A commission such as this, three times what was already extremely generous, means we don't have to worry about feeding our children."

He faced her. "Three times?"

She looked up at him. "Of course, three times. You didn't think I wanted to, well, you know, take up his offer of five times."

A relieved sigh escaped as every muscle in his body relaxed. He embraced her, squeezing her against him. "Oh, thank God! I thought you were one of them."

She laughed, hugging him back. "No, my husband, you are the only man for me. But I am willing to suffer witnessing the debauchery of Canaan and his friends if it means our daughters are fed and clothed for months to come." He kissed the top of her head and she gently pushed away. "Well, if we're going to take him up on his offer, then I better get to work recreating his last party."

He smiled at her. "Just leave us out of it, all right?"

She laughed. "Very well. But when I'm done working, why don't you join me and we'll reenact some of the scenes as husband and wife."

His robe stirred at the filthy proposition. He grinned. "Why wait?"

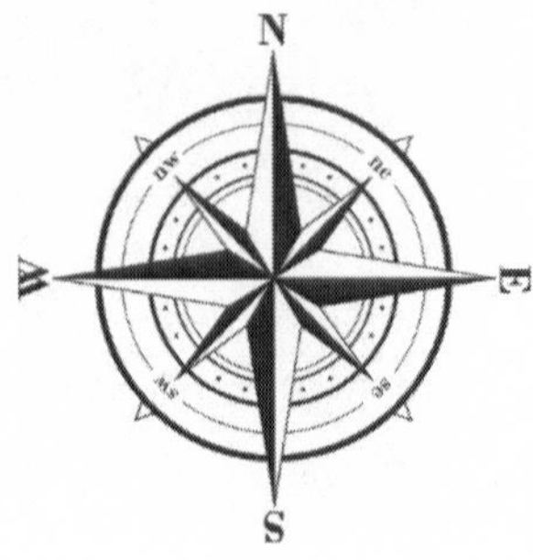

Acton/Palmer Residence, Overlook Village Gated Community

St. Paul, Maryland

Present Day

Laura had fainted with her husband's words. When she had recovered, they had both examined the photo six ways from Sunday, searching for any anomalies, any indication it was a fake, but their inexpert eyes found nothing. A call had been placed and Tommy had answered, their guests returning immediately. Laura now sat at the dining room table as Tommy set up several laptops, bringing up the photo.

His head shook. "I can't believe I didn't pick up on that. I saw this photo. I looked directly at it, but I didn't make the connection. It just never occurred to me to think that he'd still be alive."

James held up a finger. "*Might* still be alive. Let's not get any hopes up here or jump to any conclusions. Right now, we have a photo that doesn't fit the facts, and there are only three possibilities I can think of. One, is that this is a fake. Two, that this is genuine and Charles is still alive, or three, this is genuine and we're misinterpreting what we're seeing."

Laura's eyes narrowed. "How could we misinterpret it?"

"Well, for one, the marquee has 'Terminator' and then the word 'Genisys' underneath. Was there a movie called Genisys out at the same time as the original Terminator, or was there ever a rerunning of the movie, along with a movie called Genisys, and he just happened to be there and got his photo taken? I realize it's a long shot, but is it any more of a long shot than him actually being alive?"

Tommy pursed his lips. "No, I suppose not." He went to work and Laura folded her arms, leaning back, a jumble of emotions. She was excited at the prospect that her brother might still be alive but confused as to why he kept that fact hidden from her. Could he have somehow survived but lost his memory and was wandering the world, not knowing who he was? But if that were the case, why was he at a Terminator sequel? If he remembered his love for that franchise, surely he would have remembered his love for her.

Why would he make her think he was dead these past ten years? It made no sense. It had to be a fake, but if it were a fake, why? Who would create such an image then put it out on the Internet? The only person it could possibly hurt was her, and surely they would have approached her, demanding payment for further information as to where he was, then once they received it, disappeared into the ether.

James watched Tommy intently working. "Will you be able to prove conclusively whether it's a fake?"

Tommy shrugged. "If I find evidence it's a fake, I can prove that it definitely is a fake. But if I can't find any evidence, it could still mean it's a fake, but something expertly done. We're not talking Oswald here in the backyard with the shadows not matching. Fakes today can be as clumsily done as that or done so well, it's impossible to tell." He leaned back, throwing his hands up and clasping them behind his head. "I can't tell."

Laura leaned forward. "What do you mean?"

"I mean, I'm seeing no evidence of this being a fake. There's no odd pixelization around him in the background, no evidence he's been superimposed on another image, all the lighting seems to match. As far as I can tell, it's real."

"But it can't be! He can't be alive! There's no way he would hide that from me! It would mean he survived! There's no way he survived and didn't tell me!" She burst into tears, her chest aching. "He wouldn't do that to me," she murmured.

James rushed around the table and held her tight as her body was racked with sobs.

"He couldn't do that to me, James. He could never be so cruel."

James patted her head gently and addressed Tommy. "Is there any way to know for sure?"

Tommy shook his head. "Not with my equipment. The CIA might be able to tell, but even then, they might be able to determine if it's a fake, but there's no way to really know one hundred percent."

"It has to be fake," mumbled Laura, her face still pressed into James' chest. "He wouldn't do that to me."

James kissed the top of her head. “Make the call.”

“Yes, sir,” replied Tommy.

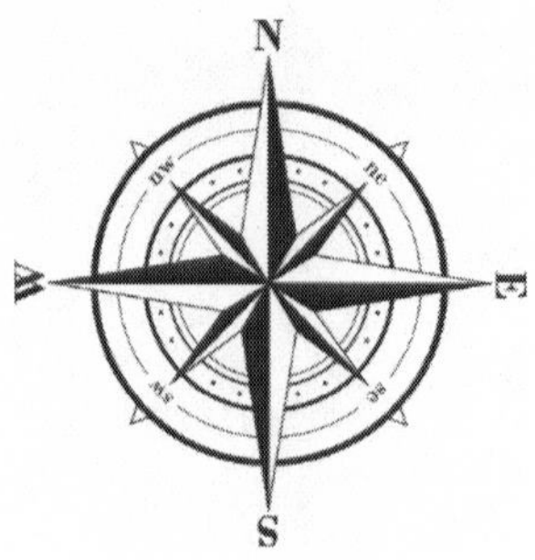

Leroux/White Residence, Fairfax Towers

Falls Church, Virginia

CIA Analyst Supervisor Chris Leroux tossed his controller on the table, ET dead yet again. He turned to his best friend, CIA Operations Officer Dylan Kane, sitting on the couch beside him in Leroux's apartment. "I can see why they buried all these in a landfill. I think that truly is the worst game ever made."

Kane agreed. "It definitely does have suck written all over it. I just can't believe you got your hands on it."

Leroux shrugged. "It's amazing what you can find on the Dark Web."

"I hope you didn't use government funds."

"Nooo, I didn't. I just found the seller, made contact, then told Randy Child about it and he took over and used his own computers to hack the guy. Less than twenty-four hours later and he's handing me a prerelease beta of one of the biggest disasters in video gaming history."

"Too bad, too. The movie was great. Before my time, of course, but I've seen it since. My parents showed it to me when I was a kid and I loved it."

"Same here. Probably one of my all-time favorites." Leroux leaned back. "Man, I can't remember the last time I actually went to a movie theater."

Kane grunted and took a swig of his beer. "Me too, except to kill someone."

Leroux chuckled. "What was playing?"

"Eternals."

"Then he was probably hoping someone would kill him."

Kane laughed. "You're probably right." He picked up his controller. "Call of Duty?"

"Sounds good to me." Leroux's phone rang. He leaned forward to see the call display. "Tommy Granger."

Kane put down the controller. "Are you two friends?"

Leroux picked up his phone from the table. "No."

"Then it must be an emergency. Where are the professors?"

Leroux chuckled then accepted the call. "Hello?"

"Hi, Mr. Leroux. This is Tommy Granger. Sorry for calling this late."

Leroux glanced at the time, his eyebrows shooting up. His girlfriend, CIA Operations Officer Sherrie White, and Kane's girlfriend, ex-Chinese Special Forces Operator Lee Fang, were on an overnight trip to a spa where they were being pampered and spoiled. It meant beer, pizza, and video games for their partners. "No problem, I'm awake. What's going on?"

"A weird one, sir. I'm here with Professors Acton and Palmer."

Leroux's eyebrows shot up and he put the call on speaker. "You said you're with them?"

"Yes."

"So, they haven't got themselves knee-deep in some shit somewhere in the world?"

"No, sir, it's not like that this time. You are aware that Professor Palmer's brother, Charles Palmer, died ten years ago at a dig site in Jordan?"

Leroux remembered reading the file, though few of the details. "Yes, I'm aware of it."

"Well, sir, I've come across a photograph taken of him years after his death. It has to be a fake, but I can't find any evidence that it is. Can I send it to you so you can use your tools to examine it?"

Kane leaned forward. "Wait a minute. Tommy, this is Dylan. Did you call on an open line, or did you use the encrypted network?"

"Open line. I didn't think there was anything classified about this."

Kane cursed. "Send the file through the encrypted network, then whatever you do, don't talk about what you found, don't even mention his name on any open line or any non-encrypted form of communication. Understood?"

Tommy's response dripped with fear. "Y-yes, sir. Why? What's going on?"

"I'll tell you when I see you in person." Kane reached forward and ended the call. "This isn't good."

"What do you mean?" asked Leroux, confused.

"I've read the classified file. You obviously haven't."

"I've read the file on him. He was a remarkable man, but I don't remember there being anything worth getting excited about ten years later."

Kane shook his head. "You don't understand. This guy has a top-secret dossier that not a lot of people have seen. The Chief showed it to me when we started dealing with the professors, just in case something odd ever came up."

"Odd?"

"Charles Palmer is supposed to be dead, but they never found his body, so that means he could still be alive. In his classified file, he's not listed as dead, he's listed as missing."

"Why would they do that? I seem to remember the witness accounts being pretty clear."

"Oh, according to all the witnesses, he's absolutely dead. He died in a tunnel collapse, but the Jordanians shut everything down almost immediately and nobody's been allowed back since to recover the body. If it were anybody else, our government would have simply closed the file on him. After all, he's a British citizen, not American, but what most people don't realize, and I'm willing to bet that includes his sister, is that he was working on a project using quantum computing technology that was way ahead of its time. The CIA got someone inside his private lab just before he died, and our analysts who examined what they found came to the conclusion that he was about to make a breakthrough that could change everything."

Leroux's eyes narrowed. "In what way?"

"You know how most people think that once we have a functioning quantum computer, because it would be so fast, it would be able to brute force attack any computer system and break people's passwords?"

"Yes, I'm aware of most people's misconception."

"Good. Then you understand it's not actually passwords that are the issue. It's encryption."

"Of course. With quantum computing's speed combined with its use of qubits, it could quickly break any encryption. And once that's broken, you don't need passwords. You can read anything they send or receive."

"Exactly. All encryption protocols, government, banking, anything, could be broken with little effort. Whoever gets their hands on this first could gain access to everything, and there's no way we would know it until it was too late. Whoever has that technology first will have an incredible advantage. There's not a government on this planet nor a criminal organization that wouldn't kill to get that tech."

Leroux regarded his friend, his pulse ticking up rapidly. "You're not saying that he invented it?"

Kane shrugged. "The analysts said that if he hadn't invented it, he was about to, and then a few weeks later he was dead." He pointed at the phone. "If Tommy's right and they've found proof that he's alive, then I'm willing to bet that in the past ten years he's not only finished it, he's perfected it."

Leroux's jaw dropped. "Holy shit! Are you saying he faked his death so that he could finish his work without anyone knowing?"

Kane held up his hands. "No idea. But if there's even the slightest chance he's alive, we need to find him first, because God help us all if the Chinese or Russians get their hands on him. What he was working on could change the balance of power. Permanently."

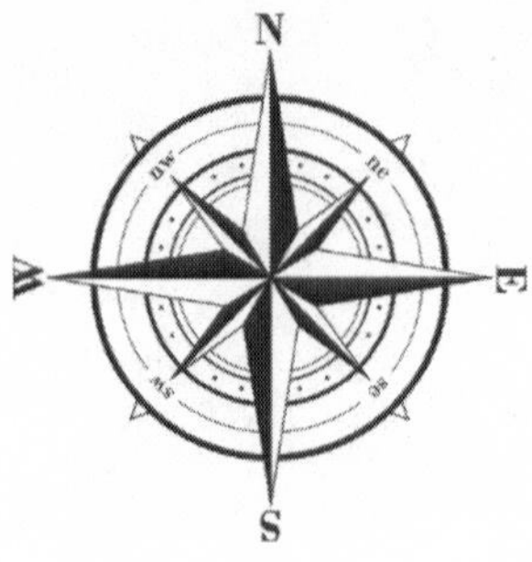

Acton/Palmer Residence, Overlook Village Gated Community

St. Paul, Maryland

Tommy put his phone down on the table and pushed away from it as if it were dangerous.

Acton eyed him. "What's wrong?"

"Dylan was there. He asked if I called on an open line or an encrypted line, and then wasn't happy when he heard it was open."

Laura eyed him, puzzled. "Why would he care about that?"

"I'm not sure, but it has to do with your brother. He said we shouldn't make any mention of him on any open line or open form of communication."

Mai leaned closer to Tommy, taking his hand. "What do you think is going on? You've worked with them before."

"I'm not sure, but we've been looking at this from the perspective of Laura's brother being alive and how that's a great thing. We haven't really been looking at it from the perspective of what are the implications."

Acton had to agree with his young friend. They had been blinded by the mystery, the intrigue, the possibility of a loved one lost actually being alive. But no one was questioning why or, more importantly, what it meant. "You're right. Let's think about this logically and not emotionally. Let's assume he is alive."

Tommy jerked forward. "Oops. They wanted me to send them the photo through the encrypted network."

"Do it."

Tommy went to work as Acton continued his train of thought. "Let's assume he's alive and ignore the remote possibility that this is all innocent, he somehow lost his memory, yada, yada, yada. If he's alive, then he faked his own death."

"But he wouldn't do that to me," repeated Laura.

Acton reached out and took his wife's hand, squeezing it gently. "He would if it meant not doing so would put you in danger."

"In danger?"

"Yes. You don't fake your own death for trivial reasons. You fake it because you want other people to think you're dead so that they stop pursuing you. Creditors, ex-wives, government, law enforcement, whatever. You only fake your death to get away. So, we know he wasn't in trouble with the law. He didn't owe people money. He had no ex-wives or family that he wanted to escape. That leaves governments and criminal organizations. And Tommy, you said he was working on quantum computing. That deals with encryption, right?"

"Well, it can, yes. The theory is that the very nature of quantum computing and the pure horsepower behind it could render modern encryption obsolete."

"Could he have created a device that could do such a thing?"

Tommy smirked. "What? Like in Sneakers?"

Acton ignored the attitude. "Exactly."

"Well, no. Well, I guess that's not right. Let's just put it this way, if he's invented a machine that's the size of an old-style answering machine, no, I don't think so, though if he has, that would be unbelievably incredible. More likely, if he has invented something, it's either a methodology that could be built using quantum computing, or if he has been working on it for the past ten years, he could have actually built a quantum computer capable of doing what we're talking about, though I doubt it's fitting inside of anyone's briefcase anytime soon."

"But the size of it doesn't matter, right?"

"No. As long as it can connect to the Internet, it can tap any feed anywhere in the world, crack its encryption, potentially in a matter of hours, at most days, then read any of the traffic it wants."

Laura, working her phone the entire time, wagged it. "But it says here that the whole idea of quantum computing rendering passwords obsolete is nonsense. Any type of brute force attack would be detected and most password systems lock you out after five tries. So how would my brother's system deal with that?"

"That's a common misconception. People are confusing passwords for encryption. A password prevents you from getting past a certain point in a computer system. Encryption scrambles the data from point

A to point B so that nobody can read it. You need the key to unscramble the data. Those keys are based on mathematical formulas. Crack the formula with quantum computing, you don't need the password. You break a company's encryption, you have access to everything. And then here's the beauty part, once you have access to their system, you have access to all their passwords. You can pull those passwords even if they're hashed, brute-force those on your own computer with nobody detecting it, and then you have full access as if you're the user. Then not only can you monitor all their data, you can enter their system through the front door and do whatever you want. Read information, insert information, transfer money, whatever."

Tommy leaned back, folding his arms. "Man, I tell you, if I had something like this back in my hacking days, I could have created havoc. If this exists, if the wrong people get their hands on it…" He didn't finish his thought and instead just shook his head. But he didn't need to. It was obvious what he was saying. This was extremely dangerous technology and if Charles Palmer had indeed invented it, they were all in danger.

"What do we do now?" asked Laura, her voice quavering with emotion.

Acton faced her. "That depends."

"On what?"

"Do you want to play it safe or do you want to find out the truth?"

She stared at them. "What do you think?"

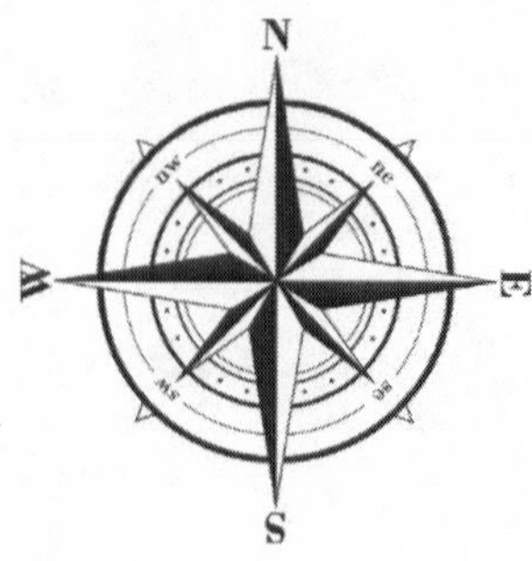

Leroux/White Residence, Fairfax Towers

Falls Church, Virginia

Leroux stared at the photo of Charles Palmer standing in front of a theater playing a movie that didn't come out until years after his death. "It has to be fake."

Kane shrugged. "You tell me, you're the expert."

Leroux dismissed his laptop with a flick of the wrist. "This isn't going to tell us anything. If whoever did it is halfway good at their job, I won't be able to tell. And the fact that Tommy wasn't able to after his own analysis tells me that either this is a really good fake or it's the genuine article."

"Then I think we'd better get some more powerful computers on this."

Leroux chewed his cheek for a moment. "Do you mean your ops center?"

"No. Even my systems are probably not powerful enough, and we don't have time to waste. The moment I was exposed to this information, my orders kicked in."

"What do you mean?"

"I mean, this is not a favor for a friend. This is now an official government operation. The United States has to obtain this technology before anyone else. You call the Chief and get your team activated and assigned this case." Kane rose and headed for the door.

"Where are you going?"

"I'm calling the girls back and getting our asses to Maryland. The professors are going to need security, and the sooner I get there the better, because if I know them, they're not just going to sit back at home and wait."

Leroux grunted. "You're probably right about that."

Kane gripped the doorknob then pointed at Leroux. "And make sure when you call the Chief, it's on an encrypted line."

"Of course." Kane left and Leroux paused as he thought about the implications of what was happening. If Palmer had indeed continued his work for the past decade, encryption might already be obsolete.

And they just didn't know it yet.

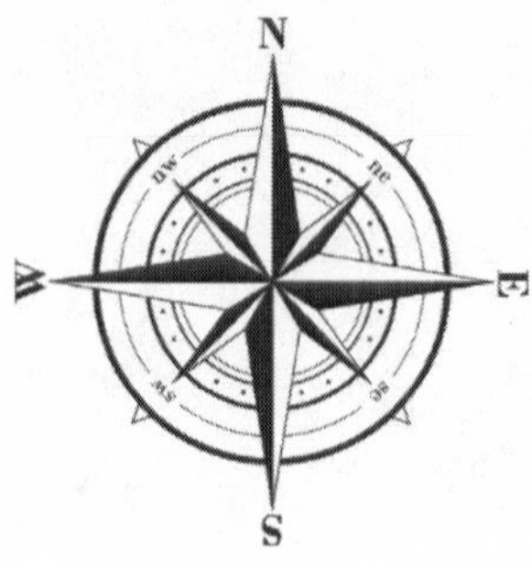

Acton/Palmer Residence, Overlook Village Gated Community

St. Paul, Maryland

"Dubai."

Acton looked up at Tommy from the tablet he had been staring at, scanning through hundreds of photos, searching for any anomalies. It was like looking for a needle in a haystack. "Are you sure?"

"Yes, the photo was taken in Dubai. Almost three years to the day after he died."

"Okay, now we have a date and place to work from. Can you tweak your algorithm to only look for photos from, let's say, two weeks before that onward, concentrating on Dubai?"

"Yes, but it's going to reduce the pool dramatically, especially for the geolocation. It would have to be set in the metadata." Tommy started working his keyboard then paused. "Um, are we good with using the university's resources?"

Acton thought about Kane's warning. "We're not using his name, are we?"

"I was, but I dropped that and now I'm just using the facial recognition component. No one should know because I grab the photo, pull it down, then do the analysis locally. Unless they've got access to one of our systems and know his facial recognition points, no one should know what we're doing. How hard do you want me to hit the network?"

Laura put her own tablet down. "What do you mean?"

"Well, I've just been having it run in the background using up no more than twenty percent of the bandwidth."

Acton checked his watch. "At this time of night and it being the weekend, there should be hardly anybody there. I say crank it up."

"That's going to set off some alarms. Whoever's on call for IT support will be notified."

"That's not you?"

"Not this weekend."

Acton cursed. "Do it, but I'll call Greg and let him know what's going on."

Laura reached out and grabbed his wrist. "But what about what Dylan said?"

"I'll be as vague as possible."

Tommy continued his assault on his keyboard. "This is where I'd kill to have the resources of the CIA. They could get done in hours what will take us days."

Acton rose, grabbing his cellphone. "Yeah, but what you find, we know about. What they find, they'll keep to themselves."

Laura leaned back, her arms folded. "You really think Dylan would hide that from us?"

"He might not have a choice. At best, he might tell us something, but we'll never see it." He headed into the next room, dialing his best friend's number. Gregory Milton, Dean of St. Paul's University, answered on the third ring, sounding a little groggy.

"Hello?"

"Hey, buddy, you hammered or did I wake you?"

"A little bit of column A, a little bit of column B."

Acton chuckled. "Listen, I need a favor with no questions."

Milton's voice perked up. "What's going on?"

"We're going to be using the university's computers for some pretty intensive number-crunching, shall we say. It's going to chew up a lot of bandwidth and horsepower, so your IT guys are going to be getting alerts. I need you to tell them that everything's all right and to just let it go."

"Just what kind of number-crunching are we talking about?"

"I can't say, but Tommy's the one taking care of everything on this end, so you know you can trust him."

Milton groaned. "Is this going to get the university in trouble?"

"I can't see how."

"Where are you?"

"Our place."

"And you can't tell me what this is all about?"

"Not over the phone."

Milton sighed. "Fine. I'll be there in twenty minutes."

"I thought you said you were drunk."

Milton grunted. "I just said that so I didn't have to admit I went to bed at nine on a Friday."

Acton laughed. "You're getting old, buddy."

"You have no idea."

Milton ended the call and Acton headed back into the room with the others. "Greg's going to call off the hounds and join us in about twenty minutes."

Laura's eyebrows rose. "Really? Wouldn't it be better if we kept the group tight? The fewer who know the better."

"Well, we're using his computer infrastructure, so if we want him to cooperate, we're going to have to let him in. Besides, we know we can trust him. He won't go blabbing about it to anyone."

Mai took a sip of her water. "Why are we being so paranoid? I mean, it's been ten years and nothing's happened. Why would we think anything's going to happen now? We discovered that he might still be alive, but no one else knows. Well, except for, I guess, the CIA now, but who are they going to tell?"

Tommy continued to work his laptop. "You don't understand, hon. If anybody out there suspected he might still be alive, they'd be monitoring for any activity." He raised his hand and circled a finger. "For all we know, this place is bugged, just waiting for any conversation about him. The phones could be tapped, cellphones could be cloned."

Acton tensed. "Do you really think so?"

Tommy shrugged. "I'd guess our phones are fine. I know mine is because I check on a daily basis. And with your CIA connections, I have no doubt they regularly inspect your lines to make sure there's nothing out of the ordinary. Bugs, however, have to be scanned for. We should arrange for that to be looked into ASAP, but if we ignore all that, when I was putting together that montage, I was using his name as a possible filter in addition to the facial recognition points. That means hundreds of thousands of queries went out from dozens of computers over a three-week period that included his name in a lot of the searches. That's going to trigger the trending algorithms. I doubt his name would've come up on any of the top ten lists, but the system would've noticed, and I was hitting search engines all around the world. And the type of people that would be looking for him would be governments. If the Chinese, let's say, had managed to get some sort of tap inside Google, for example, they might have already been alerted."

"So, what you're saying is that they might already know that he's alive?"

Tommy paused. "Not necessarily that he's alive, but that somebody's paying an awful lot of attention to a guy who's been dead for ten years. It might make them wonder why and start to look into things themselves."

Laura pointed at the laptop. "Then maybe we shouldn't be pushing our luck."

Tommy disagreed. "Like I said, I'm not using his name this time. Purely facial recognition. I'm not searching for him in a conventional sense, I'm crawling the web randomly as opposed to using search engine results to trigger starting points. It's a lot less efficient, a lot slower, but a lot safer."

Laura shivered, gripping her shoulders and rubbing. "It doesn't feel safer."

Tommy leaned away from his keyboard. "Should I stop?"

"No. I have to know. Keep doing what you're doing, but let's just be careful about it." She glanced about. "Maybe we should turn on the security system."

Acton rose. "I'll take care of it." He headed for the hallway and activated the perimeter security, wishing he had something a little more robust that included hardened elements rather than just sensors. He returned to the table and sat. "You know, there's one person who might be able to help us."

Laura regarded him, her head slowly bobbing. "I assume you're talking about Hugh?"

"You know he'd want to be involved."

Laura tapped her chin. "I don't know if that's such a good idea. If there's one organization that would be infiltrated, it's Interpol."

Mai stared at her. "Why would you say that? Aren't they police?"

"They're police from all around the world. That includes countries like China and Russia. He wouldn't be able to do any official investigation. Not even a query. Just pulling a file on a man who's been dead for ten years could be all it takes. We can't risk it."

Acton sighed. "You're right, but he's going to kill us when this is all over."

Laura started to say something then stopped, her mouth agape. She turned to Tommy. "I have a search criterion for you that might speed things up."

Tommy frowned. "Like I said, that could be monitored. I can't use his name."

She dismissed his concern. "Forget his name. Search for the latest Terminator movie. He would never miss seeing it, and the more recent you get, the more random photos there are posted on social media. He could be caught in the background again."

Tommy smiled. "Terminator: Dark Fate. I love it. That's perfect." He tapped away at his keyboard and hit the final key with a flourish. "That's going to narrow this down dramatically."

"Now what do we do?" asked Mai.

"We wait."

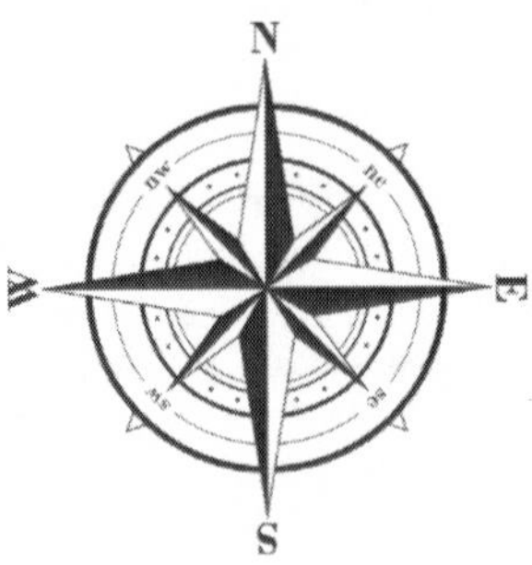

The Ritz-Carlton

McLean, Virginia

CIA Operations Officer Sherrie White sat cross-legged on the floor at the foot of her bed, sorting a handful of cards she had just been dealt by Lee Fang, probably the best female friend she had ever had, a former Chinese Special Forces officer now living in exile in the United States. If circumstances were different, the two of them might be trying to kill each other. Instead, they were overnighting at a luxury spa and now sharing a room and playing cards while gossiping and doing battle with a bottle of 18-year-old single malt scotch.

"You know, once I figure out this game, I'm going to win all my money back."

Fang grinned at her. "You're already into me for a quarter of a million. You better start learning fast. Something tells me you can't cover your markers."

Sherrie put down two cards and to her dismay, Fang snatched them up. Sherrie frowned. "Is this some sort of trick deck?"

"No." Fang gestured toward the window. "But there is a reason I have your back facing slightly opened curtains. Jill Masterson is reading your cards to me. It makes things much easier."

Sherrie couldn't resist glancing over her shoulder to find the curtains closed.

Fang snorted. "I can't believe you actually looked."

Sherrie shrugged. "Comes with the territory. We spies are naturally distrustful." She flashed a toothy smile. "Especially when we're in the hole a quarter of a million."

Fang shrugged. "You're the one who kept saying double or nothing."

"Yeah, it didn't seem like such a stupid idea when we started at a buck."

Fang's phone rang and she leaned over, glancing at the call display. "Huh."

Sherrie eyed her. "What?"

"It's coming through Dylan's secure network."

Sherrie eyed the scotch. "I hope he's not calling with a math question."

Fang snickered and took the call. "Hello, darling, can I put you on speaker so Sherrie can hear?" Fang's smile disappeared and Sherrie grew concerned. "Uh-huh. Yes, I understand, Maryland." Fang eyed the scotch. "Yes…about a quarter of the way through a twenty-sixer…we'll take an Uber, see you soon." She ended the call and sighed.

"What's wrong?"

"You know Professor Laura Palmer's brother?"

"Never met him."

"I'd be surprised if you did. He's been dead for ten years."

"Then what about him?"

"Apparently he might not be dead, and if he's not, there could be very serious consequences."

"Meaning?"

Fang shrugged as she rose. "Dylan wouldn't say over the phone, but he sounded serious."

"What does he need us for?"

"He wants us to join him to provide security for the professors."

"Sounds like fun." Sherrie corked the scotch. "Good thing we're only one sheet to the wind instead of three."

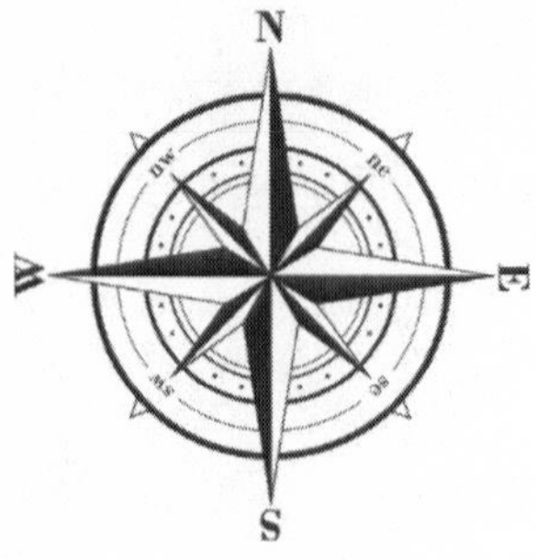

Morrison Residence

River Oaks Drive, McLean, Virginia

CIA National Clandestine Service Chief Leif Morrison entered the coded sequence into his phone, his curiosity consuming him. Chris Leroux was one of his top people, not in the hierarchy of the Agency, but in his opinion of people's capabilities. He had been one of his top analysts, a little too bookish, but Morrison had recognized his potential and pushed him into the analyst supervisor role at a very young age, perhaps too soon, but the young man had grown into it and was now thriving. Leroux was the type of person he could see occupying the Chief's position someday, and for him to call at this hour on a Friday night insisting on a scrambled line, meant something big was up.

Morrison checked the status indicator. "I'm green on this end."

"So am I," replied Leroux. "Are you alone?"

Morrison already knew the answer to the question but checked over both shoulders regardless. "Yes."

"I got a call from Tommy Granger a short while ago. He was putting together a montage for the tenth anniversary of Professor Palmer's brother's death."

"Charles Palmer?"

"Yes."

Just the mere mention of the name had Morrison's attention—he had read the file that he was certain Leroux hadn't. "I'm listening."

"Tommy found photographic evidence that suggests Palmer's brother isn't dead."

"Holy shit!" exclaimed Morrison. "Have we confirmed this?"

"Not yet."

"How contained is this?"

"It's hard to say."

"From a 'heard it from someone's lips' standpoint."

"Very. But we have no idea about electronic monitoring, intercepts. Anything is possible."

"So, the fact he's alive might not be contained?"

"It might not be. How concerned should we be?"

Morrison leaned back, scratching his chin. "Very. I need you to call in your team, get an ops center up and running, and start chasing this down. We need to know if Charles Palmer is alive, and if he is, we need to be the ones that bring him in. Our country's very future might depend on it."

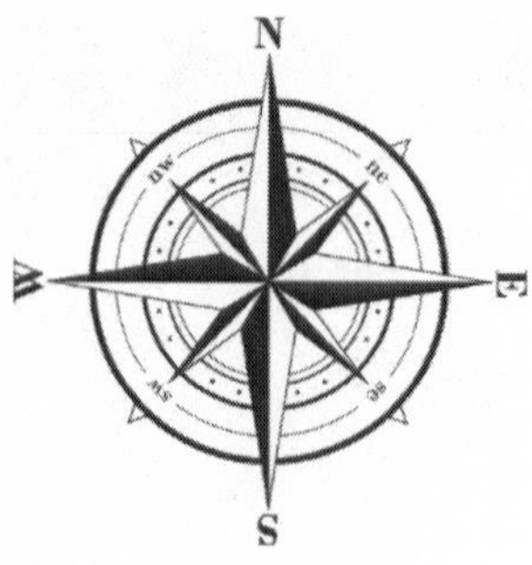

Lot Residence

Sodom

1649 BC

Lot lay on his back with Idit draped over him, both their bodies covered in sweat and lust. "That was unbelievable," he gasped. "I didn't know it could be that way."

She kissed him. "Neither did I. Do you think it was a sin?"

He stared into her eyes and thought about it for a moment. He wasn't sure. They were husband and wife, and nothing they had done went against what was taught at Temple, though such things weren't spoken of, so how could he possibly know whether anything they had done was frowned upon in the eyes of God? He finally shrugged. "I think anything between a husband and wife that brings them both pleasure without hurting anyone else would make God happy."

She grinned. "Thank God you said that. We are definitely doing that again."

He laughed. "Whenever you want."

She hopped out of bed and grabbed her wrap. "I have to get to work. I need to find that list of names Canaan gave me. I want to see if I can work them all in this time." She patted his cheek. "Since I'll have two more faces that I can use."

He rose. "I better get back to the shop. Despite this commission, the steady money comes from our regular customers." He washed up and dressed then stepped into his wife's studio, spotting a piece of parchment sitting on her worktable with a list of names as she drew on a new vase. He scanned the list, his eyebrows shooting up at some of the names, almost all of whom he recognized. There were some husbands and wives, though perhaps that wasn't the best way to characterize this list. They were all husbands and wives, just not each other's, save a few. The rest were all married men and women whose spouses were not on the list.

It was scandalous.

Even in a city such as Sodom. There were names here of the elite of the city, the ruling class, and if the wives of some of these men knew what they were up to, and perhaps more shockingly, if the men of some of these wives knew what they were up to, it could rock the city to its core.

He smiled slightly.

"What's on your mind, husband?"

"Nothing, just thinking of earlier."

She reached over and squeezed his bum. "Perhaps tonight we'll enjoy ourselves once again."

He leaned over and gave her a kiss. "I can't wait." He headed out the door and into the shop with a slight smile that had nothing to do with the incredible sexual experience he had just had and would have again tonight. He had a list of names, and once his wife completed the vase, he would have a visual image that even though it was merely a recreation of an event, it would have anyone who saw it unable to rid their memory of it. That list, if made public, could be just what he had been searching for.

Something that would shock the leaders of this treacherous society into action.

When husbands and wives of the city's most powerful discovered how deeply sin had penetrated their own homes, it could be the catalyst for change they so desperately needed.

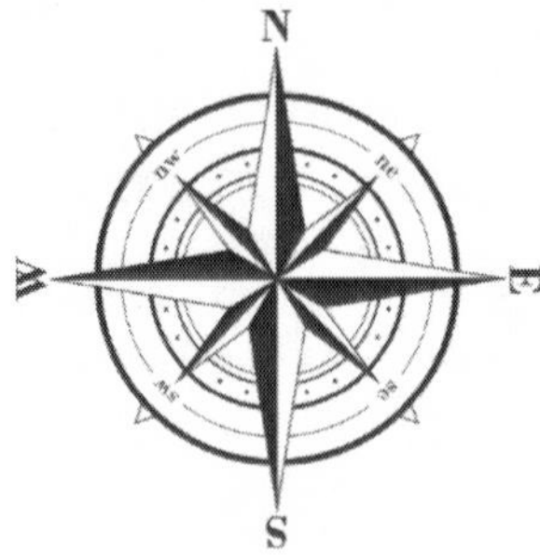

Winters Residence, Knightsbridge

London, England

Present Day

Mary Winters bolted upright in bed and looked about. The room was pitch black, just the way she liked it. Her days working for British Intelligence in MI6 had her sleeping in all manner of conditions, but now that she had left the agency behind, she enjoyed her creature comforts. Officially, she was a travel agent. In reality, she was much more, and what nobody realized was that she had only two clients. Laura Palmer was one of them, and the only one of the three people in this equation ignorant of the truth.

Twelve years ago, MI6 had assigned her a case involving a mega-millionaire genius named Charles Palmer. She was sent in to gain his trust and figure out just what he was up to and whether the rumors were true that he was working on a quantum computing device that could break pretty much any encryption out there. She had gained his trust by seducing him, but made the mistake of falling in love, an absolute no-no in her business. She had determined that he hadn't created such a device, but he was close, very close, and the ramifications of his success would be felt the world over if it fell into the wrong hands.

With her mission complete, she had ended things with him, breaking both their hearts, but worse was that he had discovered the truth of who she was. She had never wanted to hurt him, but honey traps were part of the business. Yet you weren't supposed to fall in love. It was just something about Palmer that was so compelling. He was the most intelligent man she had ever met, but he was also attractive, funny, and so attentive. When you were with him, he made you feel like you were the only person in the world, and she liked that. He was like no other man she had ever met, which is why it had hurt so much and she'd demanded she no longer be assigned such missions in the future.

And when he had called her two years later, begging her for help, there was no way she could say no.

And it had changed her life entirely.

She grabbed her phone off the nightstand, the device once again demanding her attention. It was an alert from one of the monitors she had set up. She stretched and groaned, then headed for her office, her bare feet cool on the stone floors of her luxury condo in London's tony Knightsbridge district. It was far more than someone like her could afford, but it was a gift from her benefactor, the keys delivered to her the day she retired from MI6.

She sat in her Herman Miller Aeron chair, the mesh hugging her slender, nearly naked frame as she logged into her system. She brought up the alert and cursed as her heart raced. Someone was looking into her second client far more closely than they should for a dead man.

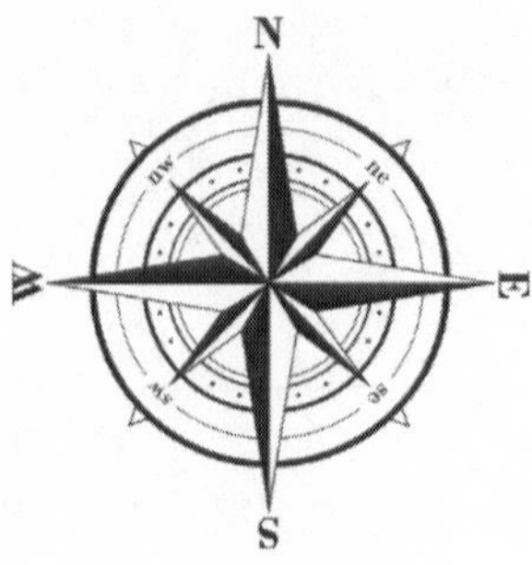

Ministry of State Security

Beijing, China

Assistant Director Yan Shengtao glanced at his screen and brought up the priority alert. He'd only been in his new position for a week, assistant director of cyber security, a respectable job in the Chinese government hierarchy, though it came with little power, and power was what he craved. With power came freedom, came wealth, came security. He had to distinguish himself and do so rapidly so he could become the next director. That was when things would really change for him and he wouldn't have to deal with such petty things as these constant alerts set up by his predecessor.

He brought up the latest indicating unusual search activity on a priority target named Charles Palmer. Who the hell was Charles Palmer? He popped over to the classified database he'd only had access to since starting his new position. It was fascinating what he had been exposed to so far. The government had files on tens of millions of foreign nationals and, depending on how important they were, those details covered every aspect of their lives. The dirt they had on politicians, military officers, police officers, teachers, everyone, was stunning, all sitting there waiting to be exploited should the Chinese people ever require something these people could offer.

He brought up Charles Palmer, quickly scanning the file, his eyes widening with each paragraph. He reread it, slower this time. The man was considered a genius, a technical wizard specializing in artificial intelligence and quantum computing. It was suspected he was working on a device capable of cracking all current encryption protocols. Orders had been given to kidnap him and steal the technology for the benefit of the Chinese people, but he had died before the mission could be completed.

Ten years ago.

Yan leaned back in his chair, his fingers drumming on the armrests. Why would somebody ten years later be hitting every search engine in the world? Could it just be that it had been ten years, so there was renewed interest? He brought up the report and dismissed the idea. There were hundreds of thousands of hits. That wasn't a reporter putting together a retrospective—these were computers programmed to execute the searches and gather the results. But to what end? And again, why ten years later? Perhaps someone with deep pockets had decided to pursue his research and was hoping to find obscure references or research papers.

He pulled the alert back up and took a deeper dive into the details. The searches had been going on for weeks, and the automated analysis showed the vast majority of the traffic was generated from a university in the United States, though there were several other computers outside of that network that also appeared to be involved. He brought up the information on the institution. St. Paul's University in Maryland. He'd never heard of it. He pulled up an analysis done several years ago as a matter of routine that classified the institution as one of little strategic importance. It wasn't known as a research center. It appeared more designed to give students a solid foundation, then they would later head to more prestigious schools to pursue postgraduate degrees. There was no evidence that this school was pursuing any type of work in quantum computing, an expensive endeavor.

He continued reading the file then stopped as he scanned a list of prominent professors calling St. Paul's home.

James Acton.

He bristled as he read the name, the memories of the incident last year flooding back, the death of his brother, the humiliation. He was certain it would end his career when Acton and his wife had escaped, but instead, those events had been purged from the records. Everything was blamed on his boss, who had perished at the hands of a traitor that had never been identified. It meant the Party put forward a fall guy, the events purged, leaving him with a clean record again, allowing him to continue his career, his climb up the ladder only slightly delayed.

He gasped and his jaw dropped as his brain finally made the connection.

Laura Palmer.

He quickly brought up the file on Charles Palmer and laughed aloud. Laura Palmer was his sister. He leaned back, folding his arms, staring at a photo in the dossier of them together. There was now a connection from Charles Palmer leading to James Acton. James Acton was the head of archaeology at St. Paul's University. St. Paul's University was a source of an Internet search on Palmer's brother. This new connection unfortunately suggested this could simply be related to the ten-year anniversary. Perhaps someone at the university was putting together a presentation in his honor. He frowned, his visions of propelling his career forward slowly disappearing.

He brought the analysis back up. The system suggested 10-20% of the university's bandwidth had been chewed up over a three-week period ending yesterday, with most of it capping out at 10% during the day. He scratched his chin. It was as if whoever was running the search was trying not to trip any indicators in their IT department. His eyes narrowed. A massive amount of data had been pulled down over weeks. This wasn't search engine results. It was too large for that. Text didn't take up much bandwidth. This had to be images and video. But why?

He sighed. Again, it suggested something being put together for the anniversary of the man's death. Images were what would be wanted, not text. But why hide this? And why the massive volume of data?

He cursed and pushed back from his desk. Nobody was hiding anything. Whoever was putting it together probably had permission to use the university's resources as long as it didn't affect the functioning of the network, so whatever was used was capped at 10% during the day and 20% at night. At worst, the network might seem a little sluggish.

According to the file, Acton was a big deal at this university, which meant his wife was as well. So, something big done for the tenth anniversary of Charles Palmer's death was certainly possible. Yet he wanted these two. They were responsible for the biggest embarrassment of his career, despite it being buried. He needed proof that this was nothing, and the key had to lie with those other computers. He clicked on the link for the most active one, the system automatically launching a search, and he was surprised at the result.

Singapore?

It had to be a mistake. He clicked the link again, and the system searched once more. Japan. He pulled closer to his keyboard, clicking again. Egypt. France. Canada.

There was no way the system was so wrong. It meant whoever owned that computer was using a virtual private network or some other means to disguise their true location, and that raised all kinds of red flags. Just who the hell was at the other end, and why were they so intent on hiding where they were if they were merely putting together a memorial for a man dead ten years?

He grabbed his phone. It was time to take a much deeper dive.

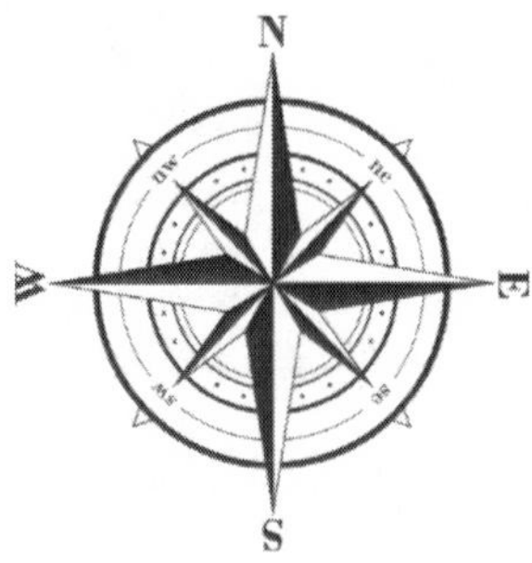

Acton/Palmer Residence, Overlook Village Gated Community

St. Paul, Maryland

Tommy's hands jerked away as an alert sounded.

Acton flinched at the high-pitched alarm. "What the hell was that?"

"Somebody's trying to locate me."

"What?"

"Well, since I started doing work for the CIA, I've made sure I've had top-level security installed on all my equipment. It makes it look like I'm in different parts of the world every time someone tries to ping me, but I also get an alert if someone's trying to find out where I am."

"Has this ever happened before?"

The alarm sounded again.

"Every once in a while, but only once. I've never had it happen twice in a row." The alarm sounded a third time and Tommy's eyebrows shot up. "Holy shit, three times." The laptop protested several more times. "Somebody's really after me."

"Shut it down," ordered Acton.

Tommy reached forward and held in the power button, killing the laptop. A moment later, he raised his hands and pushed back from the table, his mouth agape. "What the hell just happened?"

"Somebody's obviously looking for you."

Laura pinched the bridge of her nose, squeezing her eyes shut. "We should have just left well enough alone."

Acton tapped the table. "But this doesn't make sense. You said the searches you're doing don't have anything that would link you to her brother."

"They don't. They didn't. I was searching for Terminator: Dark Fate. His name wasn't involved at all."

"Then maybe this has nothing to do with what you're doing right now," suggested Acton. "Maybe it was the previous searches."

"Maybe." Tommy pulled back up to the table. "If it was the previous searches, then that means whoever is looking for me has access to the raw results. Only those would have my IP address."

"So, someone or some piece of software deep in the bowels of Google, for example, flagged your searches and got your IP address?"

"It's the only thing that makes sense."

Laura clasped her hands. "Thank God you have that software installed. Otherwise, they'd know where we are."

Tommy was about to agree then stopped himself.

Acton picked up on it. "What?"

Tommy shifted uncomfortably. "Well, I have this software installed on all *my* devices, but the bulk of the searching was done at the university.

Anybody worth their salt will know within moments where all those searches were coming from."

Acton tensed. "And if we're talking about the type of people I think we are, it won't take them long to put together the fact that his sister lives only a few miles from the university."

Mai's eyes widened. "If they think he's alive…"

Laura gripped Acton's hand. "They'll be coming."

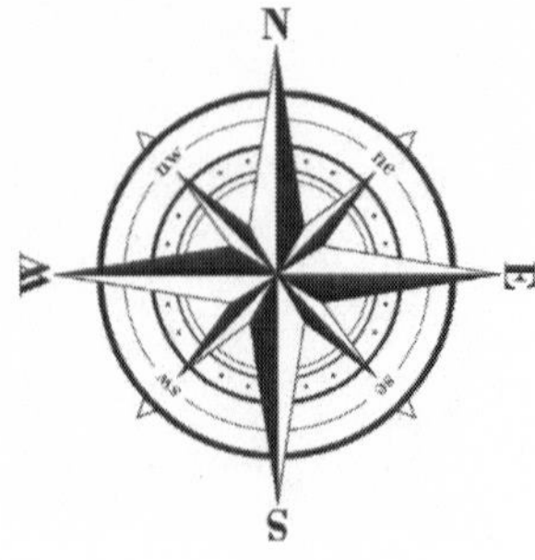

Idit's Studio

Sodom

1649 BC

Idit carefully painted in the figures she had drawn. Her heart was racing with the eroticism of it all as she recreated what her husband had destroyed. When Canaan had described what he wanted, her skin had crawled. He was a pig, what he described disgusting filth, depraved. But as she had translated his descriptions into images, it had become exciting, titillating. She had been ashamed of how it made her feel, but when she had put her face and Lot's on two of the figures, it had been transformative. Her mind was alive with the images and she couldn't stop thinking about what it would be like to do such things with her husband.

Then the stray thought had entered her mind. What would it be like to participate in something like this, an orgy of passion and lust where one's own pleasure was all that one was concerned with? Sex to her had always been a chore. She enjoyed it to a point and wanted to make her husband happy, so never denied him. But what they had done the past several days had been unlike anything she had ever felt. The rapture her body experienced at the wickedness of it all was shocking. She had heard tell of orgasmic explosions but had never experienced them before.

It had changed her.

She wanted more. Lot seemed eager and willing, and she was certain he could satisfy these needs since he appeared to take equal pleasure. But as the party grew nearer, she found herself wondering what it would be like to commit to five times the commission just this once.

But Lot would never go for it.

She leaned back, examining her handiwork.

Maybe I can convince him to let me go alone.

Her jaw dropped and her eyes shot wide at the thought. She was a married, pious woman. To think such things was sinful. She put her brush down and closed her eyes and prayed for forgiveness. Lot was right. As long as sinful temptations were so readily at hand, Sodom stood no chance. She had to get control of herself and she begged God for the strength to resist that which she had never known she desired.

And to send her husband help, for this was a battle he couldn't fight alone.

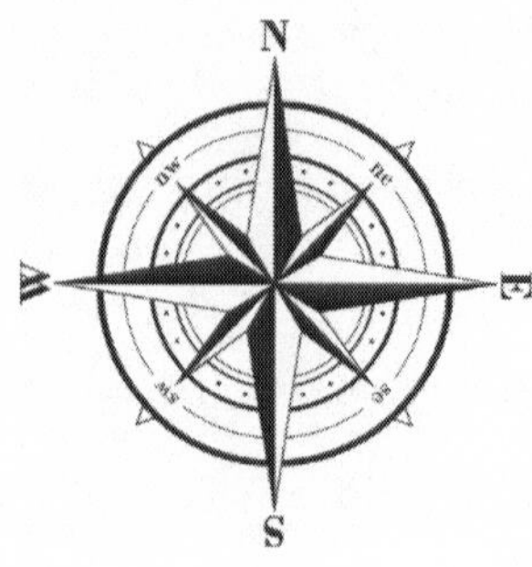

Operations Center 2, CIA Headquarters

Langley, Virginia

Present Day

Leroux stepped through the security door to the state-of-the-art operations center located on one of the sublevels of CIA Headquarters in Langley, Virginia. He smiled at the waving Sonya Tong, his second-in-command a woman he held in high esteem, whom he was aware had feelings for him that could never be reciprocated as long as Sherrie was in his life.

"How did you get in here before me?"

She shrugged. "It helps when you have no life."

Leroux laughed. "If Dylan hadn't been with me, I probably would've been in here sooner."

The door opened behind him and Randy Child, the team's tech wunderkind, entered. "You know, I can think of better places to be on a Friday night."

Marc Therrien, a constant thorn in Child's side, delivered a retort from the back of the room. "You can think of them, but you're never actually there."

Child flipped a bird as Leroux made his way to his station at the center of the room. More of the team trickled in as he situated himself. He logged in and checked for any urgent messages, both on the CIA network and Kane's private one. Sherrie and Fang had arrived back at their apartment building and they along with Kane would be heading for Maryland any minute now. That meant security for the professors within an hour.

The door hissed open and Danny Packman entered, Leroux's mental tally complete. Several members of the team had replied back that they were in no state for an op, but that they would come in the morning after they had sobered up. He had no problem with that. No one had been on call, and people were supposed to have lives outside of the Agency—he'd rather them not here than here and inebriated.

He entered a coded sequence on his keyboard and a warning indicator beeped. A light above the door turned from green to red as he stood to face his team. "Now that I have your attention," he said with a smirk, "I'll explain why I've ruined your weekend." He brought up the dossier on Charles Palmer and sent it to the main display. "This is Charles Palmer. Some of you may recognize him. He was the brother of our friend, Archaeology Professor Laura Palmer."

Therrien groaned from the back of the room. "How did I know it was going to be them ruining my weekend?"

"An understandable conclusion, though incorrect. This time it's not their fault. Here's the rundown. I'll send you the files but let me make this clear. This is top secret, and I mean it in every sense of the word. You *cannot* repeat this to anyone outside of this room." He pointed at the indicator over the door. "That's why we're in lockdown. If you need to leave, you leave with an armed escort. All devices are being scanned and any unauthorized activity will be strictly dealt with. You'll understand why in a minute. Charles Palmer was not just the brother of Laura Palmer. He was the founder of Palmer Technologies, which he sold a couple of years before his death to Meitner Telecom, a name you might recognize from the incident in Austria a little while back. Palmer died ten years ago in an accident at one of Professor Palmer's dig sites in Jordan. Now, here's the critical component. His body was never recovered. The Jordanians ordered the immediate shutdown of the site and no one's been allowed back since."

He brought up the photo of Palmer at the movie theater. "Facial recognition has confirmed that this is him. We're going to analyze the shit out of this to make sure it's not a fake, but Tommy Granger's already given it more than a once-over and he can't find any obvious evidence. Does anybody notice what's odd about this?"

Child's arm shot up. "Ooh, pick me! Pick me!"

Leroux chuckled. "Yes, Randy?"

"The last time I was at a movie theater, I didn't see a lot of dead people in the audience."

Leroux jabbed a finger at him. "Bingo. You've got it. This photo was taken at a theater playing a movie released years after his death. If it's genuine, it means either he's got a twin that his own sister didn't know about, or he's still alive."

"Why would he fake his death?" asked Tong. "Was somebody after him?"

"And that's the question, isn't it? Why would a man like that fake his death? His classified file, which I've just read for the first time, indicates no criminal history, no debts, no bad romances, no connections with any criminal elements. So why would a man like this fake his death? The conclusion the few of us in the know have come up with is that it has to do with his work."

Child spun in his chair, staring up at the ceiling. "But he sold his work. Isn't he supposed to be retired?"

"No, he apparently sold his company to pursue a passion project. Randy, you'll like this. He specialized in artificial intelligence and quantum computing. A CIA inspection of his private lab just before he died suggests he might have been close to a breakthrough in the latter."

Child's foot dropped, killing his spin. "Holy shit. That's like the holy grail if he's figured it out."

"Figured out what?" asked Tong.

Leroux waved a hand at Child, letting someone answer who understood these things far better than he did. Child eagerly leaned forward. "Well, it's like this. Most encryption systems are based on complex mathematical equations. They're so complex that without the private key to unlock them, they're nearly impossible to break. Our most powerful computers would take millions of years, so that secures our networks. But in theory, because of the potential speeds of quantum computing and how they work in entirely different ways than current computers which are limited to bits which are either zeros or ones, on or off, qubits can exist in three states—"

Tong raised a hand. "Too much detail."

Child's cheeks flushed. "Sorry, I'm just excited. If he's figured it out and come up with a stable quantum computing device that can handle the computations, he's essentially rendered all current encryption obsolete."

Therrien rose, walking down the steps to be in the direct line of the conversation. "So what? My banking password's useless?"

"Forget your banking password. This doesn't deal with passwords. This is encryption. All they need to do is intercept the data. And remember, almost all data is sent out over the open Internet, and it has identifiers saying where it came from and where it's going to in each data packet. Let's say you want to monitor the Federal Reserve to see what they're up to. You just need to know their identifier, which is easy enough to figure out, and then intercept those packages. The bank will never know because they don't care. Even if you intercepted all their data, it's encrypted, impossible to break. But if Palmer's figured it out, then they just run one of these encrypted packets against his system, it figures out the encryption key, then they can instantly read everything that's being sent.

"All emails, all communiques, all data being transferred. Everything. Who needs a password to go through the front door when you've got access to the whole damn house? And remember, no one would ever know, and this is true of any communications, even if it's not over the

Internet. Let's say burst traffic sent by our military through the satellites, those go through the open air. The Chinese intercept that stuff, and it doesn't bother us. It's encrypted. If they had this device, they could read everything. Troop movements, orders. Everything." Child shook his head. "Holy shit. Do we really think he's done this?"

Leroux held up his hands. "No idea. But it is why we think he might have faked his death. If word got out that he had created this or was nearing a breakthrough, there's not a government on the planet that wouldn't kill to get their hands on it. We think he might have faked his death to get away from what was to come."

Therrien perched on the edge of a workstation. "Wait a minute now, you said that we got into his private lab and it looked like he was close to a breakthrough. It's been ten years. Could he have still been working on it?"

"Was Doc Brown happy living a simple life in the old West?"

Child grunted. "All I can say is if I were him, with his brains and resources, I don't care if people thought I was dead. I wouldn't be able to resist continuing my work."

"Even if it was so dangerous?" asked Tong.

Child shrugged. "Somebody has to be first. Better us than them. The sooner we make the breakthrough, the sooner we make the countermeasure. And if I were him and I created this, I'd be hard at work on my next invention, which would be the one that neutralizes the first one."

Leroux ended the speculation. "For the moment, what he has or hasn't accomplished is irrelevant. Randy, we need to have that photo analyzed to see if there's any evidence of it being a fake, but in the meantime, we're going to assume it's not. I want every bit of horsepower this agency can muster searching for any more images that might have Palmer in them. We need to find him before anyone else does."

Therrien scratched behind his ear. "What's the urgency? He's been dead ten years and nobody's found him. Why all of a sudden has this become an emergency?"

"Because you haven't asked the all-important question."

"Which is?"

Leroux jerked a thumb over his shoulder at the photo of Palmer at the movies. "Where did we get that photo?"

Therrien's eyebrows shot up. "Where *did* you get that photo?"

"Tommy Granger was putting together a montage in honor of the tenth anniversary of Palmer's death as a gift for Laura. He commandeered all of the networked computers at St. Paul's University and had them running searches using Palmer's name, then used the results as jumping-off points for bots he created to crawl and pull any images that would then be analyzed by a program he wrote to see if Palmer's face was in any of them."

Child whistled appreciatively. "Damn, that guy's brilliant. He should be working for us."

Leroux agreed. "And if it weren't for his juvie record, he just might be. But can anyone see the flaw in what he did?"

Therrien raised his arm high in the air, mocking Child's earlier display. "Ooh, pick me! Pick me!"

Everyone laughed and Child delivered two spinning birds to the room.

"Yes, Marc?"

"He created a large amount of Internet traffic using Palmer's name that if anyone who knew what Palmer had been working on and had any suspicions he might not actually be dead, they might detect the increase in interest."

"Exactly. Right now, we might be the only ones looking into this, but we have to assume that the Chinese, Russians, anybody, hell, even the Brits, he's a British citizen after all, could be looking into it. We need to find him first, because we can't have that kind of technology falling into the wrong hands. Even the hands of our allies." He clapped his hands together. "Now let's get to work."

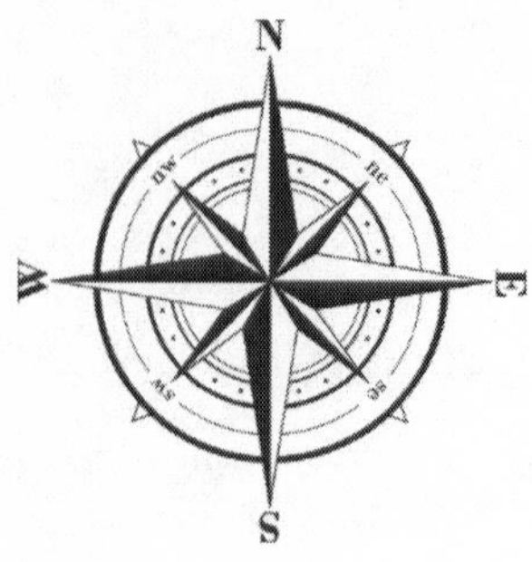

CIA Headquarters Heliport

Langley, Virginia

Kane pulled into the small airstrip just outside of Langley. Fang and Sherrie were in the back seat, still a little giggly as he hammered on the accelerator, surging them toward a chopper powering up ahead. "Just how much did you two have to drink?"

Sherrie grinned at him. "Enough that if you wanted to do a mile-high three-way, it might just be your lucky day."

Fang snickered. "Yeah, baby. What do you say?"

Kane rolled his eyes. "Now I know you're drunk."

Fang leaned forward and squeezed his shoulder. "I'm just joking. I had three fingers."

"So did I," said Sherrie. "We're just feeling a little warm. You know we train for this. We'll be fine if we're needed."

Kane brought them to a halt. "I hope so." He turned the engine off then climbed out, and the three of them headed toward the chopper with their go bags. He grinned at Fang as she squeezed an ass cheek, then his eyebrows shot up when the other cheek received similar attention, despite Fang's right hand occupied by her bag. He glanced over at a grinning Sherrie, who burst out laughing, as did his girlfriend, both cheeks released.

"You two are trouble when you've been drinking."

Sherrie leaped into the back of the chopper followed by Fang as Kane rounded to the other side and occupied the copilot's seat. He signaled for the pilot to get underway and moments later they lifted off, heading toward what he hoped would end up being nothing, but feared could be much more. He glanced back at the giggling ladies.

They'd better sober up soon.

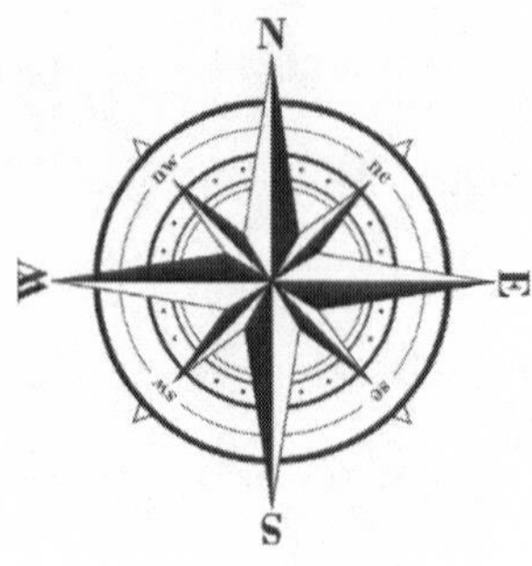

Acton/Palmer Residence, Overlook Village Gated Community

St. Paul, Maryland

Laura stared at Tommy's closed laptop. "Can they trace that to here?"

Tommy nodded. "In theory. But now that I've shut everything down we should be okay."

Acton paced by the window. "The question is, what do we do now? The fact that someone was just pinging the shit out of your laptop tells me somebody's on to us, and it can't be the good guys because Dylan's people wouldn't do that. They already know we're on this."

Tommy disagreed. "Kane's people might not have, but there are other branches of the CIA that could have. And don't forget the NSA, FBI, Homeland Security, any number of agencies we've never heard of that would do anything to get their hands on him or his design. We'd be naïve to assume it was a foreign government trying to find me."

Acton paused. "Is there any way to figure out who *was* trying to find you?"

Tommy's fingers drummed on the closed laptop. "Possibly. But if we're talking about who I think we're talking about, in other words, somebody very professional, they'll likely have security software at least as robust as mine. It's highly unlikely I'd be able to trace them without them detecting it. And it could potentially lead them directly to us."

Laura dismissed the idea. "Forget it, too risky."

Acton sat back down. "Can you send the info to Leroux? Maybe his people can do something with it?"

Tommy nodded. "Yes."

"Then do it."

He flipped open his laptop and Mai gasped, leaning forward and shoving the screen back down. "Can't they find you as soon as you turn that on?"

Tommy gently removed her hand and raised the screen once again, powering up the laptop then pressing another button. "I've disabled all the connectivity." He pointed at the button. "No Internet, no Wi-Fi, no Bluetooth, nothing."

Her shoulders slumped. "Sorry, I should have known you'd be on top of it."

He smiled and leaned over, giving her a quick kiss. "Better safe than sorry." He went to work and Acton turned to Laura.

"Perhaps we should give Cam a call."

Laura pursed her lips, her head slowly bobbing. "I think that's a good idea, but when I last spoke to him, most of his men were split between Peru and Egypt, and he was in Australia visiting his girlfriend. I don't think any of them could be here in time."

"Probably not, but he might have people here that he trusts."

"You're right." She picked her phone up off the table then hesitated. "Is it safe for us to use our phones?"

Tommy continued to work. "Oh, yeah. If they've tapped our phones we're screwed already. A phone is a hell of a lot easier to track than a laptop."

Acton wasn't sure he liked the sound of Tommy's reassurances, but the kid was right. If whomever they were worried about had access to their phones, it was already too late.

Laura dialed Cameron Leather's number. He was the head of her private security that she had hired years ago to protect her dig site in Egypt, his company's duties now extended to include Acton's dig in Peru as well as providing security for them personally when it was necessary. Leather was former British Special Air Service, and most of the men that worked for him were retired Special Forces from various branches around the world. Leather and his team had trained Acton and Laura on how to use most weapons effectively, as well as in hand-to hand-combat, survival skills, and tactics most civilians would have no clue about. That training had saved their lives countless times over.

The phone rang several times and Acton worried they weren't going to get an answer. After all, the man was on vacation. He did the mental tally on what time it was in Australia compared to Maryland and determined the man should be awake, when it was finally answered with a breathless "Hello?"

Someone giggled in the background. Tommy and Acton exchanged grins.

"Cameron, it's Laura and James. I hope I didn't catch you at an awkward time."

There was a pause. "Um, no, ma'am. Awkward isn't the way I'd put it. How can I help you?"

"We've got a situation and we might need some help."

"Ma'am, you assured me you were both staying in the United States while I was on vacation."

"We still are. We're at home. It's about—" Laura's voice cracked and Acton squeezed her hand, leaning closer to the phone.

"Hi, Cam. It's Jim. It's about Laura's brother. As you're aware, he died ten years ago, but we've stumbled across photographic evidence that he may actually still be alive."

"Bloody hell. You're serious, aren't you?"

"One hundred percent. We have a photo of him at a movie theater playing Terminator: Genisys some years after his death. He was a huge fan of the franchise."

Tommy leaned forward, interrupting him. "Make sure you don't say his name just in case automated systems are monitoring."

Acton hesitated.

Leather broke the silence. "Who's that?"

"Tommy Granger and Mai Trinh are here with us."

"Anybody else?"

"No, just the four of us."

"Good. The lad's right. Don't say the name. If I remember from his file, he was quite the genius. Artificial intelligence and quantum computing, wasn't it?"

"Yes," confirmed Laura.

"And what makes you think you're in danger?"

Tommy leaned forward. "Sir, a few minutes ago I was continuing the search for more evidence when my security software detected someone trying to locate my laptop. At least half a dozen alerts within a few seconds."

"Have you shut down?"

"Yes, sir. I've completely disconnected and I'm sending the logs to our CIA contacts so they can determine who it was."

"Stay offline. In fact, if someone's already trying to locate you, that means either they know what you know or they're suspicious as to why you're looking into a man who's been dead for a decade. I'm going to make some calls and see if I can get some trusted people to your location ASAP. For now, I recommend shutting off any Internet and Wi-Fi at the house, turning off your cellphones, unplugging your landlines, and making sure all your doors and windows are secure. Stay away from the windows and arm yourselves. When my contacts get there, they'll knock in a three-one-two pattern. Got that?"

Acton repeated it. "Three-one-two pattern. How long?"

"I'm not sure, but it could be a few hours."

Laura leaned closer to the phone. "Cameron, should we be worried or am I just being paranoid?"

"Ma'am, if you've already got somebody trying to locate Mr. Granger's laptop, then yes, you should be concerned."

"Should we leave?"

"No. You're in a gated community with excellent police response time and familiar surroundings. Remember, whoever's after you also has to position people. I'm going to let you go now. The sooner I can make my calls, the sooner I can get people to your location."

"All right, Cameron, we'll talk to you soon." Laura ended the call and Acton pointed at Tommy.

"You know where our router is. Go kill it."

Tommy held up his phone. "I just sent the logs to Leroux through the encrypted network." He turned off the phone and rose, heading for the closet where the router was located. Acton turned off his own phone as did Laura and Mai, then headed upstairs. He entered the master bedroom then opened the closet doors on the far wall, pushing aside the hangers, revealing a large weapons locker. He entered the code then pulled open the door, an impressive array of legal weapons revealed. He grabbed two Glocks each for him and his wife. They were trained, but Tommy and Mai weren't and he didn't want them carrying weapons until it was absolutely necessary. If it came down to it, the spares would be handed over—everyone deserved a chance to live. He fit his body armor in place and felt slightly safer. He grabbed three more sets, two AR-15s, and a shitload of mags for the weapons.

If anyone came after his family, they would have a war on their hands.

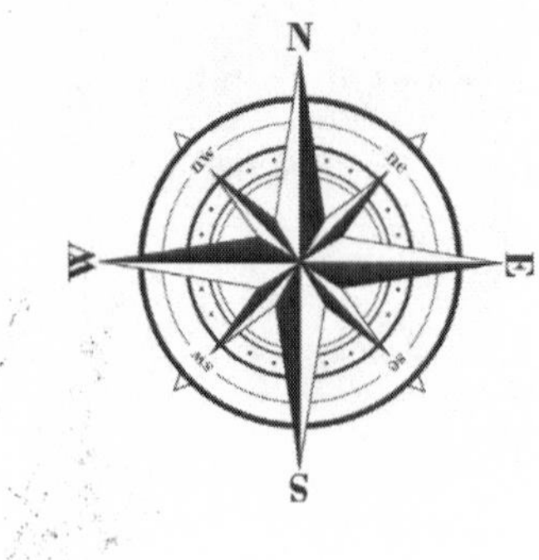

Henwood Residence

Fayetteville, North Carolina

Sergeant Carl "Niner" Sung lay in the hammock, his arms wrapped around his first serious girlfriend in a long time, Angela Henwood, one hand gripping the back of her head as their lips locked, the other with a handful of ass. This was paradise, even if it was just the balcony of her apartment. He was Special Forces, a member of 1st Special Forces Operational Detachment—Delta, or the Delta Force as the public liked to call them. Bravo Team was his family and he loved every one of his brothers. He wouldn't hesitate to give his life to save any of them, and when they were together, whether on duty or off, he always made it a point to be the life of the party. When people were laughing, even if at his expense, they weren't thinking of the dangers they were in, of the brothers they had lost.

But there had always been a hole in his heart that could never be filled by just the Unit.

And then he had met Angela, and now everything was different. What he had been craving, he now had. He had been the odd man out for so long. Dawson was now married. Red had been for as long as Niner had known him. Atlas had Vanessa and so many others had wives and girlfriends, but never him until now. He had finally found someone he just meshed with. She loved his sense of humor and had her own wicked straight-man routine that the two played off of even when they were alone.

Bliss.

Angela moaned. "You teaching it tricks?"

"What?" He kept assaulting her mouth.

"Either you've taught the little guy how to hum, or your phone's ringing."

He groaned and rolled away when she grabbed him by the ass and drew him closer.

"Just a few more rings."

He laughed and she let him go. He fished the phone out of his pocket, his eyes narrowing at who it was. He took the call. "Temple, how the hell are you, brother? I haven't heard from you in a dog's age."

"Hey, Niner, it's been too long. Listen, do you know a guy named Cameron Leather?"

"Yeah. He's Professors Acton and Palmer's security guy."

"Yes. Apparently, there's a situation."

Niner rolled his eyes, indicating to Angela their fun was over. She pouted but climbed out of the hammock. "I'll be in the bathroom with my toothbrush. If you know what's good for you, you'll be joining me before I'm done." She stepped through the sliding doors and into the apartment. Niner stared at her ass as it swayed back and forth, wondering just what the hell she was talking about.

He suddenly remembered he was on the phone. "Situation?"

"I just got a call from him. He's looking for a small security detail for the professors at their home until a situation is worked out. I can't tell you anything over the phone just in case comms are being monitored, but I understand with BD's wedding and what happened with Sweets, you guys have the week off. I was wondering if you and Atlas were interested in doing a little freelance work, just babysitting for a couple of days. None of my contacts are available on such short notice. The pay is good."

Niner chewed his cheek. "I don't take money to protect friends. Are they in real danger?"

"From what I've been told they could be."

"From whom?"

"Pretty much every hostile government on the planet."

Niner sighed. The professors had a knack for getting in trouble, but how the hell do you get every single government in the world after you when you're sitting in Maryland? "I'll tell you what, let me give Atlas a shout. If he's up for it, we'll take the job."

"And you're serious, you don't want to be paid?"

"No. Donate it to charity. Just pay my medical bills."

Temple laughed. "I think you're at greater risk of a beating from Atlas than anything else. Like I said, this should just be a babysitting job until

Leather can get his own people in place. I just need people they can trust, and there's nobody they trust more than you guys."

Niner rolled out of the hammock. "Okay, I'll get back to you in a few. I have to check on my girlfriend. She said something about a toothbrush and me helping her if I knew what was good for me."

Temple chuckled, suggesting he was in on the joke that Niner wasn't.

"What's so funny?"

"Electric toothbrush?"

"Yeah."

"Think about it, buddy. Then call me back."

The call ended and Niner stood in the doorway.

Then his eyebrows shot up, which was followed by a goofy smile.

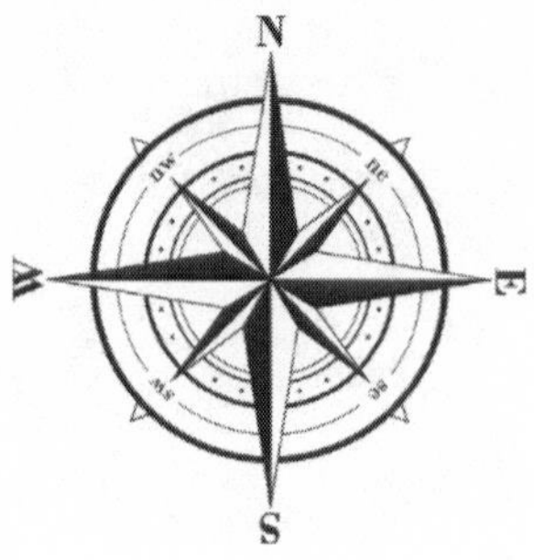

Lot's Shop

Sodom

1649 BC

Lot sat at his worktable in the shop, staring at the list of names he had written down from memory. It was an impressive list, and he felt for the innocent its release would hurt. Husbands and wives, families would be destroyed by the revelation that their partner was taking part in such debauchery. The question now was how to use the list? He could release it publicly, posting it in the town square and various other places in the hopes that enough eyes would see it, that tongues would share it with the rest.

But if someone saw him posting it, what would they do? These were powerful people. They might have him killed, and as for the list itself, wouldn't people ask where it came from? Would Canaan make the connection that he had given those names to Idit as part of the commission?

He had to disguise the source, but how? He stared at the list. None of these people would implicate themselves, yet if the list was complete, they would be the only ones who would know who had been there. He smirked. If he left a couple of names off the list, suspicion would be drawn to them, and they were all powerful enough to defend themselves and fight back, perhaps becoming the champions he needed.

He scanned the list, picking one husband and one wife whose spouses weren't also implicated. It meant they couldn't turn to their respective partner for support without admitting what they had done. He leaned back, folding his arms with satisfaction. Posting the list wasn't the solution. It was too risky. Making copies of the list with a letter that explained what it meant then delivering it to those who would be hurt most by it, and to the biggest gossips in the city, would ensure its spread and maximum effect while protecting him and his wife from any repercussions.

There was a knock at the shop entrance. Lot hid the list in a drawer then returned to the front of the shop, having forgotten he had barred the door. He removed the heavy slab of wood then opened the door to find a messenger.

"Are you the pottery merchant, Lot?"

Lot bowed slightly. "I am."

The man handed him a folded piece of parchment. "A message from Gomorrah."

Lot's eyebrow shot up. He couldn't recall ever receiving a message from Gomorrah. He took the parchment, his curiosity having him forget his plotting from moments before.

The messenger leaned in slightly. "Yours is my last message. It's been a long day. Do you know where a man can have a good time?"

Lot frowned at the lecherous look. It was clear what kind of good time this man was seeking. Lot grabbed the door. "This is Sodom. Look to your left, look to your right." He closed the door and barred it once more, heading back to his worktable. He cracked the seal then unfolded the page, his heart racing at what he read. It was from a group that called themselves The Angels of God, a name that sounded blasphemous to him. They claimed to have heard of his efforts to save Sodom from its sinful ways, and were leading a similar campaign in Gomorrah. Two representatives would call on him after the Sabbath.

He frowned. That was the day of the party, the day when he and his wife were to expose themselves to the debauchery this town's elite called entertainment. The timing couldn't be worse. They had to make their appearance at the party. They needed the commission. They needed that bonus. Yet these visitors, if they indeed were of like mind, could prove invaluable in his fight.

He looked at the drawer where he had hidden the list. It was the key. Humiliating those involved could have a huge impact. He had much to think about and little time to come to a decision.

The visitors would be arriving soon.

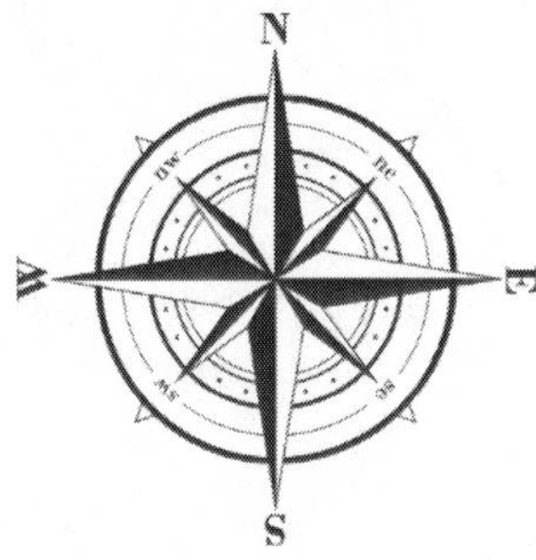

Acton/Palmer Residence, Overlook Village Gated Community

St. Paul, Maryland

Present Day

Acton sat with the others, his knee hopping as he gripped his Glock resting on his leg, his finger on the trigger guard so he didn't accidentally blow a hole in someone he loved. They were all a bundle of nerves, the conversation limited. Every sound from outside, every car engine, every dog bark had everyone flinching. Leather was sending someone, but they had no idea when that person could arrive. It could be any moment now. It could be hours from now. A thought had occurred to him earlier that had him terrified. What if whoever had attempted to find Tommy did know their phone numbers and had already been monitoring their lines? They would know the coded knock. He could open up that door and be greeted by a Chinese pistol aimed at his head. He hadn't mentioned his concerns to the others. They were worried enough.

The worst part of it was being completely shut off. Tommy had killed their Internet and Wi-Fi, all their devices were turned off, and their landline, which was VoIP through their Internet provider, was dead. If they could just make a call to find out what was going on, it could set all their minds at ease, and he was tempted to disobey Leather's instructions.

The doorbell rang and out of habit he reached for his phone to see the doorbell camera's feed, then cursed as he rose. Laura reached out and grabbed his hand as she too stood.

"They said they would knock, not ring the doorbell."

Acton tensed. She was right, but just because it wasn't Leather's people didn't mean it was necessarily bad people. Blowing several holes through the door before seeing who it was wasn't an option. For all he knew, it could be Milton. He groaned as he realized that's exactly who it was. He had forgotten his friend had said he was coming over. "It's probably Greg."

Laura closed her eyes briefly. "I forgot. Shit. Tell him to go away. It's not safe."

The doorbell rang again and Acton headed down the hallway, his weapon at the ready. He stepped into a doorway and aimed his weapon at the front entrance. "Who is it?"

"It's me. Let me in."

Acton's shoulders slumped in relief, and he was about to step back into the hallway when he paused. "Backstreet Boys or NSYNC?"

"What?"

"Backstreet Boys or NSYNC?"

"To hell with that shit. Megadeth all the way."

Acton grinned. It was his friend all right, and he was alone. He disabled the alarm then unlocked the door, opening it a crack to confirm before he pulled it open all the way. "Get in, quick."

Milton gave him a look and stepped inside. Acton closed the door behind him, but not before peering up and down the street. He locked the door and reenabled the alarm.

Milton noticed the Glock. "What the hell's going on?" He held up his phone. "You know, I've been trying to reach you. None of your cellphones are working, neither is your home line. Everything's going directly to voicemail. You're lucky the security gate was open and I didn't need the guard to call to let me through."

Acton led Milton to where the others were. "I'll explain it all to you. We're just back here in the pantry."

"Pantry?"

"It's the only room on the ground floor with no windows."

Milton eyed the gun again. "This is serious, isn't it?"

"It is. You should leave now."

"Like hell."

Acton chuckled. "I figured that's what you would say. Just make sure you tell Laura I asked you to leave."

They stepped through the kitchen, the pantry door open. Laura stood in the doorway. "Greg, you shouldn't be here."

Milton jerked a thumb at Acton. "He told me to leave, but I said no." He leaned closer to Acton and whispered, "Told you I've got your back." Milton took a seat, wincing, the man's back still a problem since he had been shot years ago helping Acton escape the very friends he wished were here now. Acton sat beside Laura on one of the chairs brought in from the kitchen.

"It's my brother," said Laura. "He might still be alive."

"Alive? How the hell could he still be alive? I thought he died on a dig in Jordan?"

"So did we. But we—"

Acton bolted upright as he finally twigged on something Milton had said. "Did you say the gate was open and there was no guard?"

Milton nodded. "Yeah. Is that unusual?"

"It should be unheard of."

Milton shrugged. "I'm sorry. I've only been here a few times at this time of night. Could he have just gone to the bathroom?"

Acton stepped over to the breaker panel on the wall. "No, that's why they work in pairs. Something's wrong."

Laura rose. "You're right."

Acton flicked the breakers, killing all the lights in the house. The battery back-up for the security system chirped.

"What are we going to do?" asked Mai, her voice quavering with fear. "Should we leave?"

Acton shook his head. "If they've breached the perimeter then they're already here."

"Then why haven't they tried to come in yet?"

"They could be getting in position, trying to figure out how many we are, where we are." He pulled his phone out of his pocket and turned it on. "There's no point in hiding now."

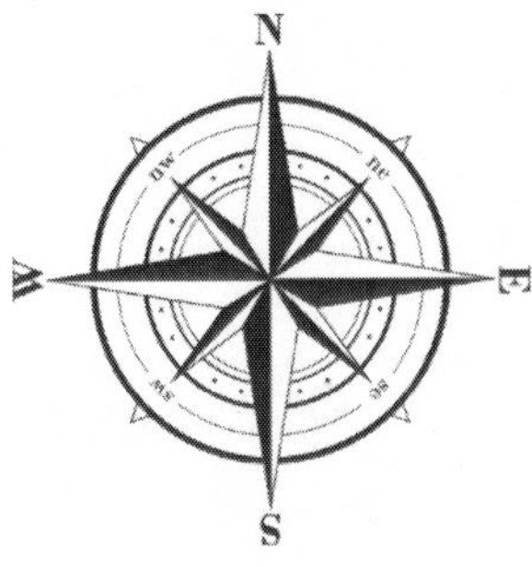

Overlook Village Gated Community

St. Paul, Maryland

"This doesn't look right."

Kane had to agree with Sherrie's assessment as they pulled up on the gated community where the professors now lived. He had always felt they needed better security because of their wealth and their history of being magnets for trouble, and was relieved to hear they had finally taken the plunge, though not for the reasons he would have chosen. They did it out of friendship for Hugh Reading, not their own safety. These were good people, and he was afraid his fears for their safety might be about to prove true. He came to a halt at the open gate.

"Let's check it out." He stepped out. Fang and Sherrie covered him as he approached the guardhouse. He peered through the window and cursed, leaving the door untouched. "Two bodies," he reported. "Sherrie, call it in."

"On it." She fell back to the vehicle, calling Leroux so he could dispatch local law enforcement. Kane checked the area, not spotting anything else suspicious.

"All right, let's go. We don't have any time to waste."

They all climbed back into their ride. Kane turned off the lights then followed the GPS instructions toward the professors' street, all the while keeping his eyes peeled for anyone or anything suspicious.

"Okay, they're the next street over. You two get out now. Head to the rear. I'll take the front."

Sherrie and Fang jumped out of the slowly moving SUV, gently shutting the doors behind them before cutting up along a hedge and out of sight. Kane made the turn onto the professors' street, taking a moment to appreciate the audacious display of wealth. He never thought he'd see the day that Acton would live in such a place, and he was happy that the two of them were enjoying their wealth beyond just taking private jets around the world and staying at fine hotels.

His eye turned to the cars on the street. There should be few, if any, all of these homes having long driveways, all occupied by even more audacious displays of wealth. Mercedes, Bentleys, and Ferraris, not necessarily assets, instead merely methods of flaunting one's success to the neighbors. There were a few notorious British automobiles in some of the driveways proving money didn't mean brains, though if they were merely meant as lawn ornaments instead of modes of transport, they did look good.

He spotted a Chevy Tahoe parked just down from where the GPS indicated Acton's home was located. It was completely out of place here, though it could be a friend visiting a neighbor or any other number of innocent reasons. He slowly pulled past, not seeing anyone inside, when gunfire erupted, his windshield splintering from the impacts. He ducked and hammered on the brakes before slamming it into reverse. He shoved the accelerator to the floor, backing out of the kill box as the gunfire continued.

His expert ear counted three distinct weapons. Two assault rifles and a machine pistol. This was where Leroux's team would come in handy, but this was an off-the-books domestic op. Kane and Sherrie weren't authorized to operate on US soil and Fang certainly wasn't. They were all technically here as civilians, which meant no satellite coverage, no Control in his ear, no backup on the way.

An alarm sounded on the dash then a handful of brightly lit warning indicators flared as the engine finally called it quits. All the gunfire had been coming from ahead. They were likely getting in position for an assault on the home when they spotted him rolling up without his lights on, paying attention to their vehicle. It could be considered a mistake, and in retrospect, perhaps it was, but his rental would have stuck out here just as the Chevy had. And even if he had his lights on, he would have checked out the suspect transport, triggering a response.

He cranked his steering wheel to the right, angling him in behind the Chevy, then popped the rear hatch. He scrambled over the two rows of seats, grabbing all three go bags, then rolled out the rear, sprinting toward the cover of a large tree as the gunfire stopped, his assailants repositioning so they weren't hitting their own means of escape. One of the guns opened up again just as he ducked behind a large oak, its century-old trunk providing him with momentary cover. And unfortunately, there was nothing else within twenty feet to hide behind. Once the enemy realized that, they would take him out.

A little help would be nice.

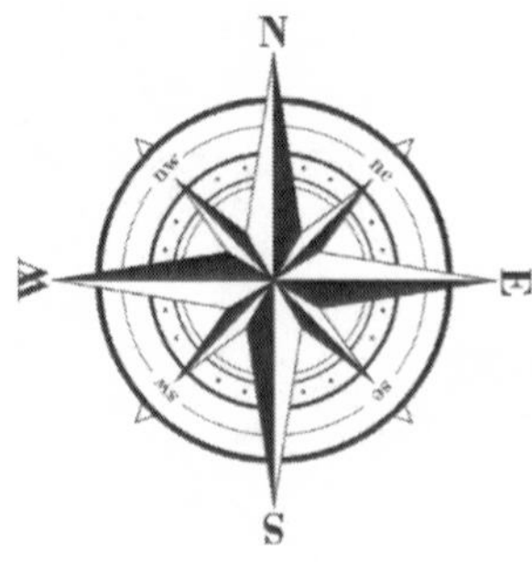

Acton/Palmer Residence, Overlook Village Gated Community

St. Paul, Maryland

Mai whimpered as the gunfire rattled just outside. Tommy held her tight as he, too, shook with fear. Acton handed Milton one of the spare Glocks plus an extra mag. "You remember how to use it?"

"Yeah. Glock. Safety's built into the trigger, so just point and shoot center mass."

"Exactly. Just try not to shoot anybody you recognize." He held out the other spare to Tommy and Mai. "Who wants it?" They both shook their heads. "Listen. If it comes down to you or them, this could be your only chance at surviving. I'm not saying you're going to have to use it, but if you need it and you don't have it, you're screwed."

Mai reached out and took it along with a spare mag. Tommy's eyes bulged. "Are you sure? I have more experience."

She gave him a look. "Video games don't count." She turned to Acton. "What are you two going to do?"

"We're just going to check things out. Dylan said they were almost here, so whoever's fighting outside could be fighting our friends."

Laura inspected her AR-15. "I wish we had MP5s."

Acton grinned at her. "So do I."

"How do you want to do this?"

"All the fun's happening out front. I'm guessing that if they had any people in the back, they would've redeployed already to help. I say we go out the back door. You go right, I go left, clear the backyard, then go up the sides of the house and figure out what's going on."

"Let's do this."

Acton watched as his wife headed for the rear door, no hesitation visible, all troubles, all fears surrounding her brother set aside so she could focus on the task at hand. He headed for the front of the house and disabled the perimeter alarm, then joined her at the back door to the patio. She slid it open. He stepped out, scanning from directly ahead to his left as she followed scanning ahead and to the right. "Clear," he whispered, and she echoed the report.

He advanced along the rear of the house toward the corner, his weapon aimed out at the backyard as the gunfire grew in volume, the well-insulated walls of their home no longer protecting them from the assault on their ears. He didn't see anybody, though there were plenty of places to hide. The fact they were both fully exposed and still alive told him that either anyone hiding back here had no intention of killing them, or they had indeed redeployed to the front as he suspected.

He reached the corner then looked back to see Laura wave at him and give a thumbs-up, then point to the front. He acknowledged it with a hand-signaled "okay," then proceeded forward, hugging the wall, his AR-15 pressed against his shoulder. As he advanced, the gunfire stopped for a moment and he feared that whoever was under attack was now dead. He peered around the corner as the gunfire resumed and spotted three people on the street advancing toward a position to his left. He craned his neck to see an SUV farther down the road, pockmarked from bullets, its rear hatch open, its engine smoking. It had to be Kane's. The question was, was his former student still inside? Were Sherrie and Fang dead along with him?

He hadn't heard any gunfire from that position the entire time. They might not have stood a chance if they had driven directly into a trap. He aimed his weapon at the target leftmost in his arc. His finger shifted from the guard to the trigger, then he stopped. What if he was misreading this? What if these were the good guys? What if this was Leather's men defending against the enemy?

He couldn't just fire blindly. He had to take a chance. He pressed against the wall, taking aim again, then did something stupid enough it might be immortalized on his tombstone. "Drop your weapons!"

The three men spun toward him and he caught a look at their faces in the streetlight for the first time. They all were Asian, perhaps Chinese, and that was too much of a coincidence. A weapon fired in his direction and he squeezed the trigger, taking down the first man. He dropped to a knee, taking aim at the second. He fired as another AR-15 joined in from the far side of the house, Laura taking out the third target.

A gun pressed against the side of his head. "Drop your weapon, Professor Acton."

His shoulders slumped as he cursed. He unslung the rifle and placed it on the ground.

"And your sidearm."

Acton pulled the Glock from his belt with two fingers when there was a whistle from behind them both.

The man gasped as the gun pulled away from the side of Acton's head. There was a sickening thud as somebody pistol-whipped his would-be captor. The man hit the ground beside him and Acton kept his hands raised, turning slowly to find a smiling Sherrie White.

"Hiya, Doc. Looks like I got here just in time."

Acton breathed a sigh of relief and grabbed his weapons as Sherrie zip-tied the unconscious man's hands and feet.

"Keep your head down, Doc. There could still be others. How many did you take out?"

"I took out two, Laura took out one. You've taken out one. That's four. I have no idea how many we're facing."

"Judging from the size of the ride it looks like they came in, I'd say that's probably all of them. You just sit tight and let us clear the area."

"Copy that. Laura's at the opposite corner."

"Let her know I'm here. And so are Fang and Dylan."

He leaned out slightly. "Hon, I'm all right! Our friends have arrived! Are you okay?"

"Peachy!"

He chuckled. "She's not in a good mood."

Sherrie grunted. "Neither am I. I'm supposed to be passed out drunk on the floor of a spa right now. Instead, I'm here with you."

"I'll try not to take that personally."

She patted his cheek. "You do that, sweetie." She pointed at their prisoner. "Watch him. If he moves—"

"I know, I know. Shoot him."

She gave him a look. "No. Knock him back out. Dead men tell no tales and we need someone to talk."

"Fine. Go ahead, I'll cover your six."

She surged forward along a hedge line toward the street. Acton scanned the surrounding area, watching for any telltale signs that someone was hiding. Something moved to his left and he flinched, adjusting his aim, his finger prepping to fire. He caught himself, relieved at the sight of Kane walking down the street carrying three good-sized duffle bags.

"I don't think we're getting the deposit back on the rental."

Fang emerged from the shadows to Acton's left and he shook his head. He was certain he had gone over that area several times but had missed her. She was good, and he was just an amateur compared to these people. Kane strode up the lawn and Acton stepped into sight, lowering his weapon.

"Glad to see you're okay."

Kane grinned. "Oddly enough, so am I." He tossed the bags by the garage door. "Everybody good?"

Acton nodded as Laura stepped into view. Sherrie checked the bodies on the street and stripped them of weapons, technology, and paper while Fang covered her. Acton jerked his chin toward his former position. "We've got one alive back there."

"Ooh, goody! Interrogation." A siren wailed in the distance, one of the neighbors obviously having called in the police. Kane pointed at the garage then at Milton's van. "How are we for vehicles?"

"We can fit everyone inside in Laura's SUV. Adding you three would be tight."

"We'll take the van. We don't have much time. We have to get out of here now before we get tied up by the locals."

Laura joined them. "You mean just leave this mess?"

"Yes. This is a four-man sleeper unit. The Chinese have them all around the world and this being the US means they've got a lot of them all across the country. More will be coming." Tires screeched at the end of the street as if to punctuate his point and Kane cursed as gunfire erupted. "Everybody fall back to the house!"

Milton stood in the doorway of the pantry, the Glock gripped in his hand pointed out at the darkened hallway, his entire body quaking with fear. He wasn't a brave man, though he didn't consider himself a coward. This just wasn't his deal. He was an academic, an academic shot in the back by Special Forces who thought he was a terrorist, beaten by South African mercenaries, and through far more than the dean of any university had probably been through in the history of the United States, all because of his friendship with Acton.

But this wasn't his friend's fault and he had a responsibility. The young man and woman cowering behind him were truly innocent in all of this, and they both worked for him at the university. It was his duty to protect them. The gunfire had stopped outside but just resumed a moment ago. Whatever was happening wasn't over.

He heard something down the hall. Somebody was coming inside. He glanced over his shoulder at Tommy and Mai. "Stay behind me."

Tommy's head bobbed rapidly, terror in his eyes as he gripped his laptop tight against his chest as if it were a security blanket. Mai sniffed hard then stepped forward, taking a knee on the opposite side of the door, aiming her weapon down the hall.

Milton glanced down at the young woman, her bottom lip trembling, tears streaming down her face. This was bravery, facing your fears despite being terrified. This young woman, half his age, was willing to fight for those she cared for, for those she loved. He thought of his wife and daughter and how horrible it would be if they were left alone. Niskha was still young, coming into their lives far later than planned, a decade-long struggle to get pregnant given up on before the miracle happened. Yet despite his burning desire to be there for his daughter, he was shocked at his silent prayer.

Please, God, should you take one of us tonight, take me. Let this brave young woman survive.

Footfalls echoed and he sucked in a breath as he took aim. "Remember, look before you shoot."

Mai nodded, quickly wiping the tears away with the back of her hand.

"Don't worry, it's me."

Milton sighed heavily, lowering his weapon at his best friend's voice. He reached out and gently pushed Mai's gun toward the ground. "We're okay," he replied. Acton poked his head into the kitchen as gunfire continued outside. "What's going on?"

"Looks like there were two teams. We took out the first one, but then a second engaged. Oh, and our friends have arrived."

"Thank God. What are we going to do?"

"Dylan wants to make a break for it." Acton beckoned them to join him. "Everybody to the garage."

Kane stepped into the kitchen, urging them to hurry. "Let's go. We don't want to give them a chance to outflank us." He looked with approval at the sight of everyone wearing body armor. "Do you have any more of that, Doc?" he asked, tapping Acton's vest.

"Four more upstairs."

"Go get them."

Acton disappeared, feet pounding on steps heard a moment later as Milton and the others joined Kane in the kitchen. "Shouldn't we wait for the police to arrive? I mean, trying to escape in a car, won't we just get shot up?"

Kane gently pushed him toward the garage door. "We *are* waiting for the police to arrive."

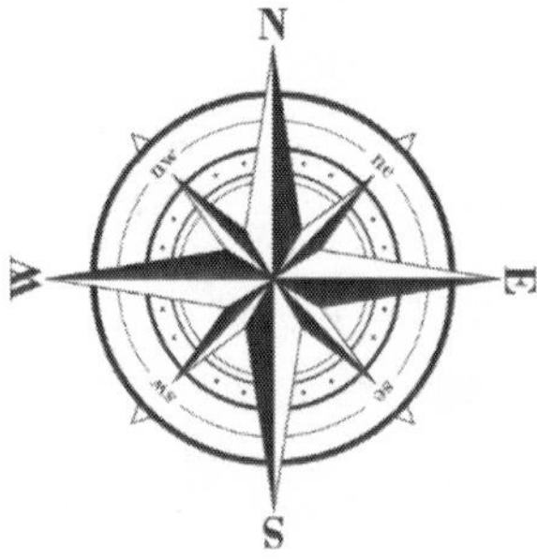

Ministry of State Security

Beijing, China

Yan's heart hammered as he listened to the report from the second unit to arrive on the scene. He had been right to pursue this. After he had gathered together all the intel he could and presented it to the director, things had moved swiftly, though that wasn't necessarily surprising considering the potential stakes. A device that could defeat all encryption could give China the edge it needed to defeat all of its enemies. But it could give the same edge to whoever got their hands on it first, and the great experiment could come to an end if the Americans were able to use such a device against them.

What was surprising was that he was given command of the operation to track down Charles Palmer. He recognized the responsibility for what it was. Should he succeed, it would be a great honor, but should he fail, he would be blamed. This could make or break him, and right now, things weren't looking too good for his future. Team One was down, three confirmed dead, the status of the fourth unknown.

"We're getting into position now, sir," reported the Team Two lead. "We've got two guns holding us back, more inside the house. Local law enforcement is also inbound. What are your instructions?"

"We need the sister. Kill anyone else if you have to."

"What about the locals?"

"They're not my concern. If they die, they die. We need the sister no matter what."

"Understood, sir, but we're going to need more firepower here."

Yan glanced over at one of the controllers. "ETA?"

"Team Three is four minutes out. Team Four is eight. We've got half a dozen more teams coming in, but they're all at least fifteen out."

"And the locals?"

"Satellite shows the first two cars about to arrive on scene."

"Any more being dispatched?"

"I'm counting at least six within five minutes. And as soon as our people engage the first units, every police officer in the region will be sent in. Whatever is going to happen has to happen in the next five minutes, otherwise this operation is blown."

Yan cursed.

And they'll never find my body.

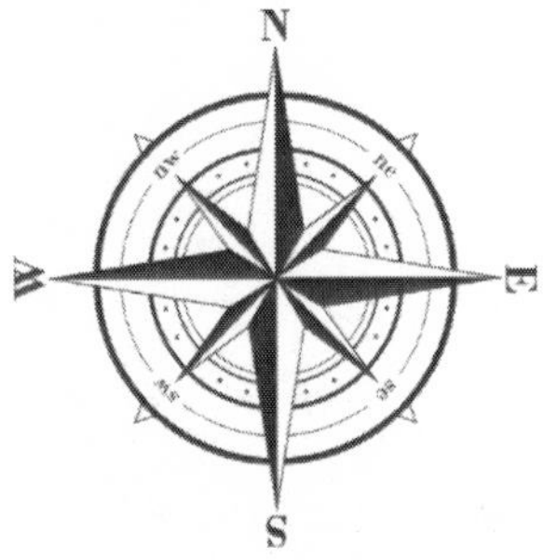

Acton/Palmer Residence, Overlook Village Gated Community

St. Paul, Maryland

Laura sat behind the wheel of her SUV, her pulse racing. Milton lay across the back seat with Tommy and Mai crouched on the floor. James sat in the passenger seat, the four extra sets of body armor draped over the open side windows. The glass wasn't going to stop anything, and unlike in the movies, the type of weapons they were going up against would slice through the skin of her car. The body armor just might absorb a few of those shots intended for flesh.

Kane gripped her arm through the window. "Breathe."

She sucked in a deep breath, holding it then slowly exhaling, remembering her training.

"You know where to go?"

"Yes. Opposite direction of wherever the police are."

"Exactly. They're going to be the target as soon as they arrive, not you. As soon as that garage door opens"—Kane held up the clicker—"you get to the end of the driveway and head in the opposite direction of the flashing lights."

"What if they come from both directions?" asked Tommy from the floor behind her.

"Then pick the one that seems to have the least amount of gunfire focused on it. I'll try to tell you which way to go if I can. Get away from the immediate area and out that front gate. Prepare to encounter resistance at the gate. They could have a team sitting there just in case you try to make an escape, though that's unlikely. This is all happening fast, so they're still positioning people."

"Do we stop if we see police?"

"No. You've got the GPS programmed for the nearest police station with a substantial force. Get your asses there. Get inside the building and tell them what's going on. We'll be right behind you in the dean's van." Kane peered into the back seat at Milton. "How does she handle?"

"Like an elephant on roller skates."

Kane chuckled. "So, no high-speed chases then?"

"None you'll win."

"Here they come!" shouted Sherrie from outside between bursts of gunfire, the police sirens loud now.

Kane patted Laura's shoulder. "You've got this. You're one of the best damn drivers I know. Just control your breathing, don't panic, and you'll be fine. We'll see you all on the other side."

She gave him a curt nod. "You be careful."

He grinned. "Who? Me? Careful is my middle name."

"Now!" shouted Sherrie. Kane clicked the button and the garage door slowly rose in the rearview mirror. Laura waited before putting the car in reverse, the backup lights beacons as to their intent. Kane ducked under then rushed out of sight.

James turned to the others in the back. "Okay, everybody stay low. No matter what, don't put your heads up to take a look. This could be the most intense few minutes of your life, but it's only going to be a few minutes. We don't have far to go to get through the gates."

A barrage of gunfire opened up and one of the sirens fell silent. "Let's go!" shouted Kane. Laura put it in reverse and crouched, giving it a shot of gas, using the backup camera to guide them rapidly out of the garage and down the driveway to the street. James poked his head up and she scolded him. "Take your own damned advice!"

"Go left! Go left!" shouted Kane and Laura cursed as she reached the end of the driveway.

"Whose left?" She had to look. She sat up then swung her head to the left and right. She gasped. Two cop cars were down the street being shot up, muzzle flashes in the bushes revealing the enemy positions. Kane was sprinting across the lawn firing, and she spotted Sherrie and Fang using trees as cover. She ducked back down, realizing he meant her left. She cranked the wheel, turning them onto the street then hammered on the brakes. She shoved it into drive then floored it, the backup camera giving her a brief glimpse of the mayhem behind them.

She rose slightly so she could see ahead, then reached up and adjusted her rearview mirror so she could see behind them. She couldn't see Kane and the others anymore, though gunfire continued, and all she could do was pray that they would be all right.

She rounded a bend in the street, putting them out of the direct line of fire, then sat up a little more so she'd have better control, for she had no intention of slowing. James was about to sit up as well when she reached out and pushed him down. "Everybody stays down until I say so."

"You're the boss."

She came to a stop sign and blasted through it, cranking the wheel to the right, sending them hurtling toward the gate that she could see just ahead. "We're almost at the gate. Everybody hang on." She continued to accelerate. She blasted past a dark SUV and cursed as its brake lights flared and it pulled a 180.

"We've got company!" she cried. Body armor hanging out the windows might have provided them with protection, but it also left no doubt as to whom they were. Muzzle flashes and gunfire erupted from behind them as two gunmen leaned out the rear windows, raining lead on them. Bullets slammed into the rear, the back window shattering.

James grabbed the bulletproof vest draped over his window and tossed it back to Milton. "Put this behind your back and head!" he ordered. Milton grabbed it and struggled with his bad back to get it in position. Tommy popped up and helped the man as the impacts continued to shudder through the vehicle. The gate was just ahead now, but it didn't matter. There was no chance they could get away in time, and as soon as a tire was hit, even if it were a run-flat, this chase was over.

Headlights ahead flicked on, high beams momentarily blinding her, and her heart sank as she spotted muzzle flashes ahead.

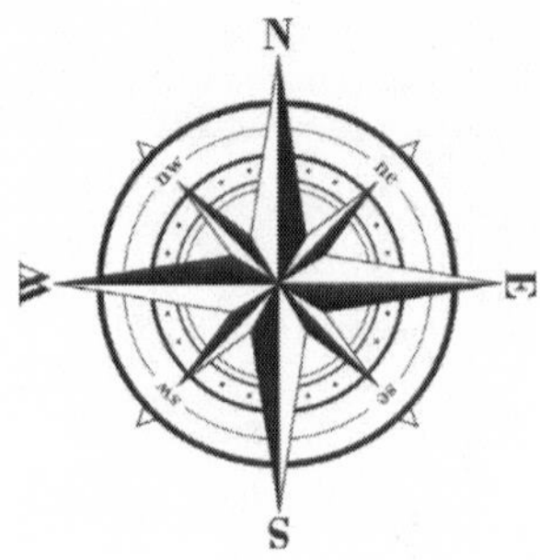

Outside Overlook Village Gated Community

St. Paul, Maryland

Niner rapidly squeezed the trigger of his AR-15, the semi-automatic hurling lead toward the pursuing SUV which he assumed was filled with bad guys. Sergeant Leon "Atlas" James, standing on the opposite side of their car, did the same.

"What I would give to have my M4 right now," rumbled the big man.

Niner agreed. "Or at least a bump stock."

The lead vehicle blasted through the gates and Niner continued firing. He spotted Laura crouching behind the wheel and his heart leaped a little. Despite being in a committed relationship, there was just something about her he found intoxicating, though he would never act on it. Not just because of Angela, but because of his respect for Acton.

Not to mention the fact the woman would probably break his neck if he laid a finger on her.

"That was Laura!" he shouted. "Looks like we're shooting at the right guys." He fired his last round then drew his Glock, emptying the mag in the engine block, Atlas taking out the gunman on the driver's side. The engine clanged, a high-pitched whine squealing as the hostiles raced past, rapidly slowing.

Niner reloaded his Glock and focused his attention on the rear driver's side tire. He took it out and the back end fishtailed, the taillights flaring as the driver hit the brakes. Niner reloaded as he sprinted toward the pursuing SUV while it careened to a halt. He broke to the right, indicating for the slower Atlas to cover the driver's side since the big man already had an angle on it. The passenger-side doors opened, two men stepping out, and Niner double-tapped both of them then followed up with single shots to the head as they no doubt were wearing body armor.

Atlas' AR-15 rang out, multiple shots firing, but none from the enemy. Niner swung around the side of the vehicle, keeping his weapon trained on the interior, watching for any movement. Spotting nothing, he advanced. "Cover me!"

"I've got you!"

Niner checked the rear seat and found one body leaning out the window that Atlas had taken out earlier, the driver slumped over the steering wheel. He groaned. Niner pressed his gun against the man's head then pulled him back, revealing a pistol in the man's lap. The idiot reached for it and Niner coldcocked him, knocking him out. "Clear in here!"

Several police cars blasted past, two of them screeching to a halt as Niner grabbed the driver and threw him onto the pavement. He zip-tied the man before laying down his weapon and lying flat on the hardtop, Atlas doing the same as police surrounded them, screaming orders.

Niner twisted his head to face Atlas. "Do you think we just created a shitload of paperwork for the Colonel?"

Atlas grunted. "I think the Colonel could be the least of our worries."

"That was Niner!" cried Laura.

"Are you sure?" Acton popped his head up to take a look, the gunfire fading rapidly behind them.

"Positive. He looked right at me."

"What the hell would he be doing here?" he asked as police cars whipped past them.

"What should we do?"

Acton wasn't sure. Kane's instructions had been clear. No matter what, get to the police station programmed in the GPS, but those instructions had never considered that any of their friends in the Delta Force would be arriving to help them. Leather must have somehow got word to them. It was the only explanation, otherwise Kane would have mentioned it.

"Those police are going in blind." Laura eased off the gas. "All they know is their people were taking fire. They could assume Niner and whoever else was with them are the bad guys. We have to help them."

Acton cursed. She was right. The variables in the equation had changed. He twirled his finger. "Let's turn around."

Laura hit the brakes and pulled a rapid 180, sending them hurtling back toward the danger. She glanced over at him. "Better let Leroux know what's going on."

Acton already had his phone in his hands, preparing to call Leather. "Shouldn't we call Cam?"

Laura shook her head firmly. "No. Leroux has all the contacts within the government. If anybody can smooth things over it'll come through him, not Cameron."

She was right as usual. He logged into the secure app, firing off one-sentence messages, not sure when he'd be cut off by a police service weapon pointed at his head. He glanced up, spotting the flashing lights ahead. "You better slow down. These guys could be a little trigger-happy."

She applied the brakes, killing most of their speed as he continued to send updates to Leroux.

"Hands! Let me see your hands!"

Acton pressed Send then dropped the phone in his lap, raising his hands as half a dozen police officers approached the shot-up SUV. Acton extended his hands out the open window and made eye contact with the closest officer. "We're the victims here, officer. They were shooting at us. We were just trying to get away."

"Come out one at a time! You first!" barked the officer.

Acton opened the door from the outside, pushing it out of the way. He stepped out, his hands still high. "Officer, we have weapons in the vehicle. They're all fully licensed and were used in self-defense."

"Gun!" shouted the officer, several more rushing over, the intensity of the situation ratcheting up.

Acton stepped away from the door. "I have a knife on my hip and several spare magazines in my pockets. There's a Glock on the front seat and an AR-15 in the passenger footwell."

"Advance toward me!"

Acton slowly stepped forward. "My wife is in the driver's seat and we have three in the back. My wallet with ID is in my back pocket. You'll see that we live here."

"Interlace your fingers behind your head!"

Acton did as told.

"Turn around and back toward my voice."

Again, he followed the orders. No matter how much you felt you were in the right, you always obeyed the man with the gun. If more people followed that simple rule, a lot of America's young men and women wouldn't be getting shot. Handcuffs were slapped on his wrists then he was patted down, his ID retrieved.

"Professor James Acton." The photo ID was held up to his face. "I'll get you to stand over here, sir, while we straighten things out. I'll have to leave you in the cuffs for now."

"No problem. You do what you need to do. Just know that the first two squad cars that were sent to our house I think were shot up pretty bad. I don't know what happened to your people, but you're probably going to need ambulances."

"It's being taken care of."

"There are three friendlies on site, a man and two women. They're with us. They're friends of ours who came to provide security."

"Security for what?"

Acton sighed. "As much as I hate to say this, officer, let's just say it's above your pay grade."

"What's that supposed to mean?"

"I wish I could tell you. All I can say is that those after us are very bad people and this is a national security issue. By the time you get everybody sorted out, I'm willing to bet you'll have a phone call telling you what you need to know."

Laura was brought up beside him, handcuffed. "There were two people here who helped us," she said. "One guy is Korean American and the other guy—"

"Was a stunt double for Black Adam?"

Acton and Laura exchanged grins at the officer's description of Atlas. "That would be them."

"They're in the back of my squad car."

"You'll probably be getting a call about them too. They're definitely the good guys."

"They might be, but they're a little more tight-lipped than you two."

"If you knew who they were, you'd understand why."

"Who are they?"

Acton shrugged. "Would you believe me if I told you it was a matter of national—"

The officer cut him off. "Security?"

"Exactly."

"Uh-huh. Why the hell do I think I'm going to have two days of paperwork out of this shit?"

Acton leaned forward, lowering his voice. "Actually, if you wait for the phone call, there might be no paperwork at all."

The officer paused. "I like the sound of that."

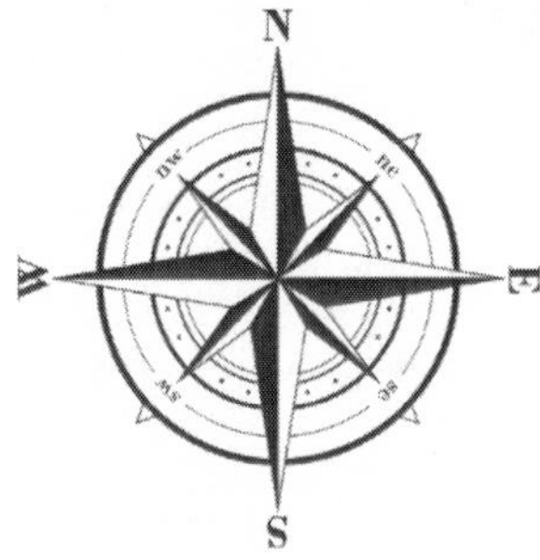

Ministry of State Security

Beijing, China

Yan slammed his fist on the desktop, everything rattling in protest. He pointed at one of the controllers. "Order the rest of the teams to hold back. Spread out around the area. Acquire and trace the target. We'll regroup for a proper attempt later."

"Yes, sir."

The orders were issued and Yan rose, heading for the door. This operation had been a colossal failure but it had proven one thing that he hoped might just save his neck—Charles Palmer had to be alive. There was no way this much security would have been brought in for his sister if he weren't. And if Palmer were alive, it meant he could have been working on his quantum computer for the past ten years, and if he were near a solution a decade ago, he surely would have found it by now.

What had just happened was confirmation something was definitely going on beyond an innocent misinterpreted search. If his career survived the next five minutes, he could have even more resources made available to him. And if he played this right, he'd still have his second shot of punishing the professors and bringing a glorious advantage to his country.

His future wasn't over yet.

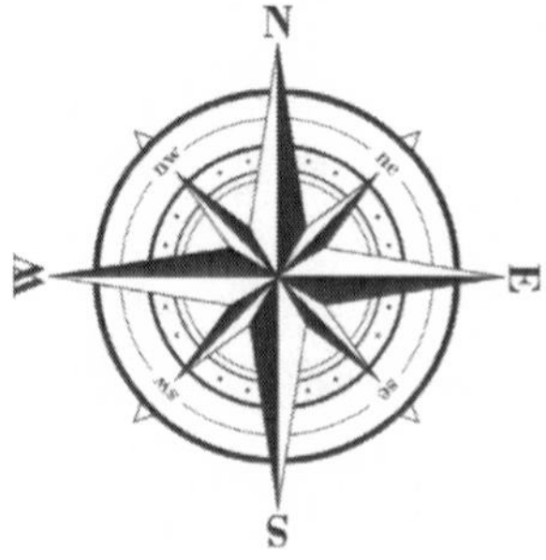

Idit's Studio

Sodom

1649 BC

Lot couldn't tear his eyes away from his wife's masterpiece. She had a way of painting that he had never seen before, her style so unique, it had her in ever-increasing demand, her commissions continually rising in value. Her contemporaries all painted or drew in a way where images simply seemed flat. They could be inspiring, moving, thrilling even, depending on the subject matter, but they never captured what his eye saw. When he had first seen his wife sketching something near where she lived, he had been immediately drawn to it. It had depth. It spoke to him enough that it had him mustering the courage to approach her. The conversation had led to a friendship, and when they got older and understood such things, to love then marriage.

Her talent was unique and developing, and as he stared at her latest creation, it no longer disgusted him like it had the first time he had seen it. And he was horrified that as he slowly walked around the finished vase, his newly perverted mind picked out the positions he and his wife had already tried over the past days, and those yet to be enjoyed. He closed his eyes and clasped his hands over his face.

God forgive me. Give me the strength to resist.

"What do you think?"

He flinched at his wife's voice behind him. He opened his eyes, finding them once again thirsting to join in and partake in what was depicted. "I think it's the perfect example of what's wrong with Sodom."

"You don't like it?" The hurt in her voice was evident and he turned to face her, taking her hand.

"The artwork is exquisite as usual. One of your finest pieces. It's the subject matter."

She frowned as she stood beside him, staring at her efforts. "Well, I didn't have much choice there now, did I?"

"No, I suppose not."

She rubbed his back. "How was temple?"

"Good. Packed as usual, filled with hypocritical sinners. You know, while I sat there listening to the rabbi, I searched the faces of my fellow man, desperately seeking those ten good souls we spoke of, and I couldn't find them. There were only two men there that I thought might fit the description."

She leaned her head on his chest. "Of course you're one of them."

"No, not anymore."

She stared up at him, concern in her eyes. "Why not? You're the best man I know."

"Not anymore. I was fooling myself. I thought I was a good man." He gestured at the vase. "But I've given in to the temptations represented here."

She placed her hands on his cheeks, drawing him closer. "You gave in to those temptations with your wife. We've brought each other joys we never imagined possible, all in the privacy of our bed chamber. Surely there's nothing wrong with that." She ran a hand along the lip of the vase. "Surely you can see that the sin is not the action but the context. It's the fact that they're doing this in public. It's the fact that they aren't doing it with their spouses. That's the sin. Sex outside of wedlock is a sin, but sex within isn't. If I drew a picture of two people making love and told you they were married, would you be offended? But if I then told you that they weren't married to each other, how would you feel? That's when you get offended because the context has changed. You're a good man, husband, and the fact that this offends you is proof of that. Just because you're a little tempted by what you see depicted here doesn't make you a bad person, it makes you a flawed person like all people are, because only God is perfect. Thinking about something isn't sinful. It's acting upon something that is."

He held her tight, taking comfort in her words, for she was right. While he might not be as pious a man as he had thought, he was still a good man. But three men in a sea of sinners could never hope to hold back the wrath of God should it be delivered upon Sodom.

He only prayed his plan worked.

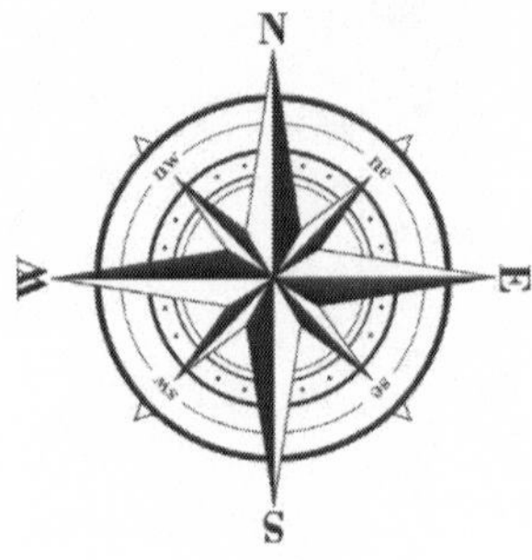

Outside Overlook Village Gated Community

St. Paul, Maryland

Present Day

Acton rubbed his wrists as he waited for the handcuffs to be removed from the others. Apparently, Laura's suggestion to send their plea for help to Leroux had been the right choice. Only minutes after their detention, orders were received setting them free. He gave everyone the once-over. "Are you all okay?"

Head bobs except from Milton who had a hand pressed into his lower back. "I'm going to be paying for this for the next few weeks."

Acton frowned, concerned for his friend. He pointed at the car Niner and Atlas had arrived in. "Why don't you go sit? It might take some of the pressure off."

Milton sighed. "I think I will."

Acton whistled at Niner and Atlas talking with the scene commander nearby. They both turned and Acton pointed at their car. "Greg's going to sit in there. His back's bothering him."

Niner reached into his pocket and pulled out the fob, unlocking the car. He gave a thumbs-up then returned to his conversation. Acton helped Milton in the passenger seat. His friend winced then stretched out, groaning in a mixture of agony and ecstasy.

"Better?"

"A bit. I just need to get home so I can lie in my own bed and Sandra can give me a proper massage."

Acton bit his lip, scrunching his face. "I'm not sure when you're getting home. And if anything, we should probably get your family some place secure until this is all over."

Milton sat upright, his pain forgotten. "You don't think…"

Acton shrugged. "I don't know what to think, but if they find out you were there, they could use them as leverage."

Milton fell back in his seat, his shoulders slumping as he closed his eyes. "I should have just stayed home."

Acton chuckled, giving his friend's shoulder a squeeze. "They were probably coming after you regardless because of the university's computers being used. They would assume you gave permission."

Milton grunted. "Yeah, they'd never believe that I have rogue staff crippling my network for weeks on end for a personal project."

Tommy frowned, glum. "Sorry."

Milton dismissed the apology with the bat of a hand. "Just ignore me, son. It's not your fault." He pulled out his cellphone and paused. "Should I risk calling them? And what do I tell them?"

Acton glanced at Laura. "What do you think?"

She pinched her chin, shaking her head. "I don't know. I wish Dylan were here. He would know what to do."

Acton looked about for Kane. The gunfire in the distance had stopped some time ago. Kane and the others were to take Milton's van when it was safe to do so, but there was no sign of them. There was only one way out of the gated community, and this was it. "They must be detaining them."

"Who?" asked Laura, Acton forgetting he had been thinking to himself.

"Dylan and the others. This will all get sorted out in the next few minutes, I'm sure." He turned to Milton. "I think it's best to maintain radio silence for now. Your phone's not secure, and your home line definitely isn't."

Milton grasped at his temples with one hand. "I don't know. Minutes count."

Niner and Atlas jogged up to the group now clustered around their ride. "You guys all right?" asked Niner.

Acton nodded. "We're all good except Greg's back is acting up."

"I'll live," said Milton unconvincingly.

Niner jerked a thumb at Atlas. "I can have the big man stretch you out. You'd be in for a treat."

Atlas rolled his eyes as Laura snickered.

Milton waved off the offer, a touch of fear in his eyes at the prospect. "I'll be fine. I'm more concerned about my wife and daughter."

"You're right. Let's get down to business," said Niner. "We're all being let go on the condition that once this is all over, we voluntarily come in to give statements. Of course, the big man and I won't be showing up, but since you all have to live here, I recommend you do and tell them everything you know that hasn't been classified."

"Where are Dylan and the others?" asked Laura.

"They've been released. They hung back to help those police officers that were pinned down. They should be here any minute."

"What do we do now?"

"We need to get you all to a secure location." Niner held up a hand, cutting off Milton. "That includes your family, sir."

"And just where might that be?" asked Acton.

Niner smirked. "I had a thought about that."

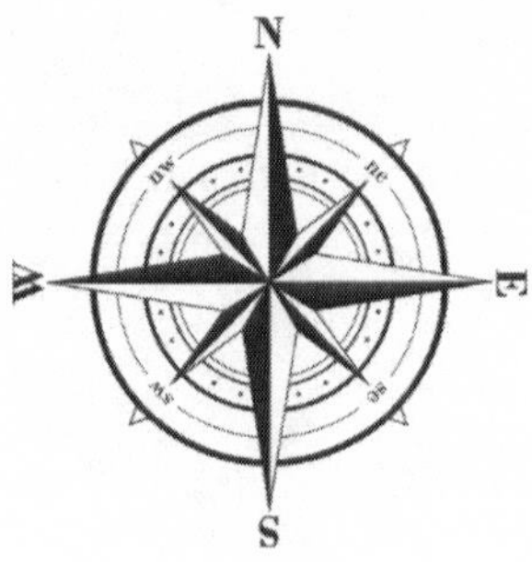

Winters Residence, Knightsbridge

London, England

Mary was fully showered, dressed, and fed, ready for anything that might come, eager for the truth to finally come out now that the biggest secret of her career had been discovered. It appeared someone was already on to it, according to the desperate phone call from Laura demanding a jet be arranged as quickly as possible. The details given to her were scant, though enough for her to know that something was wrong, and it was definitely related to her client's brother.

It had her wondering how Laura would react when she found out the truth. Would the woman understand what her job had been all these years, or would she feel betrayed? If the roles were reversed, she would think betrayal would be the order of the day, and she wouldn't blame her. For ten years, Mary had been lying to Laura, and though they rarely met, she had little doubt Laura thought of her as a friend. Mary wanted to feel the same but had never allowed herself to cross that line like she had with Laura's brother.

It was simply too difficult.

The lie was meant to protect Laura, protect her brother, and if something had happened back in Maryland, as she suspected, that lie had been necessary, and how this situation would be resolved satisfactorily was for the moment unknown. If the secret were out, there was no faking his death a second time. No one would believe it. Palmer would have to hand himself over to one of the friendly governments, likely his own British government, and agree to work for them in exchange for their protection. There were worse things, she supposed, but he would essentially be a prisoner of his own country.

She didn't envy the choice now ahead of him.

Her phone beeped with a secure message and she brought it up. It was from him, the response to her latest update about his sister requesting an aircraft. Her eyebrows shot up at his instructions.

Well, this could be interesting.

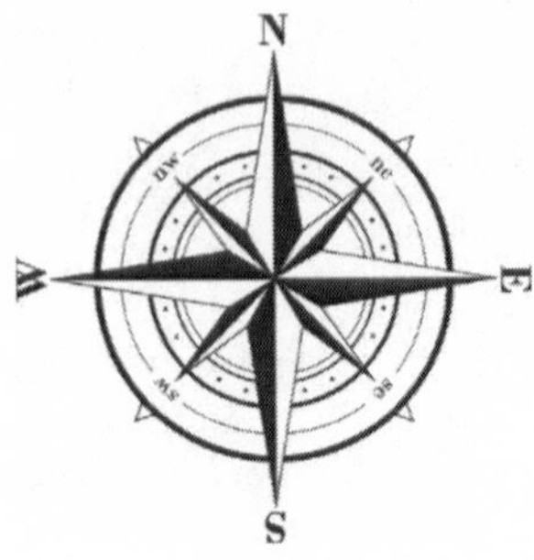

Montgomery County Airpark

Gaithersburg, Maryland

Acton took a seat in the luxurious Gulf V, part of Laura's private lease-share network of jets arranged by their travel agent Mary, a woman capable of working wonders with no notice. Kane, Sherrie, and Fang had showed up a few minutes after Laura had made the call for a jet on Niner's instructions, then they had retrieved Milton's family. Right now, in this one plane, almost everyone he cared about in the world was here. If what Kane suspected were the Chinese caught up to them now, everything he had fought for over the years could be wiped out.

Niner and Atlas stood at the head of the aircraft, its engines whining, ready to taxi to the runway. "This is where we leave you, ladies and gentlemen. Once you're in the air, you'll be safe until you land. Hopefully, before that happens, we'll have some answers. Good luck."

"Thank you, guys," said Acton, standing and shaking their hands. "You saved our asses once again."

Laura gave Atlas a hug then Niner gave her a big one, lifting her up off the floor slightly. He groaned. "That just made it all worth it."

Laura giggled and patted Niner on the cheek. "And you say hi to Angela for me."

Acton leaned in. "And when I see her next, I'm giving her a big hug."

Atlas grunted. "Now you're in trouble, little man. One hug from him and Angela will realize what it's like to be with a real man."

Niner stepped back from Laura. "Doc, you wouldn't!"

"Keep grabbing my wife like that, and I would."

Niner frowned. "You wound me, Doc. She's like a sister to me."

Atlas groaned. "That's disgusting, dude."

Kane cleared his throat. "I don't know what kind of love quadrangle or whatever is going on here, but how about we get in the air and you guys settle this later?"

Acton laughed, slapping Niner on the shoulder. "He's right. You two get out of here, and thanks again for all the help."

"Anytime, Doc," replied Atlas. "And I apologize for my friend hitting on your wife."

Niner grinned, jerking a thumb at his big friend. "I only do it to make him jealous."

Atlas headed for the door. "I'm out of here."

Niner pranced after his friend, his hips thrust out, his butt cheeks clenched, leaving them all laughing, Milton's daughter Niskha giggling at the antics. The flight attendant closed the door and moments later they were taxiing as everyone strapped themselves in. Niner's idea to get them in the air was brilliant, yet it was only a temporary solution. The pilot would have filed a flight plan, and Acton had little doubt the Chinese would have access to it. As soon as they landed, they were a target once again. Hopefully, before that happened, their CIA friends would have figured out something.

But then again, could that something save their lives?

Laura gripped his hand as they took off. She wasn't a nervous flyer, the source of her anxiety the situation. They cleared the runway and rapidly gained altitude when the pilot's voice came over the PA.

"Ladies and gentlemen, this is your captain speaking. I'm now finally able to tell you that our destination is the Azores, at which point you'll be switching to a different aircraft, the details of which will be provided to me upon arrival. I'm sorry, I don't have much more info. This is a bit of an unusual flight for me and the crew, but I learned long ago not to bother asking questions, so let's just sit back and enjoy each other's company. My understanding is we have a young lady with us tonight. If she wants to visit the cockpit, just let the flight attendant know. That goes for any of the big kids too."

Kane unbuckled his lap belt and turned in his seat to face Acton and Laura. "Azores? Did you guys have anything to do with that?"

They both shook their head and Laura responded. "No. I just told Mary that we needed a plane immediately, it was an emergency, I couldn't give her any details, and I said I didn't have a destination, I just wanted to be in the air for as long as possible."

Sherrie turned in her seat. "Why the Azores? Why would she pick a destination like that? There's nothing there and definitely nobody who can help us."

Acton grunted. "Not to mention the last time we were there things didn't go so smoothly." His eyes narrowed as he thought about it. "You know, if there's one destination within range of this aircraft that is almost definitely not going to have a pre-positioned Chinese unit, it would be the Azores. There's no strategic value."

Kane's head bobbed in agreement. "That's true. But how the hell would your travel agent know that? And she's got us switching to another aircraft. Why not just refuel this one? And where's that other aircraft heading?"

"Not to put a damper on things," said Fang. "But unless my government has become completely inept since I left, if they don't know about this flight already, they will soon. And then they'll access the flight plan and know we're heading to the Azores. Even if they don't have a team pre-positioned, they can get one there before we land."

"Then what do we do?" asked Laura.

"We have to hope we can transfer to the second plane without them intervening."

Kane shook his head. "But then they'll just trace that one. This is a game that only works for so long, and my guess is *if* it works in the Azores, it's the last time it will. It's time for some answers."

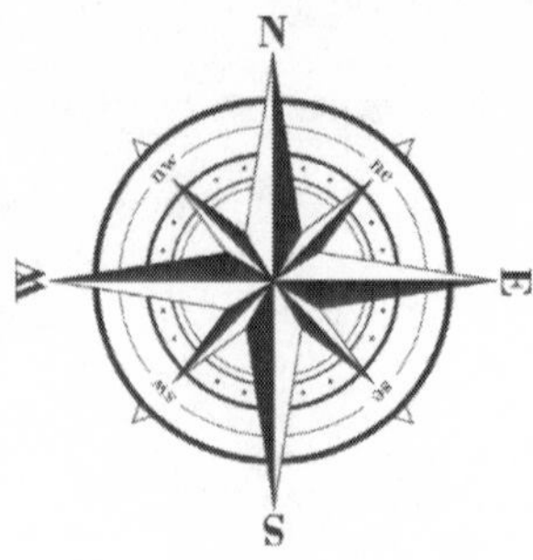

Operations Center 2, CIA Headquarters

Langley, Virginia

Leroux glanced over at Tong before returning his attention to the main display. "Anything?"

She shook her head as she continued to work her station. "Nothing. Just a couple of regularly scheduled flights. Nothing private, nothing last-minute."

Child spun in his chair. "But that doesn't make sense. If they're supposed to meet up with this second plane, there has to be a flight plan on it, doesn't there?"

Leroux folded his arms and turned, facing the young man who wasn't that much younger than him. "Eventually, yes. But we're going to have to assume for now that the plane is being held in reserve and will be sent at the last possible minute."

Tong faced him. "But isn't that level of planning a little bit beyond a travel agent? I mean, she has them heading to the Azores, which from what I can tell is about the perfect place for them to head, then swapping onto a plane that for the moment doesn't exist. That's something we would think of. But would she?"

Leroux pinched the bridge of his nose as he closed his eyes. "What do we have on this woman?"

Tong pulled up the file, displaying it on the screen, reading off the highlights, nothing particularly standing out. It appeared she had been in the travel business since she graduated from an unremarkable university in the UK, then founded her own firm a decade ago, catering to the well-heeled.

Leroux sighed. "I don't see anything here that suggests she should be this on the ball."

"Maybe she just reads a lot of spy novels," suggested Therrien.

Leroux grunted. "It's as good an explanation as any, but for now, we're going to have to try to anticipate the moves an amateur might make to hide that connecting flight, though beyond just doing everything last-minute, I don't see what else she can do. For now, let's just monitor it and focus on finding Professor Palmer's brother. What's the status on that, Sonya?"

She tapped at her keyboard then jerked her chin toward the displays, six photos shown. "This is what we've found so far where facial recognition gave an initial positive. Photos two, four, and five were false positives." They disappeared from the screen. "These three, however, appear to be him. An initial analysis suggests they're genuine, however, photo number one, despite its metadata indicating it was taken two years ago, was actually taken twelve years ago. Somebody obviously set the date wrong on their device."

Leroux stared at the screen, his arms folded as he eyed the remaining two photos. "And these ones?"

"One was taken two years ago, the other eighteen months ago. The first in Dubai again, the most recent in Qatar."

"More specifically?"

She smirked. "Well, they weren't all at Terminator retrospectives, but they were all around movie theaters."

Leroux smiled slightly. "It looks like we've found his Achilles heel. He has a weakness for seeing movies on the big screen. He also seems to be hanging out in the Gulf States. Okay, let's move the timeframe forward to that last photo, and concentrate all our efforts on the Gulf States around any movie theaters and entertainment districts. With what the Chinese just did in Maryland and the fact they lost three teams doing it, they're going to know that we suspect the same thing. Charles Palmer is alive. They're going to be throwing everything they've got at this as well. This is a race, people, and whoever wins it could control cyberspace for the next decade. Let's get to work." He headed for the door. "I'm going to brief the Chief. When we do locate Palmer, extraction could get ugly."

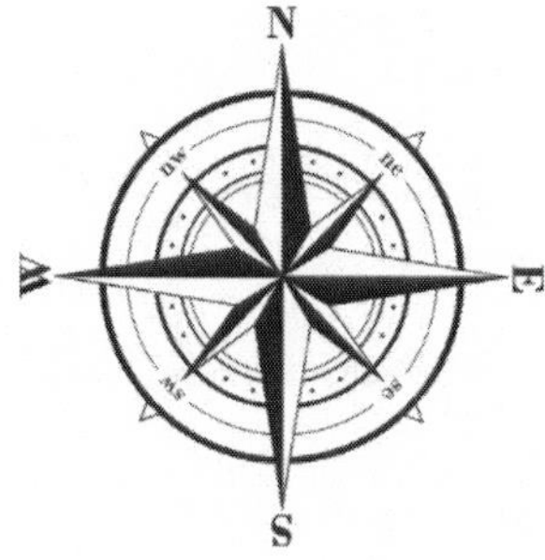

Unknown Location

Charles Palmer lay back in his massage chair, the Swedish creation doing wonders to relax his tense body. As he controlled his breathing in an attempt to steady his emotions, his eyes stared out at the images shown by his VR headset, images of his sister, some of them from when they were younger, others far more recent, depicting the life she had created for herself after his death. When he had discussed faking his death with Mary, he had proposed bringing Laura along with him. Mary had nixed the idea. Keeping two people hidden from the modern world doubled the chances of discovery. And besides, it wouldn't be fair to Laura, because she would immediately agree. She would do anything he asked of her, and it would have ended her life. Here she was successful, happily married, with good friends and a new family. She hadn't gone wild with the money he had left her, and had instead used it wisely, for good.

He was so proud of her, and every day he wished he could tell her the truth. Yet he couldn't. It was simply too dangerous. Before he made his decision to remove himself from society, somebody had broken into his private lab and discovered how close he was to succeeding. He was far ahead of everyone when it came to quantum computers, having taken a different approach from most labs researching it at the time. If his research fell into the wrong hands, it could be easily exploited and data encryption as we knew it would be obsolete. It didn't bother him if his government or the Americans exploited it. It was countries like China, North Korea, Iran, Russia, or criminal organizations gaining access that truly terrified him.

He had always known the danger, which was one of the reasons why he had sold his company so that he could focus solely on his research without having to report his progress to shareholders, or worse, government regulators. By doing what he was doing privately, he could be assured of absolute secrecy. But somebody had suspected something, broken into his lab, and it was only a matter of time before someone decided he was close enough to kidnap and force him to work for them.

That's when he had called Mary, the only person he could think of that might know a way out. He had loved that woman, probably still did, and when he had found out she was an MI6 agent sent in to figure out what he was working on, the betrayal had hurt him, a gut punch that took years to recover from. She had put together the plan to fake his death, she had sent in the team to plant the explosives that would take down the tunnel, to hide his change of clothes so that he could pose as a local emerging from the cave only moments before the explosion, detonated by one of the team hiding in the rocks nearby.

In the chaos that ensued, he merely walked out of the camp, climbed into a pre-positioned car and drove away. The team sent in to help him had no idea who they were helping and had no involvement after the detonation. He made it to Amman, boarded a private charter that took him to Dubai with all new ID. While he was traveling, Mary had used her contacts to have the Jordanians immediately shut down the dig site, yank all the permits, and put a ban on all further excavation in the area. It meant nobody could go in to find that his body wasn't there. Her plan had worked perfectly, no one suspected anything, his well-attended funeral going off without a hitch, the name Charles Palmer soon forgotten by the few who knew it.

Yet despite the success, his heart had been broken. He loved his sister so much, and had despaired that she had thrown herself at her work for so long, never finding love, never even seeking it until James Acton had yanked her out of the shell she had withdrawn into.

But now the secret was out. How, he wasn't sure. With the number of cameras everywhere, perhaps it was inevitable that somebody somewhere would catch him in public, someone would recognize him. Things were happening fast now. The Chinese had made a play for Laura, and if they knew, this entire house of cards he had built would soon collapse. The secret was about to come out, and he wanted to tell his sister in person why he had done what he had and beg her forgiveness.

Then figure out what to do next.

Her safety and that of those with her was paramount. Now that the world would soon know he was alive, every actor in the intelligence community, good and bad, would be after him. And so they should be, for he had continued his work and he was far beyond anyone out there. His quantum computer had tens of thousands of nearly error-free qubits working in tandem, over a hundred times the latest breakthrough announced by computing giant IBM.

He was generations ahead, for he had discovered a scalable methodology that, once perfected, allowed him to merely chain together duplicate constructs. If he wanted to, he could scale to hundreds of thousands and eventually millions of qubits, but he didn't need that for his purpose. He already had more than enough to crack any encryption out there, exactly as he feared was possible.

Now his life's work was devoted to defeating his own creation. He had to figure out a defense against it, then his intention was to publicly release that defense. Once it was in place, his breakthrough that would take mankind to the next level of computing would be made available free to the world, so that all of humanity could gain while protected from the harmful aspects it posed.

Unfortunately, he was years away from protecting the world from his device, and with everything unraveling around him, he could see only one solution to the problem.

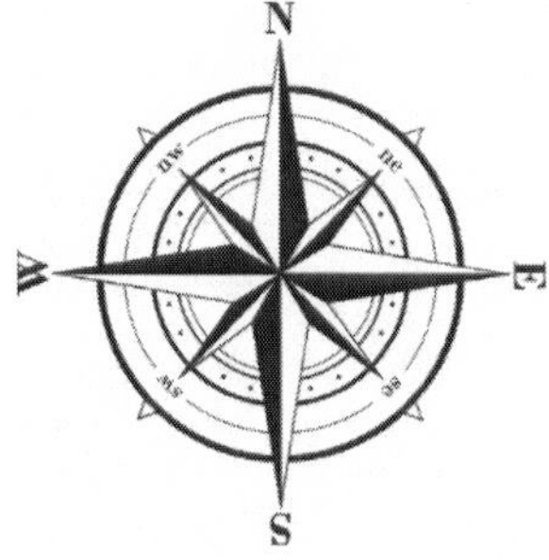

Sodom

1649 BC

Lot's heart hammered as he slipped the last message under the gate. He hurried away from the estate of one of the wealthiest families in Sodom, the wife on the list but not the husband. His message to all of them was simple. If immediate action weren't taken to rid Sodom of its sinful ways, proof of their participation in these sinful acts would be provided to the citizenry, and their reputations and their family honor would be destroyed.

As he hurried away, cringing with every step that echoed on the stone street, he found himself eager for tomorrow night's party. He was certain that many of the names from the list were invited. All except the two he had left off would receive their messages when they woke in the morning, and he had to wonder how many would still attend the debauchery. It would be a good indicator as to whether his plan was working.

He was certain it would.

It was one thing to participate in such events among like-minded individuals. It was an entirely different thing to have such things made known to friends, neighbors, and family. Yet as he continued to make his way home, it gave him the opportunity to reevaluate his thinking. He had said that it would be hard to find ten good men in Sodom. It was an exaggeration, of course, meant to make a point. He was certain that in the entirety of the city, there were scores of good men, if not hundreds, perhaps even thousands.

But where were they? They were silent, if they existed at all. The sinful acts that distressed him so much were on display for all to see. Brothels, gambling houses, and drinking establishments. None were hidden away, their doors to the world opening to the front of the street, not some rear alleyway. Every customer walked in and out without shame. Would these people he had just threatened even care that their depravity became public?

He rounded a corner and ran into a man standing with his eyes closed. "Pardon me." Lot stepped around him, nearly tripping over a woman on her knees in front of the man, and growled in frustration as his point was proven. Nobody cared. Did he suspect that the majority of Sodom citizens frequented these establishments? No, he didn't. He was sure it was a minority, though that minority was substantial. It was the fact that everyone appeared to tolerate it. Nobody said anything, which suggested acceptance.

Though it could be resignation. No one dared speak up because those behind the dens of iniquity were often violent—if anyone threatened their livelihood, extreme violence was often the response. Not two weeks ago, a rabbi had been beaten nearly to death preaching that all these establishments should be closed on the Sabbath. He was still recovering. And what had the reaction of the public been? Shock and horror at what had been done, yet no protests, no demand for justice. Instead, life just went on as it always had.

His home was just ahead, the entire street in darkness, only the stars overhead lighting the way as they always did. Something streaked across the sky and he smiled. His mother had told him as a child that when he saw something like that flying past, it was an angel on its way to God to deliver the prayers of those who saw it. She called it angel fire. He closed his eyes for a moment as he continued down the street.

Please, God, send us help, for no one more than Sodom needs it.

He opened his eyes, and as if in answer to his prayers, several more angels streaked across the heavens, and his heart swelled at the thought God might have finally heard his prayers.

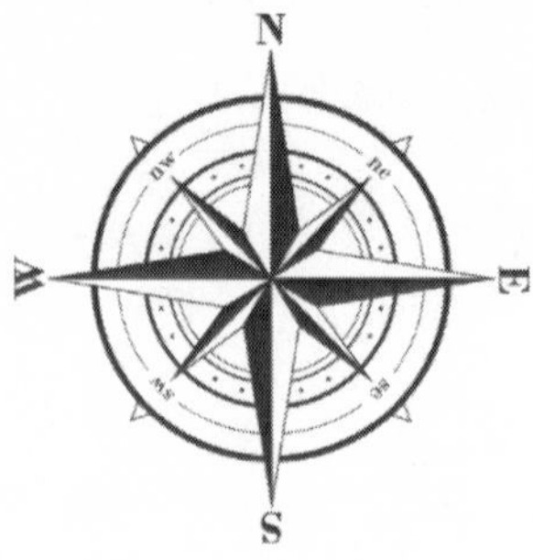

Director Morrison's Office, CIA Headquarters

Langley, Virginia

Present Day

"Qatar? Are you sure?"

Leroux shook his head at his boss, Leif Morrison. "No, sir. But eighteen months ago, he was spotted there. As soon as we narrowed our search last time to photos taken around theaters showing a Terminator movie, we started getting fresh hits. Now that we've narrowed it down even further geographically and within the past year and a half, we'll hopefully get more. But every hit so far has him in the Gulf States."

Morrison's head bobbed as he steepled his fingers in front of him, tapping his forefingers against his chin. "It makes sense. If he faked his death, it was no doubt well-planned and a lot of money would have been set aside beforehand. That kind of money buys rock-solid new identities and greases the palms of any official that needs to be greased. All of those states are very modern with stable electricity, stable food and water supplies, stable Internet. He could buy himself a floor in one of those high-rises with a private elevator, and no security cameras. Set up a luxury condo and a state-of-the-art lab attached to it and enjoy life in isolation. Let's start reviewing some footage of condos that allow long-term rental or ownership."

Leroux chewed his cheek for a moment. "That's going to be an awful lot of footage. These countries have built their entire economy around things like that."

"True, but this was planned out, and a lot of that was within the past decade. I guarantee you, the day he died on paper, he moved into a unit, so anything built since then can be filtered out. Look for anything luxury at least ten years old that allows long-term rental or ownership, and see if you can get your hands on the tenant list, see if there's somebody that showed up ten years ago that's still there. And don't just look for people's names. Chances are this was done through some sort of shell corporation."

Leroux chuckled. "You'd think you've done this before, sir."

"I haven't always just pushed paper." Morrison leaned back. "So, what's the game plan if you do find him?"

"That's the question now, isn't it? We've got the professors and their friends, along with Dylan, Sherrie, and Fang on a private jet heading for the Azores where they're supposed to be switched to another plane that we haven't been able to find yet. With this new revelation that he's most likely holed up in the Gulf States, I have a funny feeling he's bringing them to him."

Morrison's eyes narrowed. "To what end?"

"I can only think he believes he can protect them, but I don't know. Maybe he wants to tell her the truth in person, then maybe hand himself over."

"To whom?"

Leroux shrugged. "If I were him, I'd be handing myself over to the Brits. Or he might just go into hiding again."

"I don't think so, unless he doesn't care about his sister. If the Chinese know and we know, I'm willing to bet within the next forty-eight hours pretty much everyone in the intelligence community is going to know he's alive. Even if he goes back into hiding, he knows that his sister can be used as leverage against him. They're not safe until either he's dead, he's in our hands and that's made known, or he can somehow convince the world that his research was a dead end. What do you think the likelihood of that is?"

Leroux sighed. "I read the classified file. The assessment ten years ago was that he was close. If he kept working on it, he's probably already cracked the problem."

Morrison agreed. "So, let's assume his research wasn't a dead end, and maybe he's even finished it. The only two choices left is death or handing himself over to someone. Is there any indication the Brits know what's going on?"

"At the moment, it looks like us and the Chinese are the only ones on this, but if the Brits have caught wind, there's no way in hell they'd call us up and let us know. They'd want him for themselves."

"We need to get in there and extract him and the others. At least then we'll control the situation. We can let him decide where he wants to go after that, but right now, it's just too risky. If the Chinese get him first, he's not going to be given any choice, and he'll be tortured into giving up any secrets. Let's get a unit in position, ideally Bravo Team since they know all the players. The professors will trust them and they should be able to convince Palmer to go with them."

Leroux scratched his cheek. "Dawson just got married, sir, plus they lost a man in Myanmar. The team's been stood down for a week."

"Didn't you say you just had Atlas and Niner on scene?"

"Yes, sir, but that wasn't us."

"No, but it means at least some of them are willing to work. And remember, we don't need a full team. We've got two of our own assets plus a freelancer there. Not to mention the professors know how to shoot the shit out of anything. That's five trained guns right there. Let's see if we can get four from Bravo Team into position. That should be more than enough. This needs to be as covert as possible. We're not going in with Black Hawks and attack helicopters. I'll give Colonel Clancy a call and give him the heads up. I'm going to contact the Pentagon as well and see what assets we have in the region that can be put on standby just in case the shit hits the fan."

Leroux rose. "Yes, sir." He paused. "One question."

"What's that?"

"How far are we willing to go to make sure the Chinese don't take him?"

Morrison regarded him for a moment. "Tell Kane that if it looks like the Chinese are going to take him, he's authorized to eliminate Palmer."

Leroux tensed. "Sir?"

Morrison sighed. "I'm sorry, son, but we don't have a choice in the matter. If the Chinese or any of our enemies get their hands on him, it'll be open season on all of our secrets. They could take down any computer system in the country, banking, the power grid, water supply, anything, and even once we restored it, all we'd be doing is protecting it with the same type of encryption we have now. From what I've read on this technology, they could just go in after we get it back up, crack the encryption in a matter of hours and bring it all down again. Rinse and repeat. Our nation is screwed. If we can't have the technology, then nobody can."

"Professor Palmer is not going to be happy if we kill her brother, sir."

"Unfortunately, when it comes to the security of this nation, one academic's feelings aren't my concern."

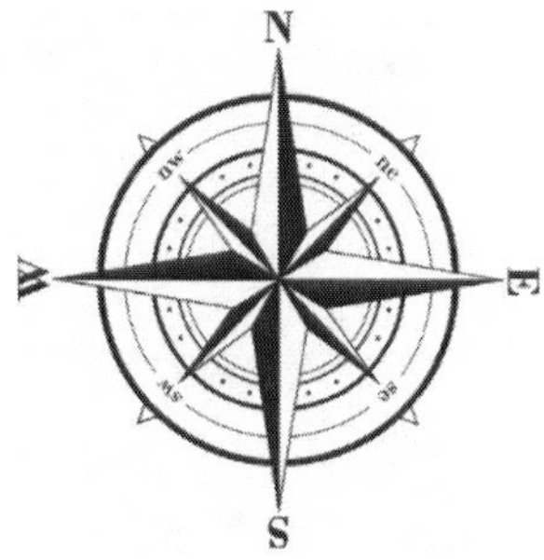

1st Special Forces Operational Detachment—Delta HQ

Fort Bragg, North Carolina

A.k.a. "The Unit"

Niner and Atlas marched down the nearly deserted corridor toward Colonel Thomas Clancy's office. They were about to be called onto the carpet for what they had just done off the books. Niner could live with that, and he was certain Atlas could as well. If they hadn't taken the job from Temple, the professors and their friends could be dead, and potentially Kane and the others as well. If his career ended on a high note like that, he'd be fine with it, though he had no desire for his career to end. He loved his job and couldn't imagine doing anything else.

"How deep in it do you think we are?"

Atlas shrugged, tapping the top of his forehead. "Up to here, I'm betting." He looked down at Niner. "Which means you're screwed."

They entered the outer office, Maggie Harris' usual domain, though not at this hour. Clancy's door was open and Niner rapped on the doorframe. "Colonel, reporting as ordered, sir."

Clancy pointed at two chairs in front of his desk. "Have a seat, sergeants."

They both sat as Clancy read something on his computer then leaned back, eying the two of them. "I understand you had a little bit of excitement earlier?"

Niner shifted in his seat. "Just helping out some friends, sir."

"I've got a report here that two of my men using assault rifles engaged unknown individuals in Maryland without authorization."

Atlas leaned forward. "AR-15s, sir. Semiautomatics. And as you know, sir, an AR-15 isn't—"

Clancy held up a finger, stopping the big man. "I know full well that AR doesn't stand for Assault Rifle, Sergeant, it stands for ArmaLite Rifle, and that an assault rifle is fully automatic. And I know damn well that two of my best men didn't go out and break every damn law in the country." He tapped the screen. "I'm just telling you what I'm reading. This is the bullshit that I now have to deal with because of what you two did." He folded his arms. "So, tell me what exactly *did* you do?"

Niner leaned forward. "Sir, it's my fault, not Atlas'. Temple called me, said he had a job. Cameron Leather, the head of the professors' security detail, had reached out to him to get some additional security put on the professors. They said it was urgent. Temple asked if I wanted the job. I took it on a voluntary basis. No pay. This is a favor for friends that we owe. I contacted Atlas and he agreed to join me. We went with legal and registered firearms, with every expectation that this was a babysitting job until Leather could get his people in place. When we arrived, we found the professors being pursued by hostiles. We engaged them, neutralized the hostiles, then surrendered without incident to local law enforcement. A call was placed by Professor Acton to his Langley contacts, and they made a call that led to our release. We put the professors and the others on a plane, then returned here where we received your message."

"We're sorry, sir, if this caused you any headaches," rumbled Atlas. "That was never our intention, but if we hadn't gone…"

Clancy flicked his wrist at Atlas. "Yeah, yeah, I know, they'd probably all be dead. Okay, here's what you don't know. The hostiles that you engaged were Chinese operatives. They lost a lot of men tonight in what I could only describe as a brazen attack on a civilian residence. What did the professors tell you?"

Niner shrugged and leaned back. "Not much. They think that her brother might actually still be alive. Apparently, he's some sort of computer genius who might have invented a device that could blow up all encryption, and whoever gets their hands on it first rules the world."

"In a nutshell, that's correct. My latest update from Langley is that they're quite confident her brother is alive and has been living in one of the Gulf States for the past ten years. And it's their belief that he continued working on his quantum computing research, and that he may have indeed created a device that could render all current encryption algorithms useless."

Atlas whistled. "That can't be good."

"The Pentagon agrees. CIA has requested a small team be sent in to assist their people."

"Where did the plane go, sir?" asked Niner. "There wasn't a destination when we dropped them off."

"The Azores."

Niner's eyes narrowed. "The Azores? You mean where I found Atlantis?"

Atlas grunted. "Yeah, *you* found it."

Niner shrugged. "Hey, he who wields the trident—"

Clancy interrupted. "Yes, but apparently they're going to be transferring to another aircraft and we have no idea which aircraft that is, so we don't know what the final destination is. I'm looking for four volunteers. I know you're all off the clock, but—"

Niner cut him off. "I'm in, sir."

"Me too," agreed Atlas.

"Very well, find two more but don't even think about contacting BD. That man is on his honeymoon and if anything interrupts that, I'll never hear the end of it."

Niner leaned forward. "He scares you too, hey?"

Clancy gave him a look. "Not at all, Sergeant. Maggie, however, terrifies me."

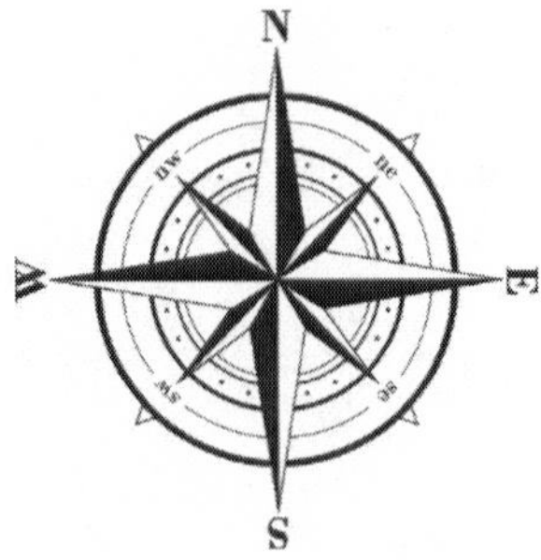

Lot Residence

1649 BC

Lot was nervous. The party was tonight, the visitors from Gomorrah were arriving later today, and everyone he had delivered a message to last night should have seen them by now. There was no turning back. This could be the beginning of his dream for Sodom reaching fruition, but so much had to go right.

His wife stepped into the room. "Can you give me a hand with the vase?"

He flinched. "What?"

"Could you give me a hand with the vase? I can't get it onto the cart. It's too heavy."

He followed her into her workshop and lifted the heavy testament to Sodom's sinful ways onto the cart. He rubbed his shoulder. "That's heavier than I remember," he chuckled as she wrapped her creation, not only to protect it, but to hide it from the eyes of those who might witness the delivery of the commission.

"Anger gives you strength, husband. You picked the original up and tossed it as if it were nothing."

He frowned at the memory. He could count on one hand how many times he had acted on his anger, and he was certain he would still have several fingers left. It wasn't in his nature. He wasn't a violent man. Was he an angry man? Yes, at times, perhaps many times. But just because one became angry, one had to become violent? Anger was an emotion like any other, and it was often valid—it was how one reacted to that anger that separated him from the heathens.

She secured the vase in place and he reached forward and gave it a shake, testing her knots. "Good?" she asked.

"Very good."

"Then let's get this over with. The sooner this is out of here and into Canaan's hands, the better." She paused and regarded him. "I think we should ask for payment of the commission upon delivery, as we normally would."

Lot paused as he eyed his wife. "We're not going to the party then? We're giving up the triple commission?"

"No, that's not what I'm saying. But after what you did last night, should someone find out, he may refuse to pay."

Lot folded his arms and scratched his chin. "I hadn't thought of that. I think you're right. We'll ask to be paid then tell him we're still coming to the party tonight when he can pay us the rest."

They wheeled the cart into the back courtyard. It wasn't far to Canaan's residence. Unlike many of the elite who lived clustered in a part of the city away from the riffraff, Canaan preferred to be in the thick of things, and with a fine home in the center of Sodom, he could walk out his door and partake in all its sinful pleasures.

They were shown in by a servant and Lot gasped at the opulence as they rolled the vase into the room. Polished stone floors, intricate columns, tapestries, works of art, vibrant colors that he rarely saw outside of his wife's creations. It was unlike anything he had ever seen, the wealth involved unfathomable.

"Ah, my favorite couple!" cried Canaan as he emerged from a side hall, his arms outstretched, his robes crisp and unblemished. His eyes widened at the sight of the wrapped vase. "Is this it?"

Idit bowed slightly. "It is."

"Let me see it! Let me see it!"

She carefully unwrapped it then stepped back as Canaan slowly circled it, his mouth agape, his eyes wide in awe. "This is unlike anything I've ever seen. It's so lifelike." He pointed, laughing. "Is that me?" Idit nodded and he chuckled at whom his artistic representation was having sex with. "And is that Lady Adah?"

"It is."

He roared with laughter and his head tossed back as a hand gripped at his chest. "That is so scandalous. I love it!" He eagerly continued, pointing out other figures from his list. "They're going to love it!" He pointed at the center of the room. "We'll put it right here. When everyone arrives tonight, they'll see it, and I have a feeling I'll be commissioning another one from you with more likenesses to be immortalized."

Lot wasn't so sure of their benefactor's prediction. He helped his wife roll the vase into position, then dared a question. "Will these people be here tonight?"

"Yes, they will. Every one of them." Canaan grabbed Lot by the shoulder and gave him a shake. "And I highly recommend you try Lady Adah. Exquisite creature." He winked at Idit. "And very open-minded should you wish to participate."

Lot wrapped an arm around his wife. "Like we said, we'll be attending, not participating."

Canaan smirked. "And like I said, you won't be able to resist. I guarantee it."

"We'll see." Lot sucked in a breath. "Are you satisfied with the commission?"

Canaan redirected his attention to his new prize. "Absolutely."

"So, the commission is fulfilled?"

"And then some."

"Then I respectfully request payment. We have bills to pay."

Canaan batted a hand at him. "You'll get paid tonight, the amount depending on what happens."

Lot bowed his head, clasping his hands in front of him. "With respect, those are two separate transactions. We'd like to be paid now for the commission, and then tonight, based upon what happens, you can pay us the bonus. It just squares everything away."

Canaan frowned, staring at him before giving an exasperated sigh. "Very well. I understand these things are thought of differently among your kind than mine." He leaned forward and wagged a finger at them both. "But I expect to see you tonight. And make sure you're here before my guests arrive so you can stand beside your creation and answer their questions. Then, God willing, earn more commissions tonight than you could possibly imagine."

Lot bowed as Canaan retrieved his purse, dropping a handful of coins into Lot's hand. "We'll try, but we have guests. We'll have to see what time they leave."

Canaan appeared far more interested in the mention of these guests than Lot had expected. "And just who are these guests of yours? Family? Friends? Do I know them?"

Lot turned toward the door in an effort to end the conversation. "No, nobody you know."

"How can you be so sure? Most of this city has passed through the doors of one of my establishments."

"I can assure you they haven't."

Canaan followed them toward the door. "Why don't you bring them tonight?"

"Absolutely not. They wouldn't…" Lot's voice trailed off. He had to be careful.

"They wouldn't partake in such things?"

"No, they wouldn't."

Canaan smirked. "Yet you would have said the same of yourself a week ago, and tonight, you're my guests. Why don't you bring them and let them decide?"

"Again, no. They have a long journey ahead of them."

"Oh, so they're not from Sodom?"

Lot cursed himself. "No."

"Where are they from?"

"Does it matter?"

"Only in that you don't want me to know." Canaan's tone had changed slightly, his veneer of friendship tarnished with a hint of anger.

"They're from Gomorrah. They're coming to discuss a commission," said Idit. "Word of my work apparently has reached them."

A smile flashed on Canaan's face as he leaned back, his hands splayed. "Now, how hard was that?" He gestured at the vase behind them. "I do believe this is the finest example of your work. Extend my invitation and leave it up to them to refuse it. Should they come with you, they can have a private viewing."

Lot bowed. "I'll ask them." He hurried Idit out of Canaan's large home. He stepped aside as a woman mounted the steps, a vile-looking creature from the way she was dressed, clearly one of the man's prostitutes.

She smiled at him. "Fancy seeing you twice in one day."

He eyed her, saying nothing as he continued down the steps, the woman cackling behind him.

"Don't worry, love. He didn't lay a finger on me."

Lot grabbed the cart and they hurried away. Idit looked up at him. "What was that all about?"

"I have no idea. I don't think I've ever seen her before in my life."

"What did she mean by twice in one day?"

He shrugged. "I've only seen you, the children, and Canaan today. You've been with me the entire time."

Idit chewed her cheek. "Perhaps we crossed her path on the way here."

"Perhaps." He picked up the pace. "Our guests will be arriving soon."

"Are you going to invite them to the party?"

"Absolutely not."

She giggled. "And are we still going?"

He felt the bundle of coins in his robe that could be triple in weight before the end of the night. "What do you think?"

She shrugged. "If we go, we get our payment, then secure the season for our children. Besides, like he said, we might get more commissions out of it."

He brought their tiny procession to a halt and faced her. "You would paint more like that?"

"Why not? It harms no one. And now that we know how much he's willing to pay, we can increase the price without any of this other nonsense. We could probably charge double or triple just for the straight commission."

"But is this how you want to be remembered?"

She stared up at him. "What? As a woman who used her talents to feed her family?"

He frowned and resumed heading to their home. "I suppose that's one way of looking at it."

"It's the only way to look at it. We're not in any position to turn down money. Certainly not this amount. While we may frown upon these people, perhaps some good can come of it. We take advantage of their depravity, feed and clothe our children, keep them warm at night, all with Sodom's ill-gotten gains. Maybe that's a good thing."

He wasn't so sure about that, but for the moment, she was right. They were poor. These people were rich. If they were willing to pay exorbitant amounts to immortalize their debauchery, then who was he to say no?

He sighed. "If my plan works, there might not be any more commissions to be had."

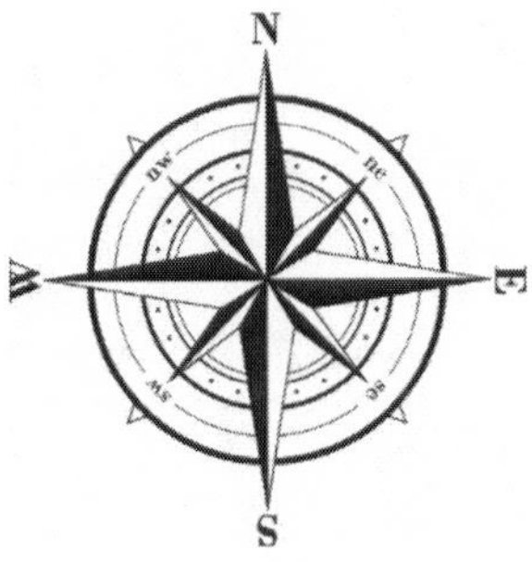

Ponta Delgada Airport

Azores, Portugal

Present Day

Mary stepped off the private charter and onto the tarmac. She had never been to the Azores and had never had any desire to do so. It was merely a curiosity, another place she could check off her list that she had visited, but it certainly wasn't a bucket list item. When she had agreed to help Palmer fake his own death, he had paid her a huge sum of money with one condition—that she insert herself into his sister's life and watch out for her. They had brainstormed just how that insertion might work. Pretending to become friends with her had been dismissed. Friendships came and went, and this relationship would have to last years, perhaps decades.

It would have to be a business relationship. Palmer had suggested travel agent, and after some discussion, Mary had set about creating her own private company, establishing a fake history for herself and the business, then after the funeral, which she attended, approached Laura and offered her services. Once Laura had inherited the unfathomable amount from her brother's estate, she had agreed and the relationship had developed over time, initially restricted to commercial bookings, hotels, the usual, but she had eventually convinced Laura to purchase a part of a lease-share, and once James Acton had entered her life, things had become truly busy.

Laura had never attracted trouble until she met him, but now the two of them were truly a full-time job. It was impressive the trouble they could get into. The job she had agreed to was to watch out for Palmer's sister in case anything went wrong with his plan. Never could she have imagined what she would end up dealing with.

The truth was all coming out now and she had to wonder, once this was over, what she would do. She rather enjoyed what she did for Laura and her husband, and their extended family, and whenever they got in trouble and she had to help bail them out, it was a thrill, reminding her of her old career at MI6. Yet it might be time to move on. Assuming everything was settled in some satisfactory way, her job was over, what she had agreed to, fulfilled.

She sighed as she stood by the terminal, enjoying the sunrise. Laura's plane would be here shortly then they would all be taking hers to their final destination, and then her life as she knew it was likely over.

And she didn't like the sound of that.

Laura rushed down the steps of the private jet and into Mary's arms, hugging the woman hard as tears flowed. "Oh, thank God you're here. I just don't know what's going on. I don't know what to think. I'm so confused!"

Mary smiled at her, her own eyes glistening. "Let's get on the other plane and I'll explain everything." She stepped back as James joined them. "Do you have any luggage?"

"Just what we're carrying," replied James. "There was no time to pack."

"Do you have any weapons?"

Kane stepped over. "Yes. Is that going to be a problem?"

"It will be where we're going."

"And where is that?"

"I can't tell you until we're in the air. I recommend you leave every weapon you have, including knives, on the aircraft. I'll have it returned to a safe location where everything will be recovered by one of my people."

Kane's eyes narrowed. "One of your people?"

She smiled slightly. "I'll explain—"

"When we're on the plane." Kane rolled his eyes. "I know, I know." He indicated for Sherrie and Fang to join him and they returned to the plane, reappearing a few moments later. "Let's get the hell out of here," said Kane. "If the Chinese managed to get a team here, we've got no way to defend ourselves now."

They boarded Mary's plane, their travel agent heading for the cockpit then joining them again a few moments later. "The pilot has confirmed we're all fueled up and cleared for immediate takeoff. I had some friends arrange a lockdown of the entire grounds and a diversion of all flights except for yours and mine for the past six hours. That's not as big a deal as it sounds since there's not a lot of overnight flights here, but it means if the Chinese didn't already have somebody in position, then they didn't get anybody in by plane, and it's too far to get anybody in by boat in time."

The plane taxied as everyone took their seats. Laura sat and James dropped beside her, buckling up. "So, what you're saying is we're hoping the Chinese didn't think the Azores was of enough strategic importance to bother positioning a team?"

"Exactly."

The plane turned onto the runway, its engines powering up. The pilot's voice came over the speakers. "Ladies and gentlemen, this is going to be a little bit rougher than you're used to, as per instructions from your hostess."

Mary turned in her seat to explain. "I told him there was a chance we might get shot down, so he should try to gain as much altitude as rapidly as possible."

Mai yelped. "Do you really think we could be shot down?"

Mary shrugged. "Anything's possible, though I doubt it. Even if the Chinese had a team here, I doubt they'd have equipped them with shoulder-launched surface-to-air missiles."

The plane surged down the runway, rapidly gaining speed. The nose gear lifted off, then the rear, the engines of the jet screaming behind them, the entire airframe rattling as the steepest incline Laura had ever experienced on takeoff continued. She peered out the window to see the ground rapidly falling away, giving way to the ocean that surrounded the small islands. The angle of ascent slowly eased into something she was more accustomed to, then the engines eased off slightly, reducing the vibrations.

The pilot's voice returned. "Ladies and gentlemen, I think it's safe to say we're out of any danger, and I'd like to thank our hostess for taking me back to my days when I used to fly Tomcats for the Navy."

Mary unbuckled and rose, standing in the aisle. "That's why I chose him, because of his military background."

Laura shook her head. It was yet another piece of the puzzle that didn't make sense. How did this woman know about the pilot's military history? How had she been able to select him to be the pilot on a last-minute flight? "Just who the hell are you?" she finally blurted out. "And don't tell me you're a travel agent."

Mary laughed. "Well, I *am* a travel agent. That's the truth, but I'm *your* travel agent and one other."

Laura stared at her blankly as she attempted to make sense of the nonsensical statement. "How the hell does somebody make a living with only two clients?" Her eyes shot wide. "Charles!"

"Exactly."

"Then he *is* alive."

"Very much so."

Laura's shoulders slumped and the tears of betrayal, relief, and confusion flowed. James wrapped an arm around her shoulders and held her, taking over the questioning that she could no longer manage.

"I think you owe us an explanation."

"And Charles has authorized me to tell you everything and to answer all questions that I'm capable of answering."

And for the next fifteen minutes, Mary described in detail why and how Laura's beloved brother had felt it was necessary to fake his own death, and it broke her heart. She now understood why he felt it was necessary. That had been made clear by the events of the past day. There indeed wasn't a government on this planet that wouldn't kill for this technology. What hurt was that he had excluded her. She would have happily disappeared with him, yet she supposed she could understand why he didn't want that life for her.

She lay her head on James' shoulder. For one, she never would have met the love of her life. Mai would still be living under a repressive regime in Vietnam, never to have met Tommy. James would have found the crystal skull in Peru and would likely have been killed by Bravo Team since he would never have fled to England to find her, because, on paper, she would be dead.

She squeezed her eyes shut, humbled at how much her being alive had affected the world around her. How many people were alive because she had met James? How many lives had been saved?

She sighed.

"Are you okay?"

She looked up at her husband. "I will be. I just can't…what's happened, it's like a dream, a nightmare."

"Where are we heading?" asked Kane.

"I've been instructed to tell you only that it is one of the Gulf States."

James' eyebrow shot up. "The Gulf States?"

"Yes, I purchased the top three floors of a luxury condominium there through a shell corporation that can't be traced back to Charles. We needed him to live in a stable regime where there was little likelihood of him being recognized, and money could solve any problem."

Laura tweaked on that statement. "But I inherited all of his money."

Mary smirked. "No, actually, you didn't. In the weeks leading up to your brother's, shall we say, accident, he made a series of very large, very risky investments that all bombed on paper. The inheritance you received was about half of what he actually had. He paid me a substantial sum to watch over you so that I could have a business with only two clients and give up my career, but the rest actually bounced around multiple shell corporations and numbered accounts. It allowed your brother to lead a life of luxury that compensated in some little way for the solitude that became necessary, and also allowed him to continue his research."

Kane leaned forward. "And that research?"

"You'll have to ask him that when you see him."

Laura perked up. "You mean I'm going to see him? I'm going to see my brother?"

Mary smiled. "In about eight hours."

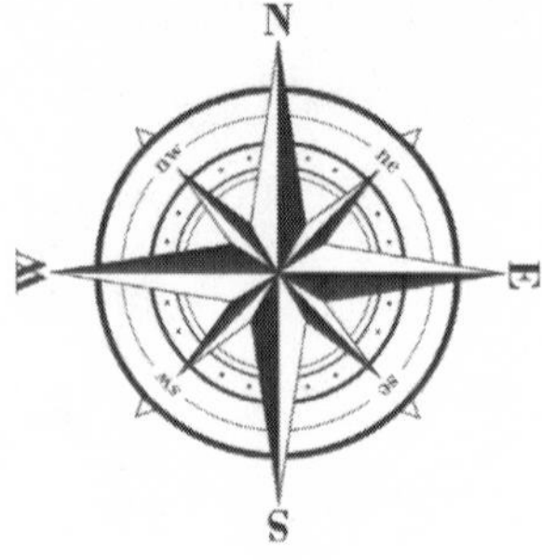

Operations Center 2, CIA Headquarters

Langley, Virginia

Leroux watched the replay of the satellite feed showing the professor's plane unloading in the Azores, the passengers immediately boarding another aircraft already waiting. He turned to Tong. "What plane is that?"

She shook her head as she continued to work her station. "I don't know. It's not supposed to be there, but get this, that airport's been on embargo for six hours. No planes in or out except for the professors'."

"And apparently one other."

Tong shrugged. "Like I said, it's not on any of the systems. It shouldn't be there."

"Get the tail number."

Tong worked her magic and pulled up the registration number from the tail of the aircraft. She ran it and threw up her hands. "It doesn't exist!"

"What?"

"It doesn't exist. It's not in the system."

"How the hell does a plane with no registration number not only get into the air, but land then take off again with nobody questioning anything?"

"Something tells me there are a lot of greasy palms around the aviation community today," muttered Child as he spun in his chair.

Leroux disagreed. "No, bribery gets things ignored, but you can't wipe the registration of a plane from existence. Can we get the data plate off the footage we have?"

"Give me a sec." Tong went to work and isolated an image from airport security, running it through an enhancement routine to clear up the grainy image. "Got it. Running it now." And again, she threw up her hands. "It doesn't exist! According to the manufacturer's registry, as well as FAA and European registrars, that plane was never manufactured and never officially put into service."

"All right, we know that's bullshit. Let's work the problem from the other end. They met a woman there. I'll bet Randy's next paycheck that she was our travel agent, Mary Winters."

"Hey!" exclaimed Child as he killed his spin. "How did my paycheck get dragged into this?"

Leroux continued. "We know she's based out of London, so that's as good a starting point as any. Let's start pulling footage to find out how the hell she got to the Azores. Find out where she lives. See if you can get a shot of her leaving because she would've had to do so in the middle of the night. There's no way she gets on a non-existent flight."

Child grinned. "Unless she's Wonder Woman."

"The plane's not invisible, you tool!" shouted Therrien in the back.

Child turned toward his taunter. "It might as well be if every system in the world says it doesn't exist."

Leroux paused, his jaw dropping as he faced Tong, his second-in-command doing the same. "You don't think?"

She shrugged, her eyebrows rising. "It definitely fits."

"What?" asked Child.

"If Palmer has invented a machine that can break any encryption, then all he had to do was remove all records about that aircraft and we'd be seeing exactly what we're seeing now. It was never built. It was never registered. It's never flown."

"Holy shit!" exclaimed Child. "You're right. No manufacturer makes a fifteen-million-dollar aircraft and doesn't register that fact."

"There's one thing we're forgetting," said Tong.

Leroux faced her. "What's that?"

"Black Ops aircraft wouldn't be registered."

"We would know about them."

"If they were ours, yes."

Leroux chewed his cheek for a moment. "That's definitely a Gulf V built by General Dynamics. They would still register it." He shook his head. "I could see it if it was Chinese-made or Russian, but not American. I think it's much more likely, knowing what we know, that Palmer has built his quantum decryption device and is using it to hide this flight."

Child looked about the room. "If that's the case, he could be monitoring everything we're doing."

"Technically, yes, though he'd have to know where to look. Just because you can break any encryption in the world doesn't mean you have automatic access to everything. You still need to know it's there to look for."

"Should we be worried?" asked Tong. "I mean, we have to trust that this so-called travel agent is on our side or at least the side of good and isn't actually a Chinese mole, but if our encryption can be broken, should we be careful what we're putting out there?"

"No. I'm not going to change the way we're doing things based on a hypothetical. And besides, he has to know we're not the ones he needs to worry about, it's the Chinese and the Russians. If anybody should be concerned about their systems being hacked it's them, not us."

"Until we fail."

Leroux spun toward Child, the kill order on Palmer something known only to the Chief, Kane, and himself. "What do you mean by that?"

"I mean, surely we all realize where this is heading. There's no way in hell we can let the Chinese get their hands on Palmer. You don't think the Chief's going to give a kill order if we can't bring him in first?"

Leroux grunted, impressed at the young man's assessment of the situation. "We're not there yet. Let's just track back this aircraft and trace where it's going. I want our Delta guys to have a shot of getting there on time."

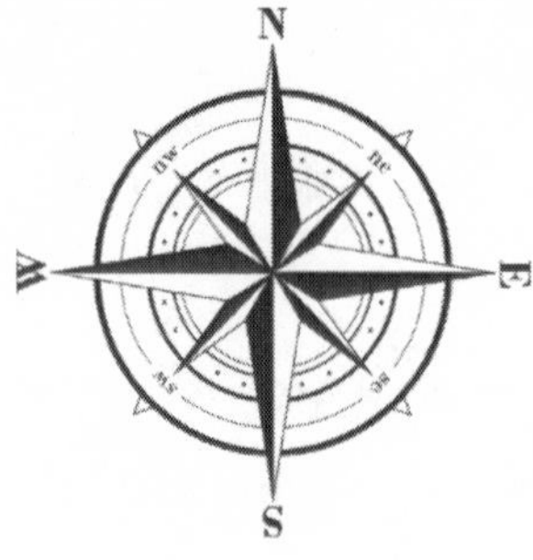

Over the Atlantic

Niner sat in the second seat of the F/A-18F Super Hornet as it blazed a trail across the Atlantic. At the moment, it was the fastest way to get from point A to point B on the planet, with refueling aircraft rendezvousing with them at points along the way. He couldn't wait for the day when Elon Musk had his Starship ferrying people around the planet in thirty minutes or less.

Dominos for everyone.

It was no wonder the US Air Force already had their tentacles into the project. If you could insert 100 or 200 troops at a time with equipment anywhere on the planet in less than an hour, the strategic advantage would be incredible. But while he was certain riding a rocket ship into battle would be a thrill, he had a feeling it wouldn't compare to a Super Hornet for the fun factor.

He leaned forward and glanced out the cockpit to see the other three planes in formation. He and Atlas had met with Master Sergeant Mike "Red" Belme shortly after leaving the Colonel's office. Red was second-in-command of the team and best able to choose who should volunteer for the mission. Niner had no doubt that every man on the team would be willing to go, but because it was only to be four of them, they needed to round out the skills.

Red couldn't go because of the beating his ribs had taken when he had been shot last week. Red had immediately recommended Sergeant Will "Spock" Lightman, the grieving widower who still felt he owed the professors for funding their off-the-books op in Moscow. Sergeant Eugene "Jagger" Thomas was Red's second recommendation because of his close-quarter combat skills, which were second to none in the Unit. It was Red's belief, and Niner agreed, that if they were to end up in a fight, chances are it would be in an urban setting, possibly inside a high-rise. Sniper skills weren't necessarily an asset in this situation, but the ability to fire blindly around corners and actually hit something after taking a split-second look just might save lives.

They still didn't have a final destination, but Langley was confident their final target would be in one of the Gulf States. His concern was that by the time they got there, it would already be too late. Traveling at Mach 1 was fast, but they had a shitload of ocean to cover, and the professors had already been in the air for several hours before the plane he was in had even left the ground.

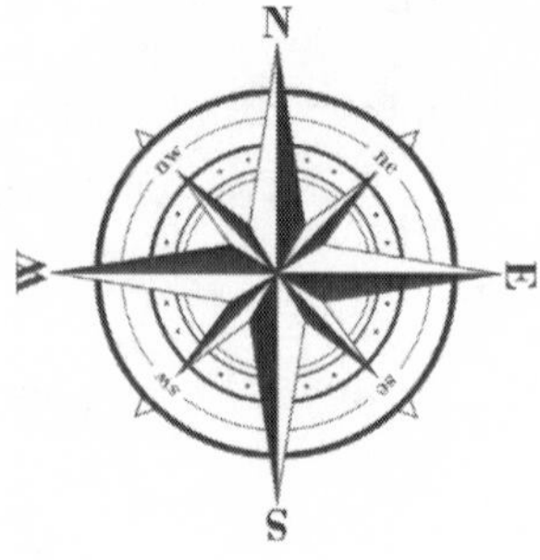

Lot Residence

1649 BC

It was rare that they had guests. In fact, Lot couldn't remember the last time someone other than friends or family had been over, neither of which he considered guests—they were always welcome in his home. True guests were rare, especially considering his opinion of most of those he didn't know in their sinful city. Because of the subject matter he expected to be discussed, they had sent the children away to Idit's sister for the night.

There was a knock at the door. He froze, slowly turning toward it as Idit rushed into the room, straightening her clothes. He reached out and clasped her hand. "Are you ready for this?"

She flashed a smile. "Whatever this is."

He pursed his lips and stepped toward the door, her words resonating. He had no idea what this was. Two people from Gomorrah claiming to represent a group called the Angels of God were here to discuss his efforts to cleanse Sodom of its sinful ways. Yet how could they know what he was doing? He spoke to his friends about how he felt, to fellow shopkeepers who complained about constantly cleaning up after the revelers each morning, yet did nothing to discourage the goings on. Could word have reached Gomorrah? It obviously had, otherwise, they wouldn't be here. That meant something he had said to someone had made an impression, enough for it to be repeated in another city. He had to admit to a touch of pride at that, and pride was sinful as well.

He opened the door and smiled at the sight of two men in crisp white robes. Both were strikingly handsome, about his age, and he found it impossible to believe they had just traveled from Gomorrah, for neither had a spot on them.

"Are you the pottery maker, Lot?"

Lot bowed. "I am. And you are the Angels of God?"

Both men bowed. "I'm Raphael," said the first.

"And I am Gabriel," said his partner.

Lot stepped back, extending a hand and inviting them inside. The two men entered. "This is my wife, Idit."

She curtsied. "May we offer something after your long journey? Food? Drink?"

Both men declined the offer, Raphael smiling at her. "A journey undertaken in the service of God is never a long one."

Lot gestured for the men to sit then indicated Idit. "May my wife be privy to what we are to discuss?"

"Of course."

The four of them sat and Lot shifted uncomfortably, uncertain as to what to say. He cleared his throat. "So, word has reached Gomorrah of my ideas?"

Raphael smiled. "You could say that."

"And what is it you wish to discuss? Collaboration?"

"Nothing like that," said Gabriel.

Lot's eyes narrowed. "Then why are you here?"

"To deliver a warning."

Lot tensed and Idit's hand darted out, grabbing his. "What kind of warning?"

"The day of punishment is at hand."

Lot exchanged a confused look with his wife. "What do you mean?"

"Have you not noticed the sky?"

"You mean the angel fire? I saw it last night when I was out."

"Yes. It is a sign from God that divine retribution is at hand."

Lot frowned. "I've seen such things since I was a child and never heard of anything happening. What makes you think this time is any different?"

Raphael smiled. "We know."

"How?"

"God has told us."

Lot suppressed the urge to roll his eyes. This was apparently a waste of time. Then a thought occurred to him. "Did someone put you up to this? Is someone playing me for the fool?"

Raphael shook his head. "I can assure you nothing of the sort is happening here."

"Then why are you here?"

"To warn you of what is to come."

Lot leaned back, annoyed. "Divine retribution?"

"Exactly."

"And what form will this retribution take?"

"That is for God to decide."

"What? He didn't tell you?"

Gabriel smiled gently. "I see you don't believe us."

"Would you? Two strangers show up at my home, claiming to want to discuss how to help each other clean up our respective cities, and instead you tell me you're here to warn me that God's going to destroy my home. What would you think?"

Raphael bowed his head slightly. "Probably much the same as you now, but there's a reason we're here to warn you. It's to give you a chance to leave and save yourself."

"Oh? I'm supposed to abandon everything I have on your word?"

"That's for you to decide. Should you heed our warning, you should head to the eastern mountains with your family."

Lot laughed. "The mountains? Are you kidding me? Do you realize how far that is? I have two young daughters. We could never make it there. And then what are we supposed to do when we get there? Live in a cave? Starve?"

"It's for your protection."

"It's a death sentence, and you should know that. If we are to escape God's wrath, then why can't we just go to Zoar? It's a fine town of good people, righteous men and women who fear God, and in general, live good lives."

Raphael and Gabriel looked at each other then Gabriel nodded. "Very well. Take your family to Zoar, but do so as soon as possible. And never look back, only forward to your life ahead."

"And will you be there?"

"In spirit. Our job is to warn the righteous."

"Warn the righteous? That God's wrath is about to rain down upon them, and that they should all head for the mountains if they want to survive?"

"Yes."

"And should they not heed this advice from strangers?"

"Then they will die along with the wicked."

"So, God would kill the righteous with the wicked? There are plenty of people who feel as I do. Are you going to warn them all?"

"No. We're here to warn *you*."

"And only me?"

"Yes."

"But I thought you said your job was to warn the righteous of God's retribution."

"It is."

"Then I don't understand."

"Lot, in the eyes of God, *you* are the only righteous man in Sodom. You and your family are the only ones deserving of saving."

Idit gasped. "But what of the children? Surely they're innocent in all of this."

Gabriel addressed her. “Children raised in wickedness by wicked people are doomed to be wicked themselves.”

“How can you possibly know that?”

“Look around you at the wickedness. It’s better the slate be wiped clean than to allow this to continue and spread like an infestation across this land.”

Idit rose and darted out of the room. Everyone else stood and Raphael bowed. “I’m sorry if we upset your wife. That wasn’t our intention. Will you heed our warning and join the righteous in Zoar?”

Lot wanted to tell him where to shove his warning. “You’ve given us something to think about.”

“Then we will take our leave and return tonight to discuss it further.”

Lot never wanted to see the men again, but there was something about them that compelled him to say yes. “Very well, we’ll see you tonight and I’ll inform you of our decision.”

“Excellent.”

The men left and Lot barred the door. He turned to his wife as she reappeared. “What do you think?”

She frowned. “I think it’s nonsense.”

“Which part?”

“All of it.”

“All of it?”

“Yes, all of it. Weren’t you listening? I think those two believe they actually are angels, that God actually sent them.”

“There was something about them, didn’t you think?”

"Oh, there was definitely something about them, but not in the way you mean. Think about it. Two strangers arrive at your home and tell you that they're here to warn you to leave before God destroys the city, and they've decided you are the only one worth saving in the entire place. Does that make any sense to you?"

He frowned. She was right. It was ridiculous, yet he had found their manner compelling. He sensed no deception from them, though he had encountered many a conman during his lifetime that he had felt the same about. And she was right. These men weren't angels, though in their defense, they had never claimed to be. The message had claimed they were representatives of an organization called the Angels of God.

He paused, struggling to remember the exact wording. He would have to reread the letter to be certain as to what they had claimed. In his excitement, he had read it quickly. Maybe they had claimed it, but then why would angels send a letter?

He sighed. "I wish I had my uncle's counsel."

Idit agreed. "I wish that as well. Abraham is a wise man. Perhaps you should send him a message."

Lot pursed his lips. "By the time there'd be a reply, I get the distinct impression it'll be too late."

She took his hand. "Only if these fraudsters are to be believed."

He flinched at the description. It hardly seemed fair. What possible motivation could they have for tricking him and his family into leaving? They could steal the contents of the home and the business, but that would lead to little profit. He paused. "Could they be enemies of my uncle?"

She seized on the idea. "That's definitely possible, but what's their goal? Do they intend to humiliate you?"

His jaw dropped. "Or kidnap me when I leave the safety of the city."

Her eyes bulged. "Or kill you!" She squeezed his hand. "Under no circumstances can we leave! It's too dangerous!"

He sat, no longer confident his wobbling legs wouldn't betray him. That had to be the explanation. These men pretending to be angels of God weren't here to save him, but were instead here to do him harm, likely because of who his uncle was. He stared up at his wife. "When they come here tonight, we must be firm and united in this. We will *not* be leaving Sodom, and they are no longer welcome in our home."

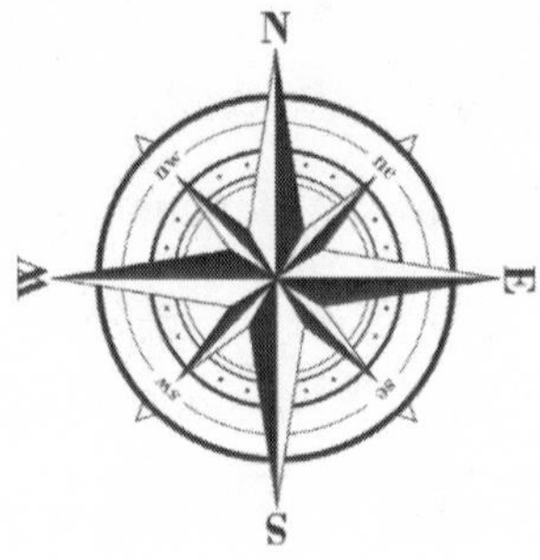

Charles Palmer Residence

Doha, Qatar

Present Day

Palmer was giddy. He couldn't think of any other way to describe it. This was a moment he wasn't sure would ever happen. After ten years, he was finally going to see his sister in person. His plan had been to finish his work, make it public, then take back his life when he was no longer a danger to those around him. He figured as long as he released the antidote to his invention, the worst that would happen is he'd piss off a lot of people in the intelligence community who would have wanted to take advantage of his creation.

And pissed-off regimes rarely killed civilians for such actions. He should be safe, and by extension, so should Laura. Unfortunately, that antidote was years away. His invention worked. He used it all the time for testing purposes, and sometimes for practical applications, such as hiding an airplane. He had no doubt the Americans were tracking Mary's charter—they were the only nation with enough satellite coverage to actually do so. They didn't worry him. While there was no doubt there were shadowy corners within the American government that might kidnap him and force him to work for them, he didn't believe they would harm his sister to gain his cooperation.

It was the Chinese that had him worried. The latest update he had received from Mary indicated the Chinese had made an attempt on Laura, but she and the others had managed to escape and nobody had intercepted them in the Azores. Over the years, he had used his invention to break into the intelligence services of most of the nations he feared. He wasn't sure how the Chinese had found out, but it was likely through taps on search engines that had flagged Tommy Granger's activity.

The Chinese knew something was up, but it also appeared that the Russians and Iranians knew as well. There was no indication they knew exactly what was going on, but messages he intercepted mentioned him by name, both the Iranians and Russians quoting sources as opposed to search engine analyses. It suggested a mole, perhaps within Chinese intelligence, or more terrifying, within the CIA. And if that were the case, as soon as Mary's plane landed with its precious cargo, that mole could reveal his location and Qatar would quickly be swimming with teams desperate to get their hands on him and his secrets.

He stared in the mirror at himself then adjusted his tie. He wanted to look his best when he saw his sister for the first time in a decade, and it was a look he was accustomed to despite his secluded life. On the rare occasions he did go out, he needed to blend in. Caucasian men in Qatar were a dime a dozen, but they almost all wore suits.

He stepped out of the bathroom and sat in the recliner occupying one corner of his large master suite. Mary had chosen well, acquiring the penthouse of a luxury condominium designed around privacy and security. His floors could only be accessed through a private elevator, or, in case of emergency, through the stairwell that had multiple reinforced doors and security features. Panic alarms located around his home would lock down everything when activated, and a security team located in the building would be dispatched to deal with any intruders while the authorities were notified. There were too many features to remember, but the fact that this entire bedroom was a panic room was one of them.

He checked his watch and smiled as he leaned back and closed his eyes. Laura would be here soon then he had to figure out what to do with his life so she could continue to enjoy hers.

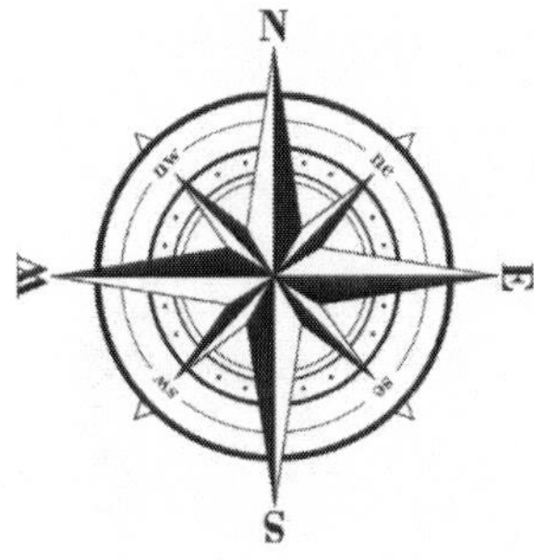

Over the Mediterranean

Kane sat in his luxurious seat, the Gulf V they were on sparing no expense when it came to its passengers' comfort. Yet he wasn't comfortable at all. He had received new orders through his CIA-customized TAG Heuer watch, orders only he was privy to. He was to kill Charles Palmer if it appeared he might fall into enemy hands. It wouldn't be the first time he'd killed someone, not by a long shot. That was his job. Palmer was nobody to him, but he was everything to a woman he considered a friend, to a woman he had fought side by side with, a woman who would do anything to help him if he needed it.

And none of that took into account his former professor, James Acton, who had provided him invaluable advice when he reached a crisis point in his life, uncertain of what to do. If it weren't for Acton, Kane had no idea what he would be doing with his life. Killing Palmer would permanently change everything and the ripple effects could be staggering. If the professors discovered he killed Palmer, they would never speak to him again, for it would be an unforgivable act.

The question was what would happen next. He didn't fear that. They wouldn't go public and blow his cover. They weren't that type of people, but they could withdraw from the world around them. They might attach Bravo Team to his actions, ending the mutually beneficial relationship that had developed out of tragedy. They might decide to turn into nesters so they didn't put any other lives at risk. The world needed more people like them, but if he killed Palmer, he might as well be putting a bullet in Laura's head as well.

Fang took his hand and moved closer. "Something bothering you?"

He hesitated. She would understand the order because she understood the job, but he didn't want to burden her with the knowledge. Yet he desperately wanted to tell her, though he couldn't speak to her about it here. If one of the others overheard, there was no telling what could happen. He squeezed her hand. "I'm fine. Just a little tired and feeling a little naked. I'm not used to not having my gun."

"Can we reequip?"

"As soon as I know where we're going, I'll reach out to one of my contacts."

She rested her head on his shoulder. "Let's try to get some sleep. I have a funny feeling that as soon as our feet are on the ground, we won't be getting any rest until this is over."

He wrapped his arm around her and closed his eyes, losing himself to the steady hums and vibrations around him. But sleep eluded him, for he was the snake in the garden about to betray everyone.

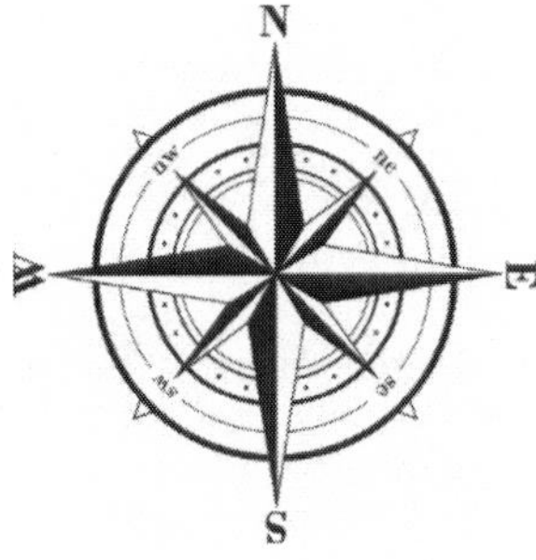

En route to Dubai, UAE

Yan sat at the front of the private jet. Eight members of the elite Beijing Military Region Special Forces Unit sat behind him, all dressed in civilian attire. Authorization for the operation had been given only hours ago by the director. They had tracked their targets to the Azores with little trouble. His team had hacked the cameras at the airport and confirmed their arrival then immediate departure on a plane that apparently didn't exist. Fortunately, his country had at least one operative near every international airport in the world, and the Azores was no exception. While it was unremarkable, many NATO aircraft passed through the area.

Their contact hadn't gained access to the airport grounds due to a lockdown, but that didn't matter. It was obvious the plane sitting on the tarmac, all records of its existence expunged, was to be used as their targets' means of escape. A drone had been used to plant a satellite tracker on it so they knew exactly where it was. They didn't know the destination yet, but based on their heading, the possibilities were rapidly dwindling, and he was willing to bet it was one of the Gulf States.

His money was on the final destination being Dubai, but he was willing to be wrong. The cluster of countries were so close together, they could reposition rapidly. They already had teams in all the major cities of the Gulf States including Dubai, but after what had happened yesterday, he wanted the best of the best on the job, and that was the team behind him. The pre-positioned units were already monitoring all the major airports, and their orders were to acquire the target and follow, not engage.

Western arrogance would lose the day as the Americans once again underestimated the capabilities of the Chinese people. And it would be that miscalculation that would have him acquiring what just might be the biggest technological breakthrough since the invention of the microchip.

And China's plan for world domination would take a giant leap forward, with him playing a prominent role.

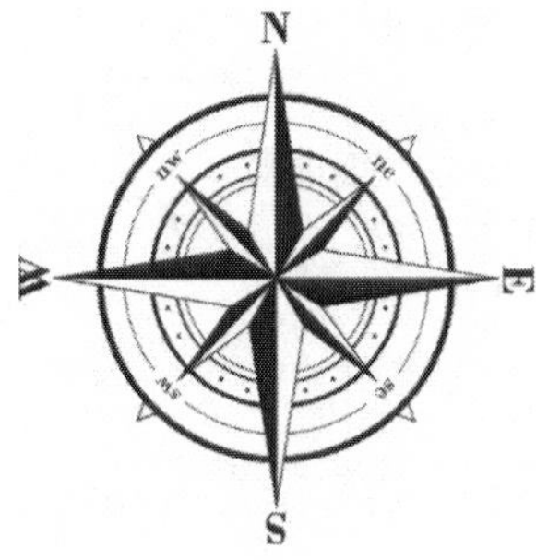

Canaan Estate

Sodom

1649 BC

The evening was proving to be as uncomfortable as Lot had suspected it would be. More critically, it was a disappointment. Every single person on the list he had delivered a message to was here, his threats of going public with their names doing nothing to dissuade them from attending and participating in the debauchery now playing out before his eyes.

He could think of nothing else to do to save Sodom from itself. Right now, as he and his wife sat on soft cushions, staring in awe at a score of people engaged in various sexual acts, making no attempt to hide their actions, he could think of no way to change their way of thinking. He simply had to look at his own reaction. What he was witnessing excited him. Yes, part of him was disgusted, part of him cringed, but too big a part of him wanted to join in, the constant invitations to him and his wife becoming more difficult to resist as the evening progressed.

His wife had been lauded for her creation, everyone delighted with her depiction of the previous party, and she had received another dozen commissions as Canaan had predicted. The wealthiest of Sodom had displayed their true colors, each outdoing the other with their offers, hoping to be the first to receive their unique creation by paying the most. If they remained in Sodom and fulfilled the commissions, their family would be taken care of for years to come just by what was offered this one night.

He glanced over at his wife and his chest tightened, his stomach flipping at what he saw. Her eyes were wide, her cheeks flushed with excitement. He had only ever seen her like this in their bed chambers. She wanted to participate as much as he did, perhaps more. He stared out at the others, performing acts he couldn't have imagined, and realized that any one of these men was a far more experienced lover than he was. He could never hope to satisfy her like them. He closed his eyes.

"What's wrong?"

"Nothing."

She took his arm and drew him closer. "This is making you uncomfortable, isn't it?"

"Yes, but it seems to be exciting you." The bitterness in his voice was shocking.

She shifted closer to him, putting her mouth to his ear. "Only in that I can't wait to get home and try some of these things with you." She patted him on the leg, apparently noticing the physical manifestation of his own shame.

"Not here!" he hissed.

"If not here, then where?"

"Ah, I see you're ready to participate."

She withdrew her hand and Lot covered himself as he stared up at Canaan, standing in front of him, naked, Lady Adah on his arm, as bare-skinned as their host.

Lot shook his head. "No, that was not what you think."

Canaan laughed. "Of course it wasn't." He gestured at the goings on. "So, what do you think? Are you ready to earn five times your commission? Lot, you can just watch if you want. The commission is your wife's if she'll join us."

Lot was terrified she would say yes, that she would give in to her temptations, not at all convinced her excitement was reserved for him and their bed chambers.

Lady Adah extended a hand to Idit. "Join us, my dear. I promise you'll have an experience you'll never forget, and I guarantee you'll be back every chance you get."

To Lot's horror, Idit took Adah's hand and rose. The delight on Canaan's face was sickening and Lot's heart threatened to burst from his chest. "I'm afraid we must take our leave of you, as we are expecting house guests." She let go of Adah's hand and turned to Canaan. "I assume we fulfilled our obligations."

He frowned, disappointed. "Yes. These guests, are they the same two gentlemen from earlier?"

Lot rose, his eyes narrowing. "Yes, but how did you know?"

"How did I know? I know everything that goes on in Sodom. One of my people spotted them entering your house. Did you extend my invitation?"

Lot could lie but that would be a sin, and worse, if caught, could cause him more trouble than the original truth. "No, I didn't. I judged it to be inappropriate considering their piousness."

Canaan gave a lecherous smile. "And their beauty."

Lot's eyebrow shot up. "Beauty?"

"I'm told they are men of an unusual quality, masculine yet not. Pure by all outward appearances. Unspoiled."

Lot was puzzled by the description, though as he thought of his visitors, he could see how someone might think they had an effeminate quality. Canaan glanced down at his nether region.

"As you can see, the thought has me excited. Perhaps I should pay them a visit so I can get to know them."

Lot was appalled at the idea. "That won't be possible. We're only meeting with them briefly then they'll be leaving. And I'm quite certain they have no interest in attending anything like this."

Canaan stepped nearer, his public display uncomfortably close to Lot's leg. "I think after what you tried to do last night, you owe me."

Lot swallowed as he took an involuntary step back, the blood draining from his face. "What? What are you talking about?"

"You were seen by a friend. Any other man out at that hour I would think nothing of it, but you, the most pious of men, the purest among us, would never be out at that hour when only the worst are on the streets, unless he was up to something. And lo and behold, most of my guests here tonight received an anonymous message claiming dire consequences if they didn't take action to clean up our city."

Lot sucked in a quick breath. "I have no idea what you're talking about. I wasn't out last night. I was at home the entire time."

Idit took his arm. "He was."

Canaan held out his arm and snapped his fingers. "Sarah!" A girl being ravished by two men extricated herself and rushed over.

"Yes, sir."

Lot's eyes widened as he recognized her as the woman from earlier who had said they had seen each other twice in one day. But who was she and how had she seen him last night?

Canaan gestured at Lot. "Is this the man you saw last night?"

She smiled at Lot wickedly. "Let me see." She dropped to her knees, directly in front of him, and stared up. "Yes, that's him, all right." She reached under Lot's robe and squeezed. "And I think *he* recognizes me too."

Lot jerked back, gasping at the indiscretion and the revelation. She was the woman servicing the man he had bumped into last night after leaving his last message. "She's mistaken," he managed.

"I think not," said Canaan. "But I'm not a vindictive man, so here's what I propose. You'll drop this nonsense or I'll make it known throughout the city that you and your wife attended this party and participated."

"But that's a lie!" cried Lot.

Canaan reached forward and tapped the proof between Lot's legs. "Your wife touched you, my girl here touched you, and now I've touched you. I'd say that's participation. Now I'll give you two options. Stay and participate fully and receive full compensation, or leave now with partial payment and begin work on your commissions. You'll attend the parties each week delivering what's been completed, and watch the goings on, hopefully eventually participating in whatever is happening." He reached out and grabbed Idit by the waist, drawing her against his naked form. "But as punishment for your attempt at trickery, I will be coming by tonight to either meet your guests with a Sodom welcome, or I will satisfy your wife who was clearly excited by what she has seen tonight."

Idit gasped and slapped Canaan, wrenching herself free. Lot put himself between the two. "You've gone too far!"

Canaan laughed, and it was then that Lot finally noticed the entire room had stopped what they were doing and were now watching the proceedings. "It's you, sir, who have gone too far. You betrayed my trust, and you tried to blackmail my friends. You threatened to destroy their reputations. I should slit your throat for what you've done, but I like you and I like your wife. This relationship can continue to be profitable and satisfying should you open yourself to that possibility. But I will be visiting your house tonight and I will be having your guests or your wife, and should that not satisfy me, then your daughters."

Idit gasped. "What kind of man are you?"

Canaan sneered. "I'm the man with the power, and you have what I want. And I always get what I want." He pointed toward the door. "Now leave before you spoil my party and all of these people come with me to have their needs satisfied by those within the walls of your humble home."

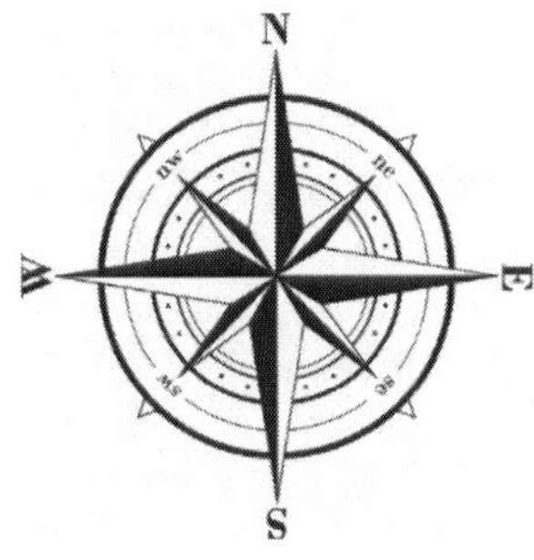

USS Ronald Reagan

Persian Gulf

Present Day

Niner stepped onto the deck of the USS Ronald Reagan then shook his pilot's hand. "Thanks for the lift, Major."

Major Chariya "Apocalypta" Em smiled. "I have no idea what you're talking about. This little trip never happened."

Niner laughed. "I suppose it didn't, but thanks nonetheless." They were led off the deck by one of the crew as Niner exchanged fist bumps with Atlas, Spock, and Jagger. "Man, I don't know if I'll ever get tired of traveling like that."

"Me neither," agreed Jagger. "Though I could do without that landing."

Atlas stretched and groaned. "Those cockpits are not designed for real men."

Niner flashed a smile at Apocalypta as she walked by with the other pilots. "Oh, I don't know. I guess it depends on what your definition of a real man is. I know mine was a hottie."

Atlas rolled his eyes. "Please tell me you didn't continually proposition the poor guy the entire flight."

Niner continued to stare at the gorgeous woman who laughed and gave him a wave before disappearing through a door. Jagger's massive lips followed. "My God, you just spent half a day confined in a small space with her?"

Niner flashed some teeth. "Yep, and the conversation was sparkling. I tell you, having a girlfriend has made me a babe magnet."

Spock cocked an eyebrow. "Monopole maybe."

Niner eyed him. "What's that mean?"

Spock shrugged. "Ask Sheldon Cooper."

An officer emerged from a door and strode over. "Gentlemen, I'm Lieutenant Commander Middleton. I've been briefed on the broad strokes of your mission, but not the particulars, so anything I don't say, assume I don't know and I'm not supposed to know."

"Yes, sir," said Niner. "What's the latest?"

"We believe your target is landing in Doha, Qatar. We've been repositioning all night to be as close as possible to the Gulf States. We can't exactly fly you in and land at the airport, nor can we risk a visible insertion. We have a submarine standing by. She'll be inserting you on the coast where a contact beyond my pay grade will rendezvous with you, provide you with equipment, and transport you to your ultimate destination. Any questions?"

"When do we leave?"

"Immediately."

Niner smacked his hands together with a smile. "That's what I like to hear." He turned to the others. "Let's get a wiggle on, gentlemen. The sooner we get in that long metal tube full of seamen, the sooner we can see some action."

Jagger eyeballed Niner. "Do you listen to yourself?"

Niner shrugged. "What?"

Atlas shook his head. "All those hours alone with a gorgeous woman and the boy is still confused."

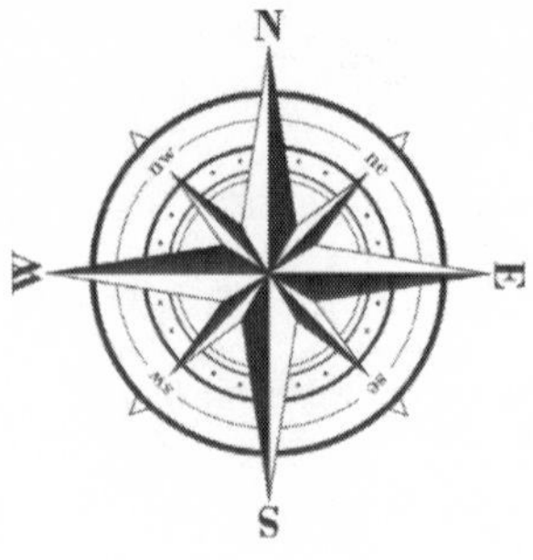

Doha Hamad Airport

Doha, Qatar

Laura's heart hammered as she stepped into the stifling heat of Doha, Qatar, their destination finally revealed to them as they descended. It reminded her of her dig site in Lower Nubia, but it also reminded her of the day her brother was supposed to have died in Jordan. Her jumbled emotions threatened to overwhelm her and she was on the razor's edge of losing control. She was beyond excited that she was about to see her brother, but also hurt and angry. She had blamed herself for ten years for something that wasn't her fault. Ten years had been lost that they could have shared. If only he had trusted her with the truth. Yet it wasn't a matter of trust. He had done it to protect her. She understood that logically, but the emotional side of her couldn't imagine doing the same to him.

She stepped onto the passenger transport with the others and they were soon brought to the charter terminal where Mary had them whisked through customs. Two large SUVs were waiting for them outside with local drivers. Mary split them up, putting the Miltons with Sherrie and Fang in the second vehicle, everyone else in the first. The doors slammed shut then the driver pulled away from the curb, sending them into the light but steady traffic of Qatar's capital city.

Mary turned in the passenger seat and addressed Kane. "There should be a couple of bags behind you." Kane reached back and pulled forward two large duffel bags. "Body armor, weapons, and comms. Everybody gear up."

Kane unzipped the bag and started handing out bulletproof vests. James helped her into hers, asking the obvious question. "Won't this make us rather conspicuous?"

Mary adjusted hers. "We're going into a private garage, then onto a private elevator. Trust me when I say, at this building, geared-up foreigners are not an uncommon sight."

"And the weapons?" asked Laura.

"The people at the building won't care. If the authorities get involved, they're not going to be happy, but things like that can always be taken care of with the right phone calls and cash. If it looks like we're going to get pulled over, all the guns go back in the bag, the bag goes in the rear, and we plead ignorance."

Laura adjusted her vest then inspected the Glock Kane handed her. "Just what is the plan here? I mean, why are we here?"

Mary pursed her lips for a moment. "I'll be honest with you, I'm not exactly sure what the plan is. None of this is supposed to be happening, so a contingency was never set up for this. Right now, the entire point of this is to get you into a safe, controlled environment, and then either your brother has a plan that he'll fill us in on when we see him, or we're all going to have to come up with one together."

Kane shoved his Glock into his shoulder holster. "Well, let me be the first to say that I hope he has a plan and it's a good one. While I agreed getting on the plane back in Maryland was the quickest way to safety, heading to the Azores and then to Qatar where we have no access to help isn't the wisest move."

"And just what would you have done?" asked Mary, the hint of condescension a mistake if Laura knew Kane.

"I would have flown us to Langley, landed at the closest airstrip, and had Echo Team escort us into headquarters."

"That would have left Charles on his own."

Kane cursed. "To hell with him. The whole point of this is to protect those who are actually supposed to be alive." He jerked a thumb at Tommy and Mai. "We've got these two, plus an entire family with a child, in danger because of what your brother, I'm sorry Laura, but what your brother did. They're the priority here, not your brother."

Laura sniffed, his words painful to hear, though he was right. She reached out and squeezed Kane's forearm. "You're right, of course, Dylan, but we're here now. What could have or should have been done is now irrelevant. We need to start thinking of next steps, and I have to think that you're right. We're safer back in the United States at a secure location like CIA Headquarters or Fort Bragg, somewhere where we have people we can trust. The question is, how do we get there now that we're here?"

Kane checked his watch then pressed the buttons surrounding the face in an odd pattern. He stared at it then cursed. "We've got a tail."

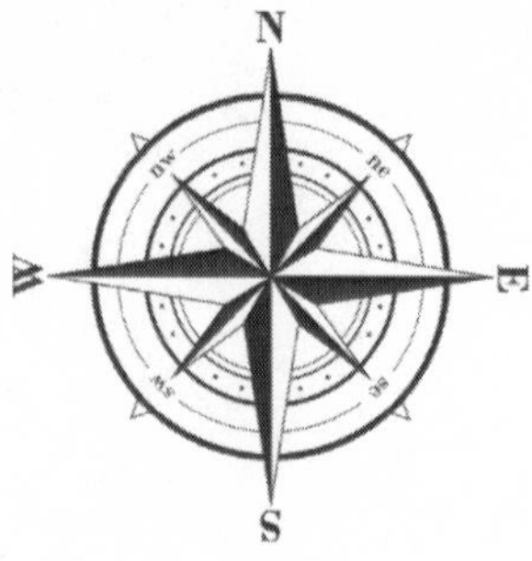

Operations Center 2, CIA Headquarters

Langley, Virginia

Leroux stood behind his station, staring at the display, satellite footage showing the two SUVs containing their people heading through the streets of Doha, Qatar. Blue indicators followed them with identifiers attached, and behind them were two red targets they had spotted following them from the terminal. There was no way of knowing who they were, at least not yet. It could be the Chinese. It could be any number of hostiles. Or, it could just be Qatari security, curious as to whom these people were that had arrived on an aircraft that didn't exist, then blew through customs in record time.

"I've got the plates." Tong brought them up on the screen.

"Run them."

Tong's fingers furiously worked her station as Leroux admired her skills. She was second to none, and he didn't know what he'd do if he didn't have her on his team. She was always level-headed in a crisis and just knew how to do whatever he asked of her. She whistled as she leaned back, jerking her chin toward the screen, Qatari vehicle registrations displayed for both plates.

"Iranian embassy?" Child spun in his chair. "How the hell did they find out? Those guys aren't exactly cutting edge."

Leroux folded his arms as he stared at the screen. It was a good question. It was possible the Iranians caught wind that something was going on, but how they could possibly be there ahead of everyone else was beyond him. Even the CIA hadn't known where they were going until the last minute. He squeezed the back of his neck in an attempt to work out some of the stress building. He turned to face Child. "You're right. They shouldn't be there, but they are. The question is how? How could they possibly know what we and the Chinese didn't?"

"We're assuming the Chinese don't know. Maybe they do."

Leroux agreed. "Let's cast a little wider net, shall we? The Chinese would definitely have teams in Qatar, so as soon as they knew where our people were landing, they would have had plenty of time to prep. And we know they'd be well-equipped, whereas the Iranians are probably using security staff from the embassy and they would have minimal capabilities beyond brute force. Let's see if we can catch sight of any drones or other vehicles being guided by satellite that are hanging farther back than the Iranians."

"How would the Chinese know they were there?" asked Child.

Leroux shrugged. "Same way we did. They have satellite capability, and if this is as important as we think it is, they would have done whatever it took to make sure they didn't lose that aircraft when it took off from the Azores. Remember, whoever gets their hands on this tech first controls cyberspace for the next five to ten years. They're not going to spare any expense."

"But the Iranians? How did they find out?"

Leroux turned back to the display. "Maybe the Chinese have a mole."

"Or we do," muttered Child.

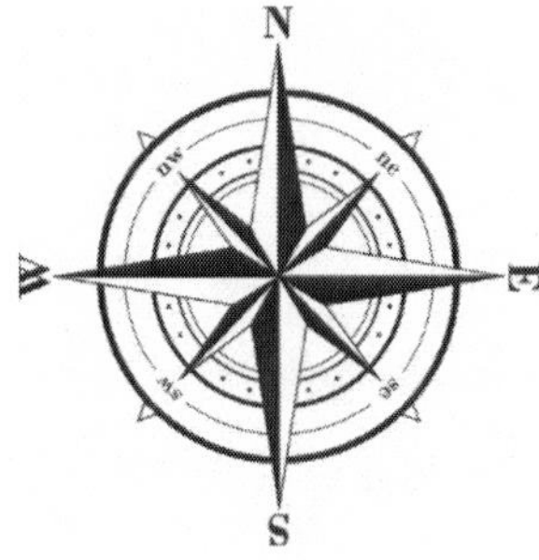

Doha, Qatar

Reza Ahmadi changed lanes as he followed the Americans. They had been sent in last minute from the embassy after a briefing both classified and minimal. The people they were following were up to something, but headquarters wasn't sure what. A paid contact within Chinese intelligence indicated the Chinese were desperate to get their hands on these people. If his country could get them first, they could sell them to the Chinese or some other higher bidder.

But they couldn't exactly grab them off the street. This wasn't Tehran, this was Doha. It would have to be done out of sight. Their contact had told them exactly where and when the plane had arrived, then they had scrambled to get into position, picking the Americans up just as they cleared the terminal. He had no idea where they were headed, he just hoped it was some place out of the public eye where they could take down the two vehicles and seize the hostages.

Once they had them secured, it was easy enough to get them out of the country. They did it all the time with wayward Iranian citizens or others that the government wanted for questioning—they just had to get to them.

He checked his rearview mirror to see the second team directly behind him, following a little too close for his liking. He leaned to his left, checking his driver's side mirror, and spotted someone right on the bumper of the trailing SUV. Doha had its share of asshole drivers like any city. Was that what was going on here? Suddenly the tailgating driver leaned out of the window, a machine pistol gripped in his hand. The muzzle flashed, the sound catching up to Ahmadi's ears a moment later as the targeted vehicle swerved out of control then flipped. He gasped as it landed on its roof then skidded along the highway.

He slammed on his brakes, bringing them to a shuddering halt, then threw open his door as did the others. He drew his weapon and opened fire on the hostiles' SUV as it rounded the upturned vehicle of his comrades. Machine pistols from both sides opened fire on them and one of his team went down. Ahmadi ducked behind the reinforced door as it took several rounds, then reached inside and drew an AK-47. He took aim and opened up with controlled bursts targeting the engine block as the others attempted to take out the gunmen. A blast of steam and smoke erupted from under the hood, killing the approaching enemy's speed rapidly.

He redirected his fire at the windshield as his men continued to fire, those in the upturned vehicle now extricating themselves and joining in. All the traffic had stopped in both directions, civilians abandoning their cars and cowering in fear, others running away from the battle. Another of his men cried out before the final enemy gun was silenced. He indicated for the others to move in then slowly advanced himself. He kicked the driver's body hanging out onto the ground, then quickly searched him for papers and removed a wallet. He flipped it open and tensed at the diplomatic ID. "Report!"

"They're all dead," replied one of his men.

"Then let's get the hell out of here."

"Who are they?"

Ahmadi held up the ID. "North Koreans."

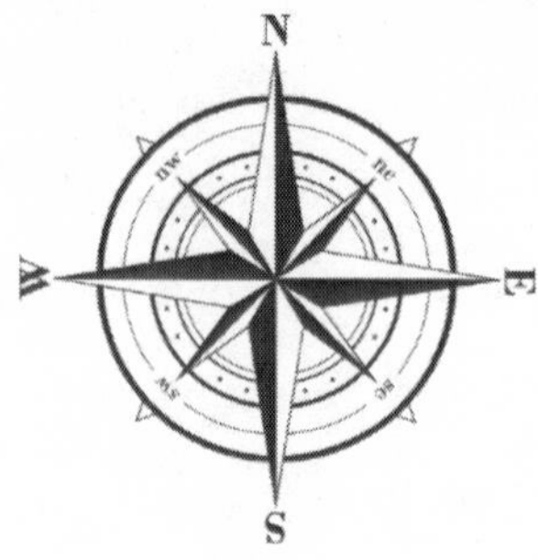

Operations Center 2, CIA Headquarters

Langley, Virginia

Leroux stared at the satellite image, his mouth agape.

"What the hell just happened?" asked Tong.

"I don't know, but we've got another player obviously. Let's see if we can trace that vehicle. It could be the Chinese."

Tong shook her head. "Way ahead of you. North Korean embassy."

Leroux dropped into his chair. "Okay, you're telling me that the North Koreans *and* the Iranians knew when and where our people would be arriving, *and* we still haven't seen any sign of the Chinese, *and* we don't even have our own people in place yet? What the hell is going on here?"

Child spun, staring at the ceiling. "I'm telling you, someone's got a mole. Either us or the Chinese. They're selling the info to the highest bidder then selling it again. If this is as important as we think it is, there are a whack of players who'd pay big bucks to get their hands on it. This could be the mole's exit plan. One last big score that's so big he can disappear and never be found, so he sells the info to everyone. Iranians,

North Koreans, probably the Russians. We could have bit players in there too that are just trying to get their hands on the people so they can resell it, not to mention criminal organizations."

Child's assessment was compelling, and too likely to be bang on. Leroux dialed Kane through the encrypted app, the operations officer answering a moment later.

"What the hell's going on?"

Leroux explained. "It looks like you were being pursued by two Iranian vehicles that were then engaged by another. North Koreans. The Iranians took out the North Koreans but suffered some casualties and are down to one vehicle. Unless they've got some sort of eye-in-the-sky support, there's no way they're catching up to you."

Kane cursed. "Do you mean to tell me that the North Koreans, Iranians, and Chinese are already after us, and we haven't even been on the ground an hour?"

"Expect more."

Kane growled. "And what about the Chinese? Where the hell are they?"

"We haven't spotted anything yet, which tells me they're using either satellite or drones to follow you."

"So, in other words, no matter what we do, they're going to know where we're going."

"Yes."

"All right, this is bullshit. We need an exfil plan and we need it now."

"We're working on one. I recommend you cancel your rendezvous with Palmer and return to the airport."

"We're here," said a woman's voice in the background.

Kane muttered something. "Too late for that now. Just get those exfil plans ready."

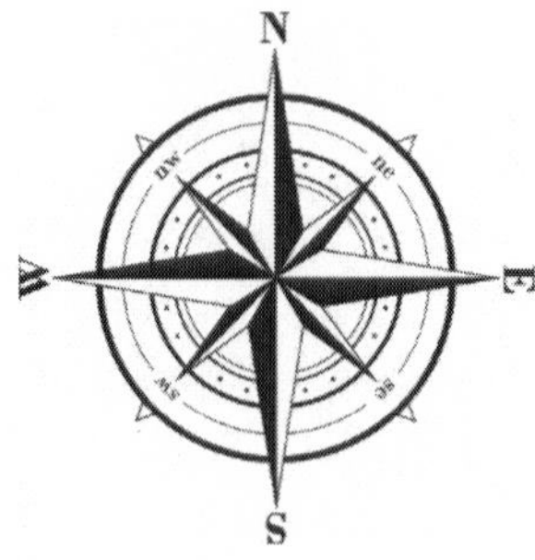

Charles Palmer Residence

Doha, Qatar

Acton held Laura's hand as the SUV tipped forward and headed down the ramp into the underground parking. He was only minutes away from meeting a brother-in-law he was never supposed to see. He was slightly nervous about the meeting. It was like meeting parents for the first time, but he was more on edge from everything going on. He turned to Kane as his former student ended a call with Langley. "So, I take it that wasn't a car accident behind us?"

Kane shook his head. "North Koreans and Iranians fighting it out."

Laura's grip on Acton's hand tightened. "North Koreans and Iranians? Is there anybody who doesn't know?"

Kane rolled his eyes. "I wouldn't count on it. I'm guessing somebody in the know is selling the information on the black market. God knows who's going to be after us, but don't be surprised if someone with borscht on their breath invites us to take a ride with them."

"This is it," said Mary from the front seat as they came to a stop. She opened her door and the rest followed. She led them to a bank of elevators and entered a code into the panel on the farthest one. It opened and they all stepped in. Acton noticed the drivers repositioning the SUVs for a rapid departure as the doors closed. Mary turned to Laura. "Your brother wants to see you first."

Laura sniffed, her eyes wide, her body's tremble felt through the iron grip on Acton's hand. "Can James come with me?"

"No, he insisted on just you."

Acton patted her hand. "It's all right. You should see him first. Remember, despite what's happened, he's still your brother and this is a happy day."

Tears pooled then escaped as the doors opened. They stepped into an impressive reception area, the Middle Eastern design distinctive and stunning.

Mary extended a hand to the left. "If everyone could wait in there, I'll show Laura upstairs. If I know your host, you'll find food and drink waiting for you."

Laura turned and gave him a hug, squeezing him hard. He kissed the top of her head.

"You know where I am if you need me."

She let go of him and followed Mary up a wide staircase that narrowed as it reached the second level of the penthouse. How much this cost, Acton had no idea, but it was clear Charles Palmer hadn't been suffering in squalor these past ten years. He hung back as the others filed into another room and waited until Laura was out of sight before joining them. Two gorgeous women in form-fitting outfits greeted him with beaming smiles, taking his drink order and directing him to an impressive array of food the others were already mounting an assault on, everyone starving, little having been eaten on either flight. His own stomach growled at the sight and he forced himself to fill a plate, though his mind was upstairs with his wife who was going through something he could never imagine.

All by herself.

Laura sucked in a breath through her nose then leaned against a wall, lightheaded. She squeezed her eyes shut as she struggled to regain control.

"Are you all right?" asked Mary, a hand gently taking her arm.

"I will be. This is all just, I don't know, too much." She opened her eyes and stared into Mary's, searching for the truth. "Is he really alive or is this just some elaborate hoax?"

Mary smiled, tilting her head toward a nearby door. "Why don't you ask him yourself?"

Laura inhaled sharply, forcing down a painful lump in her throat, her chest overwhelmed with a powerful ache. "He's really alive?"

Mary nodded.

"I'm really about to see my brother?"

"If you keep walking, yes."

Laura drew a deep breath, squaring her shoulders then wiping her eyes dry with her knuckles. "I'm ready."

Mary stepped over to the door and opened it, pushing it aside. Laura dragged her feet like lead weights toward the opening, terrified yet eager. Was she about to see her big brother, gone for so long? And how much had he changed? Was he the same man she had so admired, had so looked up to her entire life? And what about her? Would he be proud of what she had become, for she was definitely a different person than ten years ago?

She stepped through the door.

"Good luck," whispered Mary as she closed it behind her.

"Hello, Pigeon."

Laura's head spun toward the voice and she cried out, rushing into her brother's arms. She clung tightly to him, afraid if she were to loosen her grip he might be lost to her once again. She sobbed uncontrollably as he held her, his lips pressed against the top of her head as he gently stroked her hair, his own body shaking as he, too, cried.

She finally pushed back from him, still gripping his arms, and stared up into the familiar face. She laughed and reached up, running her fingers across his temples. "I see you've gone a little gray."

He chuckled. "Ten years will do that to you."

She rested her cheek against his chest. "I can't believe this is really happening. I saw you die."

He sighed. "Unfortunately, I had no choice. I knew they'd be coming after me for what I had discovered, and while I could protect myself, they'd always be able to get to the ones I loved. It was the only way I could think of to protect you."

She stepped back and he handed her a tissue from a nearby box, taking one for himself. "But they found you." She dabbed her eyes dry. "The North Koreans and Iranians were following us on the way here, but they took each other out. And the Chinese might know exactly where we are."

He frowned. "I know, everything's all bollocksed up, and I'm not sure what to do about it. It's happening too soon."

Her eyes narrowed. "What do you mean?"

"I mean, I've made an incredible breakthrough."

She thought back to what Tommy had said. "You mean you've created your quantum computer?"

He smiled at her. "What do you know about quantum computers?"

She laughed. "As much as you'd expect me to know, which is nearly nothing. But I have a friend who's very well versed in such things, and he explained it."

"And what did he say?"

"Basically, that if you did invent what the CIA thinks you did, it's a quantum computer that can break any encryption in the world."

"Essentially, yes."

She caught her breath. "And you've made this?"

He nodded. "Yes."

"And it works?"

"Yes. In fact, I've been using it for the past couple of years."

"Then if it's done, why don't you come forward? Just give it to our government or to the Americans, whoever, somebody that can protect you."

"No. No one person, no one government, should have this kind of power. There'd be no more secrets, no more security for everyone but those who possessed it."

"Then why invent it?"

"Because someone was going to eventually, and I wanted it to be the good guys."

"But you just said nobody should have that power."

"No, they shouldn't. Not unless the power can be countered. As soon as I figured it out, I began working on a method to negate my invention."

"I don't understand."

He led her to a couch and they sat. "It's like inventing fire without knowing how to put it out. Bad people could burn anything they wanted and you could never stop them. But if you revealed the secret of fire at the same time as you revealed the fact that water puts out fire, then the risk fire poses is reduced dramatically. I've invented the fire, but I don't have the water yet to put it out. Once I do, then I'll give the world both fire and water, that way people can protect themselves from the fire but also enjoy the benefits that fire can provide. Quantum computing is the future, and I've made it practical. The breakthroughs that'll be possible with the sheer computing power can't even be imagined today. The world needs this, but it has to be protected from the dangers. I'm almost there. All I need is a few more years and I'll have both pieces of the puzzle solved. And when I do, then I can come out of hiding."

Laura gripped his hand tightly. "Years?"

He smirked. "I'm not exactly laying brick here, I'm inventing an entire new way of computing. It could be six months. It could be six years. It could be never, I don't know, but I am making progress. Unfortunately, the fact that I'm alive has been discovered and I'm not sure what to do about that."

Laura tensed. "You don't have a plan?"

"I have a plan for myself. Unfortunately, I don't have one for you and the others. It's just too many people. If it was just you or you and your husband, the three of us could conceivably go into hiding. But you've got a family sitting out there plus young friends, not to mention CIA operatives who now know the truth and will be reporting everything back to their bosses in America."

"You should trust them, they're good people."

"I have no doubt they are, but would you trust their government who have proven time and again that it will abuse its power, invade the privacy of its own citizens, all in the name of national security?"

"Hear them out. It might be the only way."

He frowned. "Unfortunately, you might be right." He rose and she stood with him. "Now, let's talk about your husband."

She smiled. "What about him?"

"Is he a good man?"

She beamed, her eyes glistening. "He is."

"And he treats you right?"

"Better than I deserve."

"Then perhaps it's time I met him."

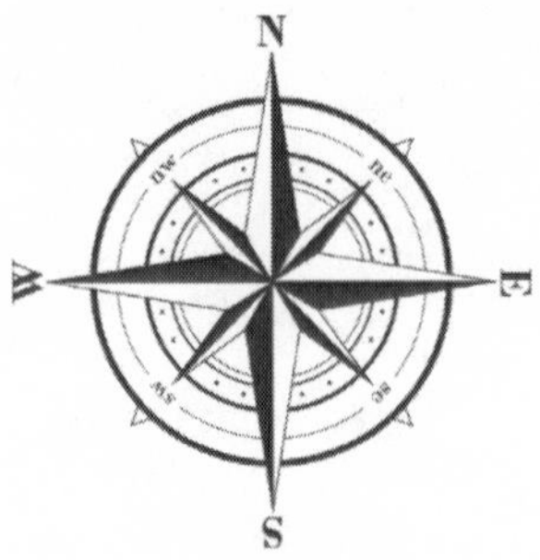

Katara Beach

Doha, Qatar

Niner emerged from the water, strutting onto the beach as if he had been there all day and not just inserted offshore by a nuclear submarine. He paused, surveying the area, enjoying his Ursula Andress moment as his perfect physique was admired by several nearby women giggling to each other. One of them gasped and pointed to Niner's left. He glanced over to see Atlas break the surface, and Niner had to admit to being a bit disappointed with the upstaging.

Atlas ran his hands down his torso, ridding himself of the beaded water. Niner glanced back at the awestruck girls, and he made a decision when he noticed Atlas was enjoying the attention.

Niner rushed over and leaped into Atlas' arms, giving him a big kiss. "You're so handsome in your speedo!"

Atlas grabbed him on either side of the chest and was about to hurl him into the water when Niner grinned.

"Now, don't make a scene."

Atlas growled. "And you're not?" He set him aside rather than hurling him then continued onto the beach, Spock and Jagger about fifty yards away. They walked past the three girls on their beach towels and Atlas nodded at them. "Ladies," he rumbled in his impossibly deep voice.

Giggles.

Apparently, these girls didn't care what Atlas' sexual orientation might be. They were just there for the show.

The team approached the parking lot and a black SUV flashed its lights.

"That must be our ride," said Niner.

Atlas grunted. "Or we're being propositioned."

Niner grinned at him. "I like the way you think."

Atlas rolled his eyes, gesturing at Niner's speedo. "You might want to rethink your choices next time. That leaves literally nothing to the imagination, and I do mean nothing."

Niner glanced down at Atlas' trunks. "Well, we can't all be you." His eyes narrowed. "Holy shit! Does that thing have a pulse?"

The driver of the SUV stepped out. "Beautiful day for a swim."

"It is," replied Niner to the coded prompt. "But I prefer Miami Beach."

"I've heard good things about South Beach."

"So have I, except don't go near it during spring break."

The man extended a hand and Niner shook it. "Right on time, gentlemen. You can call me Samir. I don't need to know your names. Langley has requested that I reequip you."

Niner smacked Atlas' ass. "And clothe us, I hope."

Samir tilted his head back and laughed. He jerked a thumb over his shoulder as he pressed a button on the fob, opening the rear hatch. "I have clothing matching your specs in the rear. I suggest you get dressed as quickly as possible, then you can gear up once we get on the road. There have been developments since you deployed."

Niner rounded the vehicle and grabbed a bundle of clothing, handing it to Atlas, then retrieved one set for himself as Spock and Jagger joined them. Atlas unfolded the pants and held them up. "I don't think these are going to fit."

Spock cocked an eyebrow. "Are those boys small?" He held up his own pants which were huge. He made a show of checking the tag. "It says Hulk." He handed them to Atlas. "Must be yours."

Atlas passed his bundle to Niner. "These things would be Bermuda shorts on me."

Niner handed his bundle to Spock as everyone continued to sort out whose was whose, then slipped into his pants. "You could have done your Incredible Hulk impression."

"Little man, I'm always doing my Incredible Hulk impression."

They were quickly dressed, all in black, each with a colorful shirt to make them appear more like tourists rather than a hit squad. Within minutes they were underway, large duffel bags hauled forward containing body armor and all manner of weapons along with comms.

Niner adjusted his vest from the passenger seat. "You said there've been developments?"

Samir nodded. "Yeah, it looks like the Iranians picked up your friends first, then the North Koreans who were none too happy to have competition. They engaged the Iranians, took out a few of them and one of their vehicles, but all the North Koreans died in the process."

Atlas whistled from the back seat. "And what about the Chinese?"

"Still no word on them. We're thinking they're better prepared. The Iranian and North Koreans were traced back to their embassies by their plates. The Chinese are going to have locally registered vehicles. There's no way they'll make themselves that easy to track. Also, Langley thinks that the Chinese might have a mole selling the location of your target to anybody who's willing to pay. Be prepared for any number of hostiles."

"Lovely," muttered Jagger. "Does anyone have an exfil plan yet?"

Samir shook his head. "None that I've been made aware of, but I've been told Langley is working on something." He gestured at the comms. "Those are already configured. You can jack directly into Control. And by the way, you're now working for the CIA."

Niner fit his earpiece in place and frowned. "The first time I was told I was going to be working for the CIA, I was all excited. I figured it meant gadgets. I haven't seen any yet."

Atlas agreed. "Yeah, our James Bond movies are totally lying to us."

Samir laughed. "We don't break out the ray guns until we really trust you."

Niner activated his comms. "Control, this is Bravo One-One, come in, over."

The reply was immediate, and Niner was pleased to hear Leroux's voice. It meant he had competence at the other end watching their sixes. "Bravo One-One, this is Control Actual. We read you. What's your status, over?"

"Control, we've rendezvoused with our local contact and have reequipped. What are our orders?"

"Our friendlies have arrived at the target's condominium building. As soon as they entered, we lost contact. It appears everything is jammed. We need you to position yourselves near the building until we can determine what's going on."

"Roger that, Control. We'll get into position. What's the status on the exfil plan?"

"We're working on it. We'll brief you as soon as we have the details."

"Copy that. One-One, out." Niner glanced back at the others. "They have no damn idea how we're getting out of this."

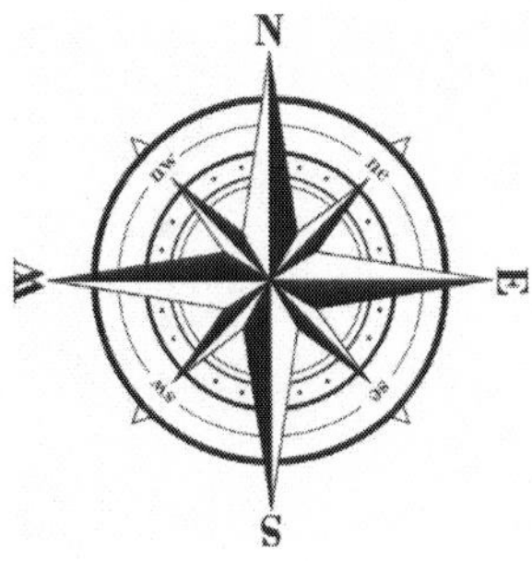

Doha, Qatar

Yan rode in the passenger seat of the lead vehicle that had met them at the private airport. Security had been disabled, the appropriate bribes paid using contacts long established who were accustomed to looking the other way, and his entire strike team was now en route to their target, fully equipped. The local teams monitoring the building with drones and satellite coverage had reported that their targets had been inside for upward of fifteen minutes now. They had no idea what floor they were on or who they were meeting, but his gut told them it was Charles Palmer.

It had to be.

The Party leadership might accuse him of jumping to conclusions if the facts weren't looked at collectively, but somebody had started a massive search for information on a man dead for ten years, and this wasn't an ordinary man. This was an extremely wealthy man, brilliant by all accounts, working on a project that could change the balance of power. A man who had died in an accident, his body never recovered, the authorities inexplicably shutting down the dig within hours and refusing to let anybody back in, a ban that held true to this day.

A man who would be a billionaire today wasn't just abandoned because of an accident. Yan was willing to bet that if they excavated the site, no body would be found. Palmer's death had been staged. The question was by whom? If he weren't here in Qatar, Yan would have thought the Americans or British helped fake Palmer's death so that he could work for them in secret. But no Western power would put him in this region. They would want him on home soil, where they could protect him and move him if necessary.

No, this was all arranged by Palmer himself. He had staged his own death and set himself up here, and Yan was convinced the man had continued his work and succeeded. The proof was the private jet that had brought Palmer's sister here. Entire planes couldn't be wiped out of existence. That required hacking into multiple systems with government-level encryption. He was positive Palmer was alive, had completed his research, and was using it to protect himself and his sister.

If his suspicions were true, mission success was critical, and there was no time to waste. The latest report he had received had Iranians and North Koreans already involved. It meant the secret was out. There could be a leak from his department, or it could be from the CIA, but that didn't matter. All that mattered was that he won the race, and that meant there was no time for sitting around waiting for something to happen.

If he wanted Palmer and his secrets, he would have to go on the offensive immediately.

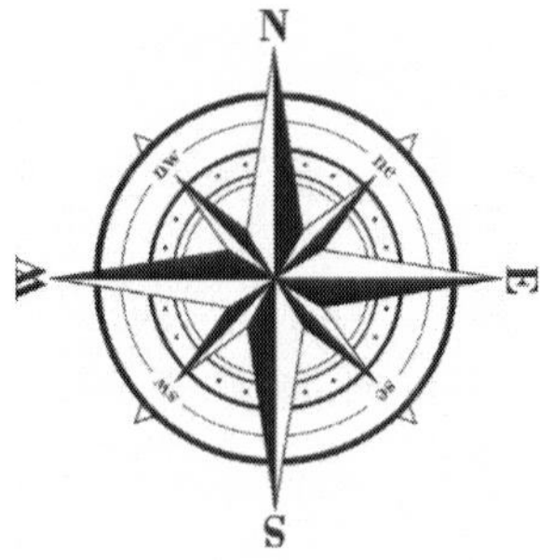

Charles Palmer Residence

Doha, Qatar

Acton smiled broadly as he shook Charles Palmer's hand. "It's a pleasure to meet you."

Palmer returned the smile. "And you. I swore if I ever did meet you I'd give you a piece of my mind for getting my sister into so much trouble over the years, but here we are with people trying to kill us, and it's all my fault. So, I suppose it would be the pot calling the kettle black."

Acton chuckled. "I suppose so." He took Laura's hand. "And in my defense, she quite often is the one getting *me* into trouble."

"Oh, James, maybe one out of every ten times."

Acton laughed. "But you always follow me willingly."

"That I do."

Acton turned to his brother-in-law. "As much as I'd like to get to know you, I'm sure you'll agree now's not the time."

Palmer did. "No, it isn't. As I explained to Laura, I don't have an exit strategy for this many people."

"Then I suggest you talk to Dylan. He's CIA and right now they're probably your best option."

Palmer regarded him for a moment, pursing his lips. "You think I should hand myself over to the Americans?"

"I think so, at least temporarily, until we can figure things out. Right now, we know the Chinese, Iranians, and North Koreans are already after you, and God knows who else. Now, I realize you might want to hand yourself over to the British—"

Palmer interrupted. "I'd rather hand myself over to no one. Let's just be clear on that point. Nobody should have this technology until I've finished my work."

Acton paused. "So, you succeeded?"

"In creating the fire, but not the water."

Acton's eyes narrowed as he puzzled out the metaphor then he smiled as everything fell into place. "That's what this has been about the entire time, hasn't it? You knew you were close to the breakthrough, so you faked your death so no one could get their hands on it. You finished your work and then have been trying to create a countermeasure to it."

"Laura, you married a smart one."

She smiled. "Yes, I did."

"James. May I call you James?"

Acton chuckled. "Laura calls me James. Everyone else calls me Jim."

Palmer laughed. "Well, then, let's go with Jim. Jim, you're right. I've completed my work and can now defeat pretty much any encryption currently in use by anyone. I'm working on the technology that would block it, but I'm years away. My intention was to release both solutions to the world so that everybody could enjoy the benefits without the risk."

Acton smiled. "Fire and water. Well, that all being said, if you hand yourself over to the Americans, you might be able to work out some sort of deal where they let you finish your work before you hand anything over to them."

"That would still leave them with the technology that they could then use against anyone. Would you trust your government with that kind of power?"

Acton grunted. "Hell, no. Perhaps an agreement could be reached where you release the water to the public and the American government keeps the fire."

"That wouldn't work. Unfortunately, in this case, the technology that the defense is built upon is the same technology as the offense. You can't have one without the other."

Acton bit his lip. "So, if you release the defense, then whoever can make it work would automatically be able to defeat current encryption methods."

"Exactly. The Americans will never agree to releasing the defense, because it'll mean handing over the ability to crack any encryption not employing the defense."

"How did you intend to get around that chicken and egg problem?"

"The intention was to release a ready-made product that governments and institutions could install on their networks and backbones to prevent their systems from being compromised. It would take time for anyone to reverse engineer it, at which point I'd be releasing the plans to the world so that all of mankind could make use of it. But none of that matters right now. All that matters is that a hostile power doesn't get their hands on it first, or their hands on me." He sighed. "Perhaps it's time I spoke to your friend."

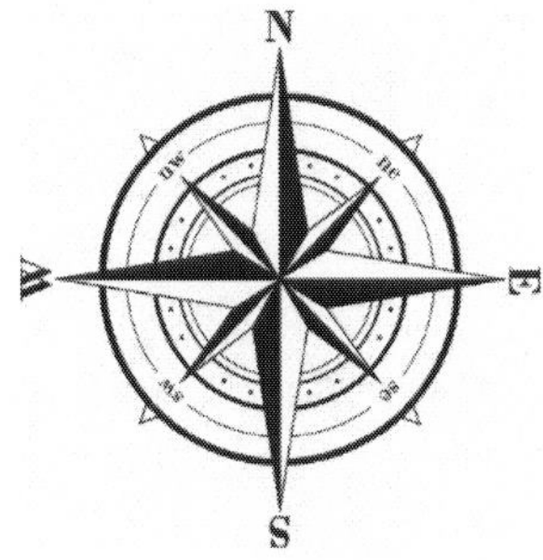

Director Morrison's Office, CIA Headquarters

Langley, Virginia

Leroux sat in Morrison's office as the agreement with Palmer was hammered out. Several department heads were in the room including the CIA director herself, plus the Secretary of State, and the head of the NSA, whom Palmer would be working for.

Morrison leaned toward the phone. "Mr. Palmer, I think we have an agreement."

"I trust you'll put that in writing?"

"Absolutely, but that's going to take some time, time we don't have. We need to get you and the others to safety immediately."

"And you have a plan to do that?"

Leroux suppressed the urge to cringe as Morrison confidently replied. "Yes, we do. It will be coordinated through our operative. Rest assured, Mr. Palmer, we'll have you, your sister, and the others safely out of there in short order."

"Very well. I look forward to meeting you."

"As do I." Morrison ended the call and looked at the others. "An inauspicious start, unfortunately."

Secretary of State Michelle Jenkins looked at him. "What do you mean?"

"We don't have an extraction plan."

She gave him a look. "What the hell is that supposed to mean?"

"It means, ma'am, that we don't have a finalized plan. But now that you're in the loop and we've made an agreement with this man to save his ass, it's your turn to do your bit."

"What do you mean?"

"We've got a carrier strike group sitting off the coast. Our people are on the top floor of a very tall building. All we need to do is put a Black Hawk on the roof, and we can get them all out. Normally we would send them in there with fighter escorts and attack helicopters, but if we do that, something tells me the Qataris are not going to be happy. But if you get permission to land that chopper on the roof to extract our people, then we have an extraction plan."

Jenkins cursed and shot to her feet, heading for the door. "My God, Leif, you could have told me this sooner."

Morrison shrugged. "We didn't have an agreement sooner. Everything is in place. We just need sign-off from their government and it's a go."

"I'll see what I can do." She headed out the door, her phone already pressed to her ear as CIA Director Gladys McQuay chuckled.

"If you ever did that to me, Leif, I'd have you gelded."

Leroux involuntarily winced.

"She's not in my chain of command, ma'am."

McQuay rose. "Well, Leif, you'd better hope this works out, or you might have made an enemy of the White House."

Morrison gestured at Leroux. "It's his plan, ma'am. Anything goes wrong, shit rolls downhill."

The others in the room laughed as they headed out the door. Leroux rose, not sure how he felt about being hung out to dry. Morrison indicated for him to wait. The door closed, leaving the two of them alone.

"You do realize that was a joke, right?"

Leroux shifted uncomfortably. "Yes, sir. But do they?"

Morrison roared. "They do, son, they do." He pointed toward the door. "Now, get out of here. I want you in the ops center. Secretary Jenkins is very good at her job and just might have that permission sooner than you think."

"And if they won't agree?"

"Then we switch to Plan B."

Leroux sighed. "Plan B sucks, sir."

"That may be, but it's better than Plan C."

"We have a Plan C?"

"No, we don't, which is why Plan B is better than nothing. Just be prepared for both scenarios and pray we get that permission before it's too late."

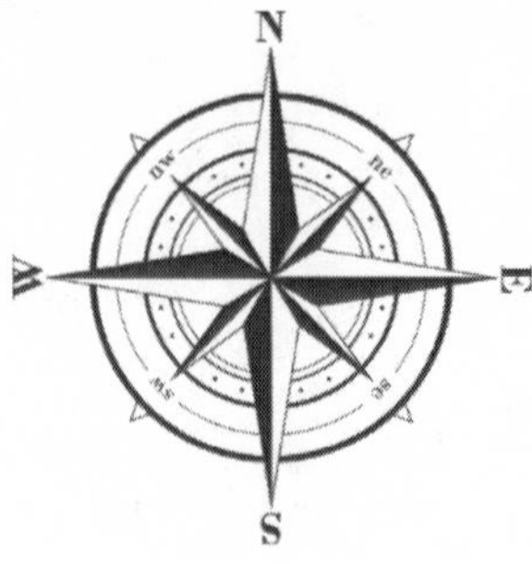

Charles Palmer Residence

Doha, Qatar

Palmer pushed back from the table and rose. His sister gave him a hug. "You got everything you wanted."

He disagreed. "No, but I got the best I could get. Now, before we leave I have a few things I need to take care of, but there's something I think you'll like to see."

"What is it?"

He smiled and jerked his chin toward a nearby door. "It's through there. Jim, you're going to want to see it too since you're an archaeologist."

Laura took his hand. "Now you've got me really curious."

He laughed. "Then go satisfy your curiosity. I'll be back in a few minutes."

Laura and her husband headed for the door. She opened it and tentatively poked her head inside then exclaimed, "Oh, my God! How did you manage this?"

He flashed her a smile as he headed for his lab. "I'll explain later." He entered his code then the system scanned his retina, the door hissing open after his identity was confirmed. He stepped inside and closed the door, heading directly for his computer. He logged in and brought up the recording of the call he had just had with the Americans. He ran it through a voice stress analyzer as he pulled several drives from one of the racks that contained all of his latest research. He placed them in a hardened case, then closed it, entering a code that activated the security features which would wipe the drives if the wrong code was entered three times.

His computer beeped, indicating the analysis of the conversation was completed. He stepped over and was disappointed that it confirmed what he suspected. He had been lied to. The Americans seemed sincere about the agreement but were lying about the extraction plan. The question was, what was the lie? They obviously had an extraction plan of some sort, so why the deception?

He initiated a wipe of all his systems. There was no going back now. He entered a code on the wall panel and the robotic arms behind the glass leaped into action, pre-programmed for this day. Four arms rapidly dismantled his creation, placing each piece into specially designed cases.

He checked the computer to see the progress of the system wipe, then sat, the fingers of his left hand drumming on his chest. The computer analysis of the phone conversation had indicated deception. Deception wasn't necessarily a lie. Since they absolutely had to have an extraction plan, the only thing he could think of was that they didn't have confidence in the plan or that the plan hadn't been finalized. Both made sense, considering the CIA had known for barely an hour where he was and where the others would be. The Chinese, Iranians, and North Koreans were already after him. Even if he hadn't reached an agreement with the Americans, he couldn't stay here.

His cover was blown.

His secret was out.

He had planned for this, but never had a solution for how to protect Laura, though that wasn't necessarily true. There was one solution, though he considered it the nuclear option.

The panel on the wall beeped and two large briefcases emerged containing his life's work. His computer chirped, indicating the wipe of the system was complete and that it was now overwriting everything with random zeros and ones. It would continue the process until stopped, and the longer it was given, the less any data restoration was likely. He was ready to go. He had everything he needed to continue his work in the United States.

But there was one last thing he had to do.

Laura slowly circled the tall vase, shoulder height. Several large pieces of it were missing, as was to be expected, but the restoration job was as expert as any she had seen, and she recognized it the moment she saw it. It was from Sodom. It was the artifact she had been excavating when her brother was supposed to have been killed.

James was on a knee staring at the artwork painted on its surface. "This is incredible. The depth, the realism. I've never seen anything like it from this time period."

Laura agreed. "Whoever the artist was, they were far ahead of their time. Millennia. To think that someone with such skill lived in a place like Sodom is mind-boggling."

Milton leaned in. "How can you be sure they were from Sodom? Maybe somebody purchased it elsewhere?"

James disagreed. "Just look at the subject matter. If that's not an orgy, I don't know what is."

"Whoever painted this might not have been from Sodom. Perhaps Gomorrah or one of the other city-states believed destroyed by God or an asteroid impact," said Laura.

This piqued Tommy's interest. "Asteroid?"

"Yes, there's evidence to suggest that the entire area where Sodom and Gomorrah were believed to exist was wiped out by an asteroid impact, which back then was interpreted as the wrath of God, so a narrative was created around it. There's no actual proof that Sodom and Gomorrah were sinful, since all the recorded history is hearsay. We were only a couple of weeks into our dig, and I was quite confident that from what we were seeing and from historical records that it very well could be Sodom." She indicated the painted figures, their bodies entwined in erotic embrace. "And this would certainly suggest that we were right, considering the subject matter." She stepped back, shaking her head. "But how did he get it?"

"After the dig was shut down. I had a team sent in to recover it."

Everyone spun toward the voice. "I can't believe you did that."

Her brother shrugged. "I knew how excited you were by finding it and how you said it was solid evidence that you may indeed have found Sodom. I didn't want that lost because of what I was forced to do."

"But how?"

"I had Mary send in a team to retrieve it. They shipped it to an address they were given by her. It was then forwarded to a team that did the restoration work, then the end result was finally shipped to me. It took a couple of years, and my intention was to give it to you as a gift when we were finally able to reunite. Unfortunately, my work took far longer than I expected, and now it's too late."

Laura's eyes narrowed. "What do you mean?"

He waved his hand, dismissing the question. "It doesn't matter. What does matter, however, is the proof you were seeking."

James rose. "Proof?"

Her brother smiled. "Proof that you found Sodom, proof that this is from Sodom. I found absolute proof."

Laura exchanged an excited glance with James. "How could you possibly have found proof? All we can do is surmise that this was from Sodom based upon where it was discovered and its subject matter."

Her brother wagged a finger. "Ah, but you're forgetting one thing."

"And what's that?"

"Ego."

"Ego?" asked James.

"All artists sign their work."

Laura gasped. "Wait a minute. What are you saying?"

Her brother stepped forward then took a knee beside the vase, pointing near the bottom at a cluster of ancient Hebrew letters. "Do you know what that says? I know I didn't."

Both Laura and James dropped to their knees and she gasped. "Idit. Oh, my God. That's Lot's wife!"

"What you can't see there with the naked eye are the other characters that were worn away. But my people were able to scan it and detect slight pigmentation." He pointed at a photo hung on the wall that Laura hadn't noticed before. Her jaw dropped as she rose. Idit's name was much larger, and next to it were three more words, the full inscription reading 'Lot and Idit Pottery.'

Laura's shoulders heaved with a cathartic release, her suspicions proven ten years later.

"This is unbelievable," said James. "You've proven it. You found Sodom."

Tommy stepped closer to the photo. "I've heard of Sodom and Gomorrah, but who's this Lot and what's her name?"

James gave Tommy a look. "Maybe you should attend some of my classes on Bible history."

Tommy held up both hands. "Hell, no. Why don't you just jump to the end of the semester and give me the answer?"

Laura dried her eyes. "According to the Bible and several texts, Lot was the nephew of Abraham and was sent to Sodom to preach God's ways to the sinful citizens there, but they rejected him. God decided to wipe the slate clean and sent the angels Raphael and Gabriel to warn him and urge him to leave Sodom before it was too late. There are all kinds of different accounts, some saying his wife opposed leaving, some saying he had two daughters, some four. Some that they were young, others married. You have to remember, this story is thousands of years old. But Lot was married to Idit, that part is not really disputed, and for both those names to be on this is simply too much to be coincidence. Whatever happened all those years ago, we'll never really know. How accurate the stories surrounding it are, it's impossible to say. But now, we have proof that two people named Lot and Idit made pottery, and that matches up too perfectly with what was handed down over thousands of years."

Mai examined the vase. "I wonder who the artist was, Lot or Idit?"

Laura turned back toward the vase. "We'll likely never know, but whoever they were, they were a rare talent, far ahead of their time. I'm guessing it was Idit, because all the history has her dying and Lot surviving. If he were the artist, you would think there'd be more examples of his work, and he would have taught his techniques to others. It could have advanced artistic capabilities by thousands of years if she had been given the chance to take on apprentices." She turned toward her brother. "We have to get this to a museum."

Kane stepped into the room. "There's no time for that. I just got word the Qataris have agreed to our extraction plan. A Black Hawk is being sent in, ETA fifteen minutes on the roof."

An alarm sounded and her brother cursed.

"What is it?" asked Laura.

"Building security has been breached. We may not have fifteen minutes."

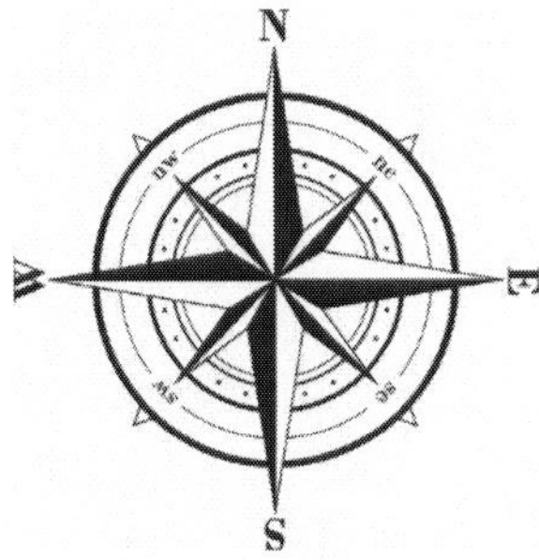

Charles Palmer Residence Lobby

Doha, Qatar

Yan stepped through the front doors of the luxury condominium. The lobby was impressive, everything you would expect in a place such as this. A handsome young man smiled from behind the reception desk, but before he could say anything, Yan put two bullets in his chest. Yan jogged over as the rest of the strike team rushed through the entrance, executing the team lead's plan. They already had files on the building as there were several Chinese nationals of interest to Beijing living here, and so far everything matched. He grabbed the pass key off the dead man's belt as his team raced out of sight, down a nearby corridor that led to where the on-site security team waited on standby.

Someone shouted in Arabic and two shots rang out. A small explosion followed a moment later. More shouting then a large explosion followed by sustained bursts of gunfire that then fell silent. If all had gone according to plan, his team had blown the door, then used a grenade to incapacitate the enemy before eliminating them.

"This is Team Leader. Security team has been eliminated."

Yan smiled at the voice in his ear then headed for the security booth with the camera feeds. An alarm sounded and he cursed as he broke into a sprint, several of his strike team joining him. They had to review the footage to see where the Americans had gone when they arrived. The building was far too big to search unit to unit, and with the sounding of the alarm, they were now on a tight clock.

The authorities would be here soon.

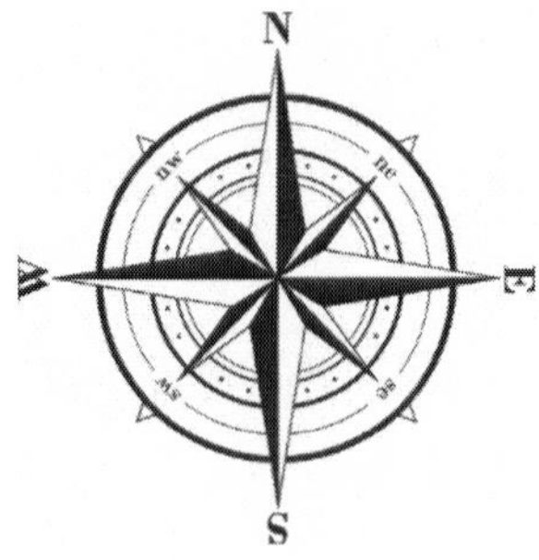

Charles Palmer Residence

Doha, Qatar

Palmer turned to Mary since security was her area of expertise. "What do we do?"

"I assume the security protocols I set up are still in place?"

"Of course."

"Then as soon as that alarm sounded, Alpha Protocol kicked in. This floor is now isolated."

"What does that mean?" asked Kane.

"It means no elevators will come up to this floor, and all stairwell doors have been electronically locked."

"How strong are those doors?" asked Sherrie.

"Strong, but the right amount of explosives will take them out. It depends on how well-equipped whoever's coming is."

Fang frowned. "If it's the Chinese, expect them to be as well-equipped as any American military unit. Just like the Americans, we have weapons caches all over the world. We can send in a team and have them fully equipped for any mission."

Acton cursed. "So they'll definitely have explosives?"

"Absolutely."

"Then the best we can hope for is a couple of minutes' delay."

Kane pulled out his phone. "I'll see if there's any way we can speed up that chopper." He stepped out of the room as Mary led everyone toward the elevators.

Palmer pointed at the two cases. "Can someone take those?"

Acton stepped over and picked them up. "What are they?"

"It's a deconstructed prototype. Whatever happens, that can't fall into enemy hands."

Laura reached out. "You better give me one of those. You're going to want to have a free hand in case this turns ugly." Acton handed one over then drew his gun as Laura did the same.

Palmer shook his head at the sight. He couldn't believe this was his little sister. She had changed so much and he was incredibly proud of not only how competent a woman she was, but how confident. And the fact her husband appeared to treat her as an equal warmed his heart.

He just wished he could have had the chance to get to know them both.

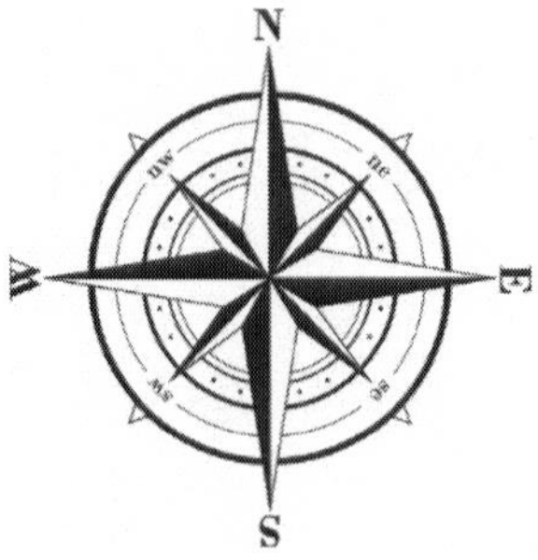

Outside Charles Palmer Residence

Doha, Qatar

Niner peered up at the building where Palmer and the others were. It was no Burj Khalifa, but it was pretty damn tall. And with their people on the top floors, he really had no desire to climb ninety flights of stairs. He checked his watch. "That chopper's twelve minutes out."

Atlas frowned. "So, what do we do? It'll take us longer than that to hike those stairs."

The alarm sounding in the building could be heard from their vantage point, and two local police officers were out front, directing people to the opposite side of the street, though they appeared to be taking no action.

"This place is going to be swarming any minute now. If we're going in, now's the time," said Spock.

Jagger pursed his monster lips. "Keeping in mind that once we're inside, the only way we're getting out is on that chopper or in the back of a Qatari paddy wagon."

Niner threw his door open. "That's paperwork. Let Washington worry about it. Right now, we've got a Chinese team in there determined to kill our people. At a minimum, we can be a distraction. Maybe buy them some time."

The four of them headed directly toward the front entrance of the building. One of the Qatari police officers spotted them, his eyes bulging at the sight. Niner fired a taser into the man before he could say anything, Atlas doing the same to the second officer. This had the civilians panicking and getting out of their way as sirens in the distance grew closer. Niner reached the front door and pulled it open. Spock and Jagger advanced, breaking left and right.

"Clear!" they both announced.

Atlas followed then Niner. They spread out across the lobby, advancing.

"One DB over here," announced Spock as he rounded the reception desk. Niner followed Atlas down a corridor to the left as Spock and Jagger took the right. Atlas kneeled beside a body, checking for a pulse. He shook his head. Niner continued toward a scarred door where it appeared a charge had been used to blow the lock. He reached out and pushed the door aside. "Is anyone alive in there?"

There was no response. Atlas darted across the door, taking up position on the other side. Niner poked his head in for a brief look then jerked back. He had spotted at least half a dozen bodies. He raised his MP5. He didn't want to take anybody out, but he wasn't going to die because of mistaken identity.

"Is anybody alive in there? We're friendlies," repeated Atlas in Arabic.

There was no reply. Niner stepped inside, Atlas covering him, and he slowly rounded the room. Six dead, all wearing uniforms indicating they were private security. A rack of weapons on the wall, untouched, suggested not only was this some sort of rapid reaction unit for the building, but also that whoever had taken them out was well-equipped enough not to bother taking any of the team's weapons.

"One-One, Zero-Five. We found a security booth, two staff dead, over."

Niner replied to Spock's report. "Acknowledged, Zero-Five. We found a security team. Six dead. No survivors. Looks like a grenade then automatic weapons fire. Do you have access to the building cameras?"

"Negative. It looks like they shot up the system after they got whatever they wanted."

Niner began checking the bodies. "Look for any type of passkey. We need to be able to use the elevators to get into position."

"Roger that," replied Spock as Niner continued to check the bodies while Atlas stood at the door covering him.

The big man cleared his throat. "You wouldn't happen to be looking for that, would you?"

Niner twisted to see Atlas indicating a lanyard hanging on the wall with a passkey attached, a Post-it note stuck beside it with a six-digit number scrawled on it. "Great security."

Atlas shrugged. "Well, at least the password wasn't 123456."

Niner grabbed the pass and the Post-it note from the wall then headed for the elevator. "Zero-Five, One-One, I think we've got what we're looking for." Spock stepped out into the corridor and Niner held up the pass. "Let's see if we can get ourselves into this fight."

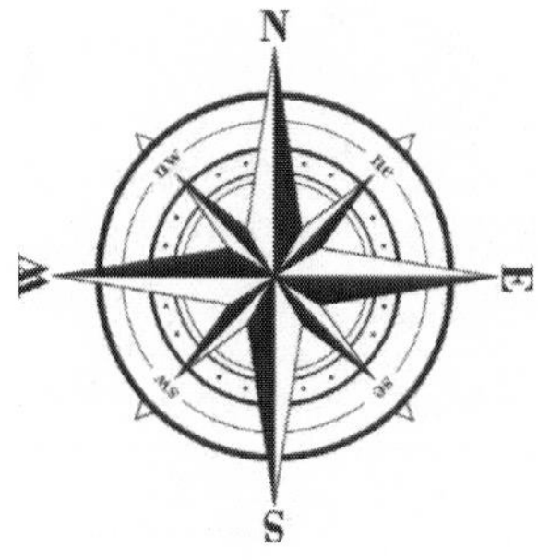

Charles Palmer Residence

Doha, Qatar

Acton stepped out onto the roof, the warm breeze off the Persian Gulf stiff. Kane and Mary had gone ahead, making certain no one was lying in wait for them, before giving the all-clear. He held the door open and Milton and his family emerged, his poor friend wincing as Niskha quietly sobbed, not understanding what was going on around her only that the adults were scared. Kane and Mary returned to the door and Mary pointed to a spot over to the left where part of the building's HVAC system stood.

"Everyone over there and stay low. It'll provide you with some cover if the hostiles make it to the rooftop." She pointed to the right. "The helicopter will be landing there. As soon as it touches down, get on board. Don't worry about trying to stay low. None of you are tall enough for those blades to hit you. Just run as fast as you can and get on board so that we can be off this roof in less than sixty seconds. Understood?"

Head bobs were the response and Acton led everyone over to their designated waiting area. Milton groaned, driving a fist into his lower back. Acton regarded him with concern. "Are you going to be all right?"

"My back is spasming something fierce."

Sandra frowned. "I haven't had a chance to give him his proper massage in two days."

Acton pointed at the ground. "Then do it now."

Milton's eyebrows shot up. "Are you nuts?"

"The chopper won't be here for seven minutes. In those seven minutes, she can provide you with some relief just in case you have to run."

Sandra shrugged, looking at her husband. "He's right. Even just a few minutes could help."

Milton cursed and Niskha giggled. "Daddy swore."

"Sorry, sweetie." Milton lay down on the ground and his wife straddled him, going to work on his lower back, having taken the proper training after he had been shot. He groaned in relief. "You have no idea how good that feels."

"Jim!"

Acton turned to see Kane beckoning him. Acton put the case down beside Laura. "I'll be back in a sec." He joined Kane by the door. "What is it?"

"Sherrie, Fang, and I will be holding this door. Your job is to make sure the civilians and those two cases get on the chopper."

"What about Charles?"

"He's Mary's responsibility."

Acton's eyes narrowed as he looked about. "Where the hell is he?"

"He's still downstairs doing something. I'm not sure what. Mary went to check."

Acton cursed. "Don't they realize what's going on?"

An explosion from below emphasized his point as Fang glanced over her shoulder at them. "*That* will be the Chinese arriving."

Sherrie agreed. "Let's hope that lights a fire under the dynamic duo's asses."

Acton leaned into the doorway then shouted, "Let's get a move on!"

But there was no reply.

Yan's team surged up the stairs, the door blocking their way now hanging off its hinges. They were going in blind. None of the plans for this building showed anything for the top three floors, all apparently owned by a holding company they couldn't get any information on. He had no doubt it was a company owned by Charles Palmer.

Gunfire erupted ahead and he took several involuntary steps back before he smiled slightly, all their suspicions confirmed. Footage from the parking garage showed the Americans from the flight had taken the private elevator that only led here. And while back home the average American might be armed to the teeth, they had cleared customs with no weapons, but boarded the elevators fully armed. It meant they were definitely CIA or equivalent, or the weapons had been supplied by somebody living here, meaning somebody worth protecting.

And that had to be Charles Palmer.

The last team member disappeared through the door, the gunfire continuing in short bursts. He forced himself up the final steps to the door and peered through to see one of his team down, gripping his shoulder. The rest of the team was continuing up the next flight of steps where they were meeting heavy resistance. He grabbed the wounded man and dragged him back past the blown door.

"Are you all right?"

The man winced. "I think so. A ricochet caught me in the shoulder. Just get me on my feet."

Yan pulled the man upright and helped steady him. "Apply pressure to the wound."

The man did as told.

"Go back down and help hold the lobby."

"Yes, sir." The wounded man slowly made his way down the stairs then out of sight as Yan grew bolder. And worried. With this amount of gunfire, Palmer could be hit by a stray bullet, and they needed the man alive.

And he still wanted a crack at the professors.

Kane cursed. This was ridiculous. They were holding back the Chinese two flights down, but there was still no sign of Palmer. He turned to Sherrie and Fang. "Can you two hold them while I go check what the hell's going on?"

Sherrie nodded. "You go do your thing. We ladies have this."

Kane ducked through the doorway into the corridor that led to the main reception area of the home. They couldn't hold the stairwell for long. All it would take would be an unnoticed flashbang to be tossed up and they would be overwhelmed. They didn't have time for this shit. The cases with the device were on the roof, and Palmer had indicated he had already wiped all the data, so what the hell was going on?

Mary emerged from the door leading to the lab, wiping away tears.

"What the hell's going on?"

She flinched, not having noticed Kane standing there.

"I'm not coming with you," said Palmer as he stepped through the door.

"What do you mean you're not coming with us? We have an agreement."

Palmer indicated the gunfire rattling just down the corridor. "And you've already proven you can't protect me and my sister."

"The chopper is going to be here in three minutes. All we need is your ass on the roof and this is over. We'll have you on an aircraft carrier in less than half an hour, then on a flight to the United States where you'll land at a secure airfield and be brought to a top-secret facility that very few know about, and those who do have no hope in hell of getting through the security perimeter. You stay here, you're dead or they take you. Neither is acceptable."

"To you, perhaps, but I've always known this was a possibility."

Mary turned to Palmer. "You're sure you won't change your mind?"

Palmer shook his head. "No, it's made up. Tell my sister that I love her and that I'm sorry to put her through so much pain once again."

An explosion rocked the room and Kane spun toward the sound of a grenade detonating. "Status!"

Sherrie replied. "We're good. Fang world-cupped it right back at them, but we got lucky. We have to get out of here and we have to get out of here now. That chopper's two minutes out."

"On our way." He faced Palmer. "Final answer?"

"I'm not going with you."

"Very well." Kane looked at Mary. "Get to the roof."

Mary turned to Palmer who gave her a nod. "Go." She sprinted toward the stairwell and Kane stepped closer to Palmer.

"One last chance."

"Don't worry about me, Mr. Kane. It's better this way."

Kane frowned and drew his weapon, putting two bullets in Palmer's chest. The man collapsed and Kane closed his eyes. "I'm sorry, but I had my orders." He jogged back toward the stairwell, wondering just what the hell he would tell Laura. She deserved the truth, but the truth would change everything.

Yet Palmer was right, it was better this way.

The doors to the elevators opened and Niner squeezed the trigger of his MP5, taking out a wounded Chinese operative waiting for a ride down.

"He could have been one of the security guards," rumbled Atlas as they stepped into the hallway.

Niner disagreed. "Not with that weapon. You saw what the security team was armed with." Gunfire thudded from down the hall, suggesting the action was a couple of floors above them.

"That doesn't sound good," said Jagger.

Spock cocked an eyebrow. "You think?"

Niner led them toward the stairwell, the main elevators taking them up to just below the floors occupying the penthouse suite. He activated his comms. "Control, One-One. What's the ETA on that chopper?"

"Less than two minutes."

Niner reached the stairwell door and opened it, the weapons fire increasing dramatically in volume. "We're not going to be able to make that ride. Once our people are on board, have them lift off. We'll keep the Chinese engaged until the chopper is clear, over."

"Copy that, One-One. We'll relay your situation."

Niner advanced up the stairs. "Control, tell the Qataris that I'd like a prison cell with a view."

Leroux chuckled on the other end. "We'll try to do a little better than that, One-One."

"That would be appreciated, Control. One-One, out." Niner rounded the bend to the next flight of steps and spotted a hostile just ahead, peering through a blown doorway. He indicated to the others what he saw then handed his MP5 to Atlas as he scurried up the last few steps and took the man from behind, plunging a knife under his ribs and twisting as Niner covered the target's mouth so he couldn't warn his comrades. Niner dragged him down the stairs as Atlas and Spock advanced past him toward the door. Niner lowered the man to the ground and his target stared up at him, wide-eyed, gasping for breath. A hand reached up and grabbed Niner by the vest.

"Tell me, is Palmer alive?"

Niner figured there was no harm in revealing the secret to a man who would be dead in seconds. "Yes."

"And did he invent his device?"

"Yes."

The man's eyes closed. "I was so close." He sighed heavily, his final breath leaving his body, and Niner followed Jagger up the stairs as the MP5s of Atlas and Spock engaged the enemy while the thunder of the massive rotors of the Black Hawk helicopter made their presence felt.

This would all be over in the next two minutes for those on the roof.

But he had a feeling his team's suffering was only about to begin.

Acton huddled with the others against the side of the HVAC unit as the massive Black Hawk landed nearby. The moment its wheels touched down, the side door slid open and two of the aircrew stepped out, beckoning them.

"Okay. Let's go! Let's go! Let's go!" shouted Acton. He grabbed one of the cases containing his brother-in-law's invention and herded everyone toward the safety of the chopper as Laura hauled the second case. They reached the open door of the Black Hawk and two of the crew helped Milton's family on board. Tommy and Mai followed then Laura. Acton shoved the case on board then jumped on, turning back toward the door Kane and the others still defended. "Let's go!" he shouted.

Kane glanced back then tapped Mary, Sherrie, and Fang on the back. He shut the door then shot out the security panel. The four of them sprinted toward the chopper. Fang dove on first and Acton grabbed her by the belt, hauling her in the rest of the way. Sherrie hurdled in, slamming into the opposite side of the chopper as Mary then Kane hopped on.

Kane turned around, aiming his weapon at the door. "Let's get the hell out of here!"

The pilot lifted off, the heavy beast straining against its own weight. The door opened and Kane fired, Sherrie and Fang joining in as they repositioned. The door snapped closed and the pilot banked away, eliminating their line of sight.

Kane rose and poked his head into the cockpit. "We've got four team members still back there."

The pilot tapped his comms. "New orders. Your special unit indicated they wouldn't be able to make the roof and we were to leave without them."

Mary overheard what the pilot said and grabbed Kane by the shoulder. "You have to tell your friends to get out of there now!"

"Why?"

"Trust me. They have to get out of there now!"

Kane cursed and activated his comms. "Control, Diggler. Tell Bravo Team they need to evac immediately. No delays."

Laura cried out. "Where's my brother?"

Acton's chest tightened as he realized in all the confusion, the entire point of this exercise had been forgotten. He turned to Mary, the last person with his brother-in-law, and she avoided eye contact but responded.

"He refused to come with us." She reached out and took Laura's hands as tears erupted. "His last words were of you. He wanted you to know that he loved you and that he was sorry for putting you through so much pain yet again."

Laura rushed toward the still-open door of the chopper and Acton grabbed her. "Charles!" she screamed. The chopper leveled out and Acton looked over to their right, what remained of the Chinese team now on the roof, firing at them uselessly as they were now out of range.

Suddenly the entire upper floors of the building erupted in flame, a massive fireball clawing at the sky, quickly replaced by thick acrid smoke billowing from the remains of what no doubt was Palmer's final solution to his problem—complete and utter destruction of his past ten years.

Acton held Laura tight as she sobbed. Her brother had obviously decided the only way to protect her was to kill himself and destroy his research. This was over, finally, but his wife's pain was about to begin anew.

An alarm sounded from the cockpit and the pilot cursed as he banked hard to the right. Laura tumbled toward the open door and Acton grabbed her as he fell as well. He reached out with his free hand and a crewman grabbed it, holding on to him with one hand and cargo netting with the other.

"Brace for impact!" shouted the pilot. Acton had no idea what was going on as he desperately held on to Laura and the crewman, but they were losing this battle, gravity coming out on top as the pilot continued to evade whatever it was about to impact them. Somebody grabbed him by the belt and hauled him back inside. He collapsed onto the floor, Laura atop him, and he looked back to see Milton's tortured face, his best friend having tipped the balance in their favor.

"Here it comes!"

Acton held on to Laura, squeezing his eyes shut as what he assumed was a missile slammed into them. But it wasn't the twisting metal or the whining engine that he heard, it was the terrified screams of everyone he loved in this world as they plunged to their deaths.

Niner and the others held on to the railings in the elevator as the entire car shook. The power flickered but the backups kicked in and they continued their rapid descent to the basement level.

"What the hell was that?" asked Atlas.

Spock cocked an ear. "That wasn't a grenade unless they tossed it in the shaft. That sounded like they just took out a whole floor."

Jagger looked up warily. "I'm not so sure staying on this thing is wise."

Niner activated his comms. "Control, One-One. What the hell just happened, over?"

"It looks like some sort of self-destruct mechanism was triggered. It took out the top two floors of the building."

"Our people?"

"On board the chopper, but be advised, Palmer stayed behind."

"Are you kidding me?"

"We don't know the details yet…stand by. We've got some sort of mayday from the chopper."

Niner cursed. If they had been caught in the explosion, they could have been taken out by debris. He stared at the numbers counting down as Jagger repeated his concern. Niner pressed his hand against the wall, feeling for unusual vibrations. "Palmer's one of the good guys. That detonation would have been controlled so it would minimize damage to the lower floors. It was probably designed to destroy his lab and any of his work."

"And kill himself," added Atlas.

Niner frowned. "Probably. Man, what Laura must be feeling right now. To lose her brother twice."

Atlas sighed as the elevator chimed, indicating they had arrived at the parking garage. "I can't imagine."

The doors opened and Niner's comms squawked. "One-One, Control. The chopper's been shot down, I repeat, the chopper's been shot down."

Laura was oblivious to what was going on around her. Niskha wailed at the top of her lungs as Tommy, Mai, and Sandra screamed in terror. But all she did was stare blankly into nothingness, her entire body numb, her brother dead yet again.

And again it was her fault.

She squeezed her eyes shut as an inner voice shouted at her. "But how could it possibly be your fault? Not this time!" But it *was* her fault. It was Tommy's fault for having put together the montage that triggered all of this. If she didn't know Tommy, then he never would have done that and her brother would still be alive.

It was a ridiculous argument, and she knew it. This wasn't her fault, and the sooner she accepted that, the sooner she could recognize the incredible gift she had been bestowed. She had been able to be with her brother once again, to see the man he had become, for him to see the woman she now was, to meet the man she loved.

Those minutes were precious.

And though she would go through the tragedy of his death once again, she had to remember that he had spent ten years alive when she had thought he was dead, and he had spent those ten years working on what he loved, sacrificing his freedom for all of humanity.

"Brace for impact!" shouted the pilot, snapping Laura back to reality as James continued to hold her tight while they spun through the air.

A crewman leaned over them. "As soon as we hit the ground, get clear of the chopper, but watch for the rotors!" He pointed overhead. "Make sure they've stopped completely!"

She rolled off her husband and crawled to a safer position, grabbing onto a handhold.

"Five seconds!"

She reached out and squeezed Mai's hand. The young woman flinched, staring up at her, her screams abruptly halting. Laura gave her a comforting smile.

"Everything will be all right." A warm, tingling sensation surged through her. She was a woman of science and had never really believed in Heaven and Hell, but right here, right now, should they all die together, she knew everyone she loved, everyone she cared about, would be with her on the other side, including her brother.

"This is it!"

Laura closed her eyes and let go of the netting, instead embracing the only man that she had ever loved as they slammed into the ground, ready for whatever might come.

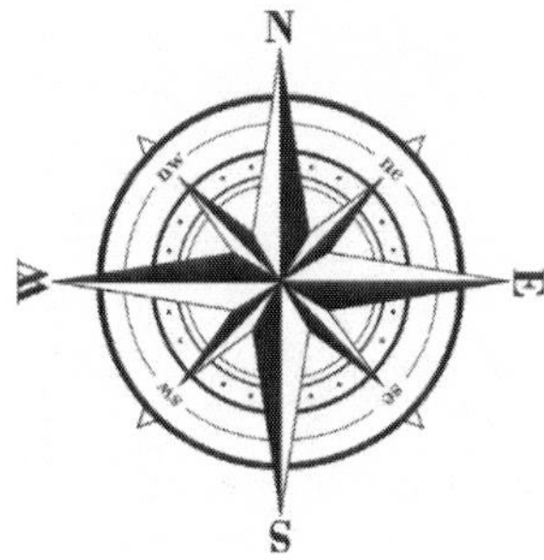

Charles Palmer Residence Parking Garage

Doha, Qatar

Niner sprinted toward the parked SUVs that had brought the professors and the others to the building. The drivers were nowhere in sight, but if they had been trained properly, they should have left the keys in case their employer needed to make his escape. Niner pointed at the second SUV and Spock silently executed the implied order. Niner hauled open the driver's side door of the first vehicle, the fact it wasn't locked a good sign. He smiled at what was on the seat. "I've got keys!"

"So do I!" reported Spock.

Niner pointed at Jagger. "Thunder lips, you're with Spock. Thunder thighs, you're with me." He fired up the engine as Atlas groaned, climbing into the passenger seat.

"I'm filing a sexual harassment suit when we get back."

"Oh, you keep promising that, but then you'd have to admit we have a sexual relationship."

Atlas gave him a look. "I don't think you know what sexual harassment is."

Niner guided them up the ramp toward the daylight, and activated his comms as he checked the mirror to see Spock was directly behind him. "Control, One-One. Sitrep, over."

"One-One, Control. The chopper is down. What's your location, over?"

"We're coming out of the parking garage now. Am I going left or right?"

"Take a left. If you go right, you're going to hit the police cordon that's being set up. Go left half a klick then you'll be taking a right. I'll guide you in."

"Any sign of survivors?"

"Not yet, but there was no explosion on impact."

"Copy that. Do we know what happened?"

"Looks like a shoulder-launched missile was fired from a building across the street."

"Chinese?"

"No way to know at this point. It could be pretty much anyone."

The hood dropped as they left the ramp, giving Niner his first full view of the chaos around them. He turned left as instructed by Langley. "Everybody look scared now," he said over the comms so Spock and Jagger received the instructions meant for all of them. He dropped his jaw and widened his eyes as they approached a police position. An officer waved them through as they struggled to clear the area of civilians. Niner checked his rearview mirror to confirm Spock had been let through as well, then whistled at the lack of debris on the street, confirming it had been a controlled detonation like he suspected.

"Take your next right," instructed Leroux in his ear.

Niner did as told and minutes later they were pulling up on the crash scene, several local emergency personnel just arriving. The Black Hawk was smoldering and could erupt at any moment. There was little time to waste, not to mention the fact whoever shot down the chopper could be on their way to finish the job.

Niner hopped out and rushed around to the opposite side of the chopper, breathing a sigh of relief at signs of activity. A child wailed, tearing at his heart. "Friendlies approaching!"

"Acknowledged! Is that you, Niner?"

Niner climbed inside, recognizing Kane's voice. "The one and only. Sitrep."

"I think we're all alive, but I'm not sure how many pieces we're in."

"We've got the two SUVs that you arrived in."

"Take the Milton family first, then Tommy and Mai."

Niner lifted the little girl, examining her. She was scratched up and had a cut under her eye, but other than that she appeared fine. He handed the wailing child to Atlas then turned his attention to her parents. "Are you two all right?"

Sandra Milton extended a hand. "I'm fine, but my husband has an old back injury."

Niner hauled her to her feet, well aware of the cause of that particular injury. He took a knee beside Milton as the flight crew around him jumped into action, sirens growing in intensity outside. "Dean, do you think you've reinjured yourself, or is it just acting up?"

"I think it's just acting up." Milton extended both his arms. "Just get me the hell out of here so I can be with my family."

Niner and Acton helped him to his feet then out of the stricken chopper.

"Have you got him, Doc?"

"I've got him."

Niner helped Laura down then Tommy and Mai. A woman he didn't recognize hopped down, warily eying the situation, her own handgun held expertly. She had to be the mysterious travel agent. Niner leaned back in and Kane pointed at two large cases.

"Don't forget those. They might be the only way to salvage anything from this shit show."

Niner grabbed them then rushed back toward the SUV being loaded with the civilians. He handed the cases to Atlas then activated his comms. "Control, One-One. No injuries that require immediate treatment. We need an evac plan now, over."

"One-One, Control. We've got choppers inbound, but there's no room for them to land where you are, and you've got locals closing in rapidly. There's a large square five klicks south of your current position. Get everyone in the vehicles and head south. We will guide you in."

"ETA on those choppers?"

"Less than ten."

"Copy that."

Gunfire rang out to his left and he dove forward, executing a shoulder roll that ended with him pressed against the front driver-side tire of the SUV, his MP5 raised, searching for the source.

"Your three o'clock!" shouted Atlas. "Black SUV! Four gunmen!"

Niner squeezed the trigger, sending a burst of lead toward the enemy. "Well, we were wondering who fired that missile." He did a shoulder check to see that the Miltons, Actons, and their young friends were all inside. "Laura, darling, are you good to drive?"

"Yes."

The reply was curt, emotionless. The woman was clearly struggling with the loss of her brother, but he had seen her under fire before, under pressure, and there was no better driver. He pointed at Jagger. "Give her your comms."

Jagger squeezed off several more rounds then did as ordered. Laura scrambled into the driver's seat, fitting the comms in place. "Do you know how to use them?" asked Jagger. She nodded. He reached forward and activated the gear. "You're on live now with Control. They're going to guide you to the extraction point. We're going to be right behind you. Understood?"

"Understood."

"Just keep your head down. We're going to provide covering fire!" yelled Niner as they kept the enemy pinned. He smacked the side panel. "Let's go! Let's go!"

Laura put it in gear and hammered on the gas. The SUV shot forward then veered to the right as she cranked the wheel. Niner and the others poured heavy fire on the hostiles, providing cover for the escaping civilians, then repositioned, their own cover now lost. He indicated for Spock and Jagger to break left while he and Atlas headed right. Kane, Sherrie, and Fang continued to fire as the flight crew and the unfamiliar woman climbed into the second vehicle.

Niner and the other Delta operators advanced, holding their fire, not revealing to the enemy what was about to happen. When the first hostile caught sight of him, it was already too late. Niner put two rounds in the man's chest as Atlas swung wide, taking out another, Spock and Jagger doing the same on the opposite side.

And then there was silence.

Though that wasn't true. Approaching sirens wailed loudly, civilians screamed as they fled the area, but all Niner cared about was weapons fire.

"Let's go!" ordered Kane, climbing into the driver's seat.

Niner turned to the others. "You heard the man. Let's get the hell out of here. I don't want to be guests of the same regime that killed thousands of workers building World Cup facilities."

They sprinted toward their lone remaining means of escape. Atlas climbed into the passenger seat wisely reserved for him, the biggest package of man meat on the scene, and Jagger dove into the rear. Niner and Spock climbed onto the running boards on opposite sides of the SUV.

Niner smacked the rooftop. "Let's move!"

Kane put it in gear and they were soon heading in the same direction as the professors. They took the turn hard and Niner's grip broke. "Oh, shit!" he cried as he fell away. Something gripped his belt and hauled him back. He grabbed on to the roof rack.

"Sorry about that!" apologized Kane as they straightened out.

"Don't worry about it. Thanks to whoever saved my ass."

"You owe me one," replied Sherrie.

Kane floored it and they surged through the nearly vacant streets, blowing past several squad cars heading for the scene, some of them spotting their fleeing vehicle with two armed and armored men clinging to the sides. Two turned to give chase, but Niner wasn't concerned—they just needed to rendezvous with that chopper.

He had no intention of being a guest of the Qataris when there was a hammock back home with his and Angela's names on it.

Laura eased off the accelerator, heeding Leroux's advice in her ear. They were away from immediate danger and now the goal was to rendezvous with the choppers and not draw any attention to themselves unless it was absolutely necessary. She checked her rearview mirror but there was still no sign of the others. Worrying about them took her mind off her brother, if only slightly. He was dead, again, this time for real. Nobody survived an explosion like that.

And it was intentional.

He could have escaped with them, he could have been safe.

"Why did he do it?"

James reached over and squeezed the back of her neck. "You know why."

She gave him a quick glance. "What do you mean?"

"It was the only way he could protect you. He knew they would never stop pursuing him as long as he was alive, even if he was under Washington's protection you'd have to be in hiding as well. I'd have to be, maybe everybody in this car would have to be. Maybe for the rest of our lives. By killing himself, and doing it in such a public way, it's over. There's no longer any reason to come after you or anybody close to him."

She wiped away the tears as she continued toward their destination. James' explanation had to be right. Her brother had sacrificed himself for her. He obviously had seen no other choice. He had killed himself once he was certain she was safe and preserved that safety by taking himself out of the equation, just like a big brother should for his little sister.

She glanced in the rearview mirror and cursed at the sight of flashing lights and the second SUV hurtling toward them. "This can't be good." She activated her comms as James spun. "Control, it looks like we've got trouble coming up behind us."

Leroux immediately responded. "Affirmative. Just ignore them. Pull over like you normally would and let them all go past. Our main goal here is to get you civilians out."

She didn't like the sounds of that but understood the thinking. "Copy that, Control." She eased off to the side of the road and watched in her mirror. Kane was driving, and as they blasted past, she could have sworn Niner grinned at her. Two police cars followed, their lights flashing, their sirens wailing. She pressed on the accelerator, resisting the urge to catch up, instead sticking to the speed limit with a slight buffer to keep any asshole tailgaters off her rear end.

"Next left," instructed Leroux.

She put on her signal light and made the turn, losing sight of the others as they continued on straight.

"Do you see the square to your right?"

She spotted it, the massive expanse of concrete hard to miss. "Yes."

"Park anywhere you can then wait for my signal."

There were scores of empty spots, hardly anybody here at this time of day, the sun at its peak, the concrete radiating waves of torture back up at anyone foolish enough to walk on the unforgiving offering. She turned to the others. "He said to wait." She held up a finger. "Control, what's the ETA?"

"Two minutes."

"Two minutes," she relayed to the others. "Remember what they said on the rooftop. As soon as it lands, we go as fast as we can and get on that chopper. Don't worry about the blades, none of us are tall enough. Just get on." She tapped the cases. "And let's make sure we don't forget these, otherwise my brother died for nothing."

Tommy and Sandra helped Milton into an upright position. James reached back and grabbed one of the cases, hauling it forward with him.

Laura held her hands out. "Give me the other one." Tommy handed it to her and she rested it atop the center console.

"Sixty seconds," reported Leroux. "Everybody get out now."

"Copy that, Control." She opened her door. "Sixty seconds. Everybody out." The SUV emptied, the heat oppressive, the air conditioning they had been enjoying going unnoticed until now.

"I hear it." Tommy pointed. "There it is!"

They all turned to see another Black Hawk heading directly toward them, this time accompanied by four smaller attack helicopters. She faced the others. "All right, as soon as the wheels touch down, we go." She gripped the case containing a life's work and the tears flowed. The chopper bounced to the ground.

"Let's go!" shouted James as he and Tommy helped Milton. Sandra carried Niskha as the rest of them sprinted toward what she prayed would be safety. The side door opened then two crewmembers hopped out, urging them forward. It was a replay of the rooftop, sans the gunfire. This time they were going to make it.

Tires screeched to her right, fear filling her heart as her eyes darted toward the sound. She breathed a relieved sigh to see it was Kane and the others leaping over the curb and racing toward them, four police units now in pursuit. She focused on the task at hand. They all had to get on the chopper without delay. She reached it first and handed the case over then helped Mai up. She climbed in then took Niskha, handing her back to Sandra as soon as she was situated. Milton was helped inside then the rest climbed on board as Kane's SUV shuddered to a halt twenty yards away.

Niner and Spock stepped off the running boards as the doors flew open, everyone scrambling out then sprinting toward the chopper. The four Delta team members aimed their weapons at the arriving squad cars that all peeled off, not wanting to risk being caught in the line of fire.

"Let's go!" shouted Kane as he leaped inside. Niner and the others sprinted toward the chopper and climbed in. The moment the last boot cleared the ground, the pilot applied power and they lifted off. The attack helicopters hung back just in case the police got any ideas, then as the Black Hawk gained altitude and speed, she saw the other choppers take up escort positions through the windows. They were soon over the water and her shoulders slumped.

It was over.

But her suffering had just begun.

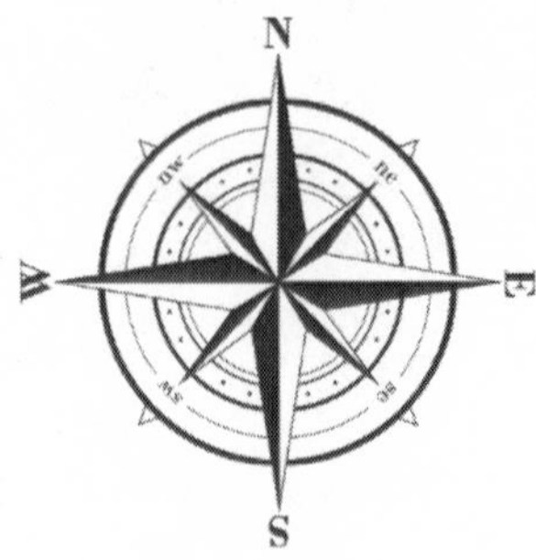

Director Morrison's Office, CIA Headquarters

Langley, Virginia

Kane sat in Morrison's office, speaking to his boss in person not exactly common. Leroux and Sherrie were with him, and it had him wondering just what was going on that had this particular combination of resources called in. The exfil hadn't gone as planned, but in the end everyone except Charles Palmer had survived relatively unscathed, and from all outward appearances, any pursuit of him or his technology had ended when worldwide headlines proclaimed that Palmer was back from the dead then dead again.

Palmer's plan had worked. His sister was safe. The pursuit was over.

So why was he here?

Morrison finished reading something on his laptop then leaned back, his eyes fixed on Kane. "We opened the cases."

Kane eyed him. "I should hope you did."

"They were empty."

Sherrie's eyes shot wide and she leaned forward. "Empty? What the hell are you talking about?"

Morrison continued to stare directly at Kane. "I noticed you weren't surprised."

Kane shrugged. "Should I be? He obviously never intended to go with us so why would we expect him to hand over his research?"

"You're saying that he died and took his research with him in the explosion, destroying his legacy?"

Leroux held up a finger, coming to his best friend's defense. "With all due respect, sir, with only half the puzzle, his legacy could have been one of chaos. He'd rather die than see his invention abused."

Morrison kept his eyes on Kane. "That's what I told the director. Washington is none too pleased, but are satisfied that if we don't have it, at least no one else does either." He leaned forward, his eyes still fixated on Kane. "Did you execute your orders?"

Kane nodded. "I did."

Sherrie turned to him. "What orders?"

Morrison replied. "I ordered him to eliminate Charles Palmer if it looked like he might fall into enemy hands."

She gasped. "Holy shit! You mean you killed Palmer? That's why he didn't come with us?"

Kane shook his head. "No. He had already decided he wasn't coming with us, that's why he gave us the empty cases. I gave him multiple chances to change his mind, but he refused, so I put two in his chest then returned to the rooftop and got on board the chopper."

Sherrie and Leroux both stared at him, slack jawed. Leroux was the first to recover. "Do the professors know?"

Kane shook his head. "Nor will they ever, agreed?"

Leroux agreed, as did Sherrie. She reached out and squeezed Kane's forearm. "But you have to live with it. Are you going to be okay?"

Kane shrugged. "I never knew the man. He was just a job."

Morrison still stared at Kane. "You're sure he's dead?"

"I put two in his chest, sir."

Morrison sat back and flicked his wrist toward the door. "Dismissed."

Kane rose and headed for the door, opening it, letting Sherrie and Leroux through. They headed down the corridor in silence then stepped onto one of the elevators. Someone else approached and Sherrie held out a hand.

"Take the next one." The doors closed and she faced Kane. "I can't believe you lied to the Chief."

Kane regarded her. "Did I?"

"You said you were sure he was dead."

"No, I said I put two in his chest."

Leroux stared at them both. "What are you two talking about?"

Sherrie eyeballed Kane. "Are you going to tell him, or am I?"

"You tell him, that way it's only speculation."

Leroux reached out and hit the emergency stop button, an alarm sounding. "What the hell's going on?"

Sherrie turned to him. "Charles Palmer was wearing a vest under his suit jacket. Two to the chest is not standard procedure. It's two to the chest then one to the head."

Leroux's eyes bulged. "What are you saying?"

Kane reached out and removed Leroux's finger from the button. The elevator resumed. "She's saying nothing. There's no evidence to suggest Charles Palmer is alive. As far as I'm concerned and the world's concerned, I put two in his chest after he had already decided to sacrifice himself, and then his self-destruct mechanism destroyed the evidence." He pointed a finger at Sherrie. "Agreed?"

She smiled. "Agreed. But what about Laura?"

"What about her? There's nothing to tell. There's no evidence out there that proves things either way. Remember, I did shoot him twice in the chest. Those bullets might have penetrated, it could have knocked him out so he didn't have time to escape his own explosion."

Leroux shook his head. "But he might still be out there, working on his invention?"

Kane shrugged. "He could be. Or he could have been vaporized in that explosion. We'll never know unless he wants us to know."

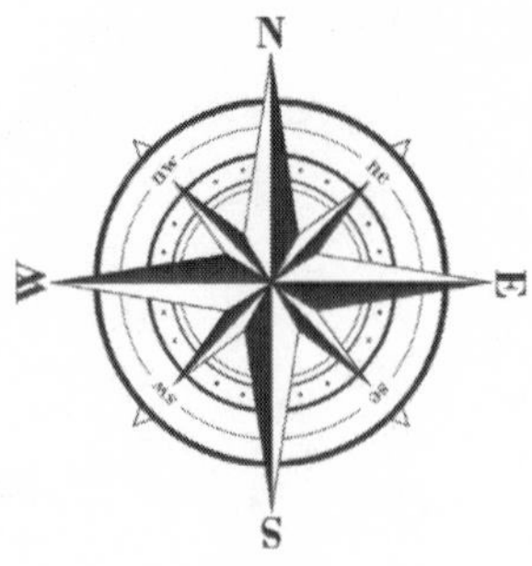

Acton/Palmer Residence, Overlook Village Gated Community

St. Paul, Maryland

The funeral had been well attended, though the crowd was lighter than last time. Ten years was a lot of time for most people to forget who her brother was. There were a lot of cameras there, since it was an interesting story, and she had no doubt quite a few of them were from various foreign governments. Her brother was dead, this time for real, and she had made her peace with that. She was happy to know he had led ten good years on his own. She didn't like the fact he had spent most of it alone, but that was when he was happiest. Alone with his research.

Seeing him, even if only for a few minutes, had been a miracle, and she would cherish those memories. But right now, she was exhausted. The past week had been a whirlwind of activity, the press hounding them, government officials demanding statements, the funeral, Hugh Reading scolding them both for not calling him.

She smiled at the man who had accompanied them back from London after the funeral. "I'm so happy you decided to spend some time with us."

Interpol Agent Hugh Reading shrugged as he pulled off his shoes. "You looked like you could use some friends."

She hugged the man who was like a father to her, and her eyes burned as James passed them, carrying two large pieces of luggage. "Oh, don't worry, I'll get these," he complained with mock annoyance.

Their maid, Rose, rounded the corner. "I thought I heard someone. Welcome back, professors, Mr. Reading. A package arrived for you yesterday that I think you're going to want to see."

James disappeared around the corner with the luggage and he whistled. "What the hell is this?"

Laura wiped her eyes dry with a knuckle then followed him into the living area, a curious Reading on her heels. She rounded the corner and gasped. There was a large crate, her height, sitting behind the couch. "Who's it from?"

James rounded it. "Some numbered company." He cursed. "In Dubai."

She tensed. That was too close to Qatar to be a coincidence.

Reading immediately took charge. "All right, we don't know what this is, so everybody just step back. Jim, get me a hammer."

Rose held one up. "I already have one, sir."

Reading smiled at the woman, taking it from her. "You continue to amaze me."

Rose blushed, batting a hand at him. "It's nothing, sir."

Reading jerked a thumb over his shoulder. "Everybody back into the hallway."

"Nuts to that," said James. "This arrived at my house. I'm opening it."

Laura stepped forward, pointing at the shipping label. "It's addressed to me, so all of you back off." She grabbed the hammer and popped the top before anyone could stop her, Reading and James both taking involuntary steps backward. She shoved the lid out of the way then yanked one of the sides free, revealing something wrapped inside.

"I don't hear any ticking," observed James.

Reading gave her a look. "Fortunately for us."

James pulled away the three other sides and Rose reappeared with a pair of scissors. Laura carefully cut away the bubble wrap then gasped at what was revealed inside, tears flowing as James and Reading finished removing all the wrapping. She stumbled back and leaned against the wall, staring at the vase her brother had restored, the proof she had located Sodom and proven part of the Bible story.

James stared at it, his head slowly shaking. "How?"

Reading glanced at him. "How what?"

"This is the vase that Charles showed us from the dig site. He retrieved it after the dig was shut down and had it restored. How did it survive the explosion? Who shipped it to us?"

Reading stared at him. "You mean this vase, thousands of years old, was in the building when it exploded?"

"Yes. At least, well, I guess, no. I mean, we don't know, right? We saw it before the explosion but then ten or fifteen minutes passed. "There's no way it could survive the explosion."

Laura gasped. "Which means it was removed." A smile spread and she grabbed James by the hand. "If this survived…"

James' jaw dropped as his eyes shot wide. "Charles could have too!"

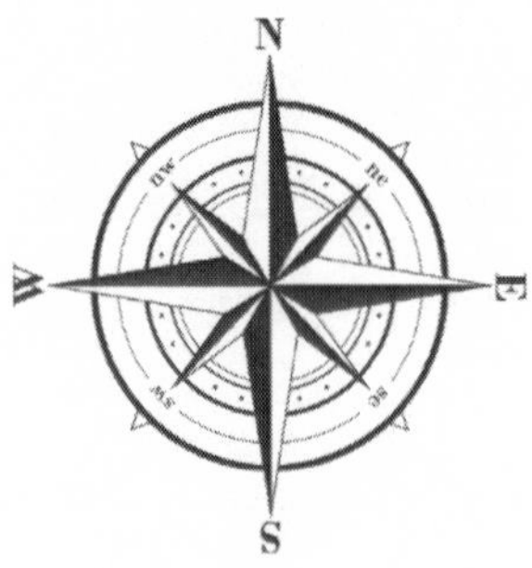

En Route to Lot Residence, Sodom

1649 BC

Lot hurried through the streets, gripping his wife's hand, his heart filled with terror at not only what had happened at Canaan's party, but at what was happening in the sky above. Angel fire streaked across the heavens, scores of them flashing past, casting long, jarring shadows that shifted rapidly, the effect unholy, unnatural.

"What's happening, husband?"

Lot had no explanation. It was far worse than what he had seen last night. Last night was merely a curiosity. This was something far more. This had to be a sign from God, a warning of what was to come, and he thought of what the angels had said. "I don't know."

They reached their home and he was dismayed to find the two visitors standing out front.

"We've been waiting for you," said Raphael.

"We were detained," replied Lot, following his wife inside. He turned to her. "Go get the girls." She nodded, not questioning him, and returned outside, her rapid footfalls fading in the distance.

"What is your decision?" asked Raphael. "As you can see, it's already begun."

Lot grabbed at his hair and pulled, trying to think straight. Something roared overhead and the ground shook. "What is that?" he cried.

"It's God's wrath." Gabriel stepped forward and placed a hand on Lot's shoulder. Lot looked up into the face with a new appreciation of its beauty. There was a feminine quality to it, though he was clearly a man. Perhaps it was that his skin was so smooth, so perfect, not a blemish visible.

He was beautiful.

Lot gasped. He was angelic. Were these indeed angels? Servants of God? Was this God Himself taking the form of angels to deliver His message? Or were they simply two men who had noticed what had been happening in the night sky for days now, and decided to take advantage? Could these still be enemies of his uncle Abraham?

The rumbling stopped and he was shocked to find himself holding on to Gabriel, the man's arms wrapped around him, comforting him.

"There isn't much time to save you and your family," said Raphael. "The righteous will be destroyed with the wicked if they remain. You must escape to the plains. Go to Zoar where you'll be safe."

Lot still wasn't certain what to do, though between what was happening outside and the threat of what was to come tonight from Canaan and possibly the man's guests, he could see no option that had them staying in Sodom. While he still was uncertain as to whether anything happening had to do with the wrath of God, the wrath of Canaan and the city's elite was real. There was no denying it. The threat had been made in person, and Canaan was exactly the type to follow through on it.

Everything Canaan had said suggested he intended to come here and rape either these men, his wife, or their daughters. He wasn't concerned about these men, they could defend themselves, though as guests in his home he had a responsibility to protect them. It was his wife and his daughters that had him concerned. There was no doubt his wife would sacrifice herself to save their daughters, but once Canaan was finished with her, would he be satisfied, or would he continue his debauchery? And if he brought his friends, then what?

No, they had to leave Sodom. That was clear now.

He let go of Gabriel and stepped back, ashamed at his display of cowardice. "We'll be leaving."

Both men smiled. "We're pleased to hear that, and God is pleased."

Lot batted a hand, dismissing the statement. "I'm not leaving because of Him or your claims. We're leaving because Canaan has threatened to come here tonight and rape my wife and daughters if he can't have you."

Raphael cocked an eyebrow, exchanging a bemused look with Gabriel. "Us?"

"Yes."

"The depravity of this place knows no bounds, it would appear."

Gabriel agreed. "Indeed. Don't concern yourself with us. We're more than capable of protecting ourselves from the likes of Canaan."

The door opened and Idit burst in with their daughters. He rushed forward and embraced them all. "Oh, thank God you're all right! Quickly, each of you pack a bag. Just the essentials. Food, water, clothing, nothing more."

"But Father, what's going on?" asked his eldest.

"I'll explain on the way. Just hurry up. Help your sister."

The three people he loved most in this world hurried to fulfill his orders.

Raphael turned to him. "You must leave at once, otherwise, we can't guarantee your safety."

The strange rumble began again, everything shaking, everything rattling as whatever it was rapidly passed overhead. It had to be God's wrath. What else could it be? Only God controlled the heavens. Only God could rain hellfire across His dominion.

Yet none of that mattered. Whether this was the wrath of God or mere coincidence, was irrelevant. Canaan could be here at any moment and they had to be gone before he arrived, otherwise, there would be no escaping the horrifying consequences.

"Lot, we're here to meet your guests!"

Lot's heart nearly stopped at Canaan's taunt. He rushed to the window and peered through the cracks in the shutters. Canaan stood outside, and he wasn't alone. All the men of the party were here, plus others they must have gathered along the way.

He faced their guests. "They're here. What are we going to do?"

Raphael turned to Idit as she entered the room, tossing two bags on the floor. "Are you ready to leave?"

She glanced over at their daughters, the eldest replied. "Yes."

Canaan hammered on the door. "Lot, let us in or we'll break the door down! No matter what happens, we're getting to know your guests or we're getting to know your wife and your daughters. There are a lot of hungry men out here, and your wife won't be enough."

"Leave us alone!" screamed Idit, the terror in her voice obvious. Their daughters burst into tears, unaccustomed to seeing their parents scared.

Canaan and the others laughed. "I hear your wife and I hear your daughters, but I don't hear your guests. Are they still here? Are they prepared for a Sodom welcome?"

Lot faced his guests. "I don't know what to do."

Raphael smiled. "You're under God's protection now."

Lot threw his hands up in frustration. "Would you stop with that nonsense? Even if God has something to do with what's going on, you're just men from Gomorrah. There's nothing you can do but submit to their demands should you wish to protect us."

The ground rumbled once again then there was a crack overhead unlike anything he had ever heard. A bright light flared briefly, every slit and gap in the home revealed in a brilliant flash. Those outside cried out in horror and Lot rushed to the window, peering out to see them all stumbling about, gripping their eyes. "What happened?"

"The power of God has rendered them blind," replied Raphael, "though it is only temporary. I suggest you take your family now and head for Zoar."

Lot grabbed the bags his wife had packed, his eyes darting over to the remnants of the shattered vase piled near the hearth, wishing they had never taken the vile commission. They had to get out of here while those outside who would do his family harm were no longer a threat for the moment. "What of you?"

"You need not worry about us?" Raphael pointed to the rear of the house. "Now go out the back way and whatever you do, don't look back. Just go and never return."

"Never?" asked Idit. "But this is our home."

"When God has exacted His vengeance, the cities of the plain will be no more. No one and no thing will ever live here again. Now go before it's too late and the only righteous man among this city of the damned is lost as well."

Lot herded his family toward the rear entrance and Gabriel called after them, "Tell this story wide and far, Lot, for it must never be forgotten what happens when man goes against God."

They rushed out the rear door and down the alleyway. He glanced up at the sky, the streaks of angel fire now nonstop, some so large he swore he could see the angels themselves. The houses were emptying into the streets as people stared up in a panic, uncertain as to what to do. But none were fleeing.

Lot continued forward with his family and reached the outskirts of this condemned city. He resisted the urge to look back as they raced across the lush plains that fed the prosperous city states, and he wondered how history would remember Sodom and the small part he had played during its demise.

THE END

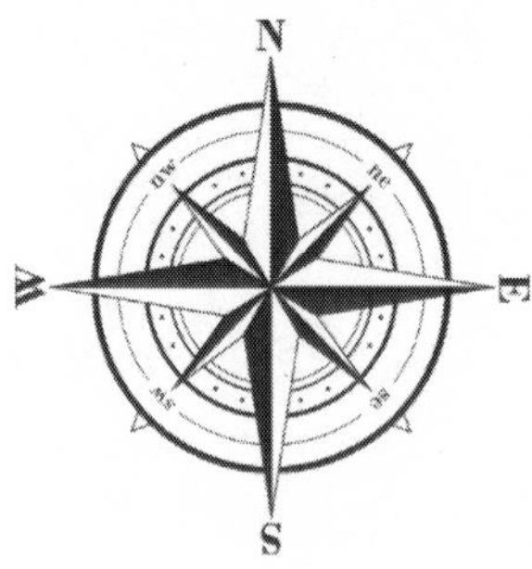

ACKNOWLEDGMENTS

This book has been in the works for over a decade. I just didn't know it. When I created the character of Laura Palmer for the first book I ever wrote, The Protocol, I gave her a brother. He had owned a tech company that he had sold for a fortune, then died at one of her dig sites in Jordan, leaving his fortune to her.

And his Porsche.

And that was all that was known about him.

I made reference to him over the years, with a few more details sneaking in the novels No Good Deed and Lake of Bones.

And then there was Mary.

An innocent travel agent who had once worked for Charles Palmer and offered her services to Laura after his death.

She was where things developed further in a more obvious way. How could a travel agent do the things she did? She's been impressing us for years now, and we finally know why.

The idea that Charles Palmer was still alive and in hiding came to me many years ago, and I've been slowly laying the groundwork for his return, waiting for the right moment.

I guess this was the right moment.

As usual, there are people to thank. My dad for all the research, and, as always, my wife, my daughter, my late mother who will always be an angel on my shoulder as I write, as well as my friends for their continued support, and my fantastic proofreading team!

To those who have not already done so, please visit my website at www.jrobertkennedy.com, then sign up for the Insider's Club to be notified of new book releases. Your email address will never be shared or sold.

Thank you once again for reading.

Made in United States
North Haven, CT
09 October 2023

42553601R00188